BLUE INK

BLUE MOUNTAIN SERIES BOOK 3

TESS THOMPSON

4kids5cats
EDITIONS

For my soulmate, Clifford Paul Strom.
I will always find you.

...and when one of them meets the other half, the actual half of himself, whether he be a lover of youth or a lover of another sort, the pair are lost in an amazement of love and friendship and intimacy and one will not be out of the other's sight, as I may say, even for a moment...

— PLATO

What greater thing is there for two human souls than to feel that they are joined to strengthen each other, to be at one with each other in silent unspeakable memories.

— GEORGE ELIOT

CHAPTER ONE

Charlotte

The herd of elk appeared out of nowhere on a dirt road outside of Peregrine, Idaho. One second, I was squinting into rays of morning sun that reached through thin clouds in beams of blinding light. The next, they appeared, brown and beastly, directly in the middle of my path. I cursed and slammed on the brakes. My forehead smacked against the steering wheel and bounced back up like a rubber ball on concrete. Black spots danced before my eyes. Pain shot through my head. I winced and touched the tender spot on my forehead.

I blinked. Were they real?

Yes, still there. A herd of elk, and me, Charlotte Wilde, a city girl in a Volkswagen Bug wearing skinny jeans and black pumps, were at a standoff in the middle of a muddy, soggy meadow.

Seemingly unconcerned with my unexpected arrival, several dozen female elk nibbled on tufts of grass that grew alongside the road. The lone male, with antlers as wide as my car, lifted his head and stared at me with curious eyes. The patchy quality of his coat told me he was in the process of shedding his winter warmth. How I knew this I can't say, other than it was probably one of those useless facts about animals my father collected to share with his young patients at his pediatric dental practice. Or rather, his *former* dental practice. Right now, he and my mother were gliding down the freeway toward Florida in their brand-new Airstream.

Despite his uneven pelt, the male was magnificent. I shivered as a current of energy passed between us. Did he sense my trepidation? Could he smell the shedding of my former skin?

I was the first to break eye contact. Notwithstanding the beauty in front of me, I had to get to Ardan Lanigan's house by 9:00 a.m. From our brief email correspondence, I suspected he was a man of precision. I had exactly three minutes to get there.

How *did* one get past an entire herd of elk?

Grassy meadows stretched out on either side of the overgrown road. I opened the car door to inspect my chances of running for it if the elk decided to surge the car. No good. At least an inch of water lay on the muddy road. Neither my Volkswagen Bug nor my black pumps were worthy opponents against the rugged terrain of Idaho.

Were elk aggressive creatures? I had no idea. They were slow. They hadn't moved an inch in either direction and didn't seem inclined to do so anytime soon.

There was only one thing to do. I had to call Ardan Lanigan and tell him the trouble.

I pulled up his number on my phone and prayed for him to answer.

"This is Ardan."

"Hi. It's Charlotte Wilde. I'm almost to your house, but I've run into some elk. They're blocking the road."

"Are you hurt?" His tone was one of concern. All right, then. He was a sensitive man despite being richer than God.

"No, no. I stopped before I hit them. But they're giving no indication of interest in moving along their merry way."

"They're like that here. It's my brother Kevan's fault. He treats them like domesticated animals, so they're not afraid of humans." I couldn't discern if that fact amused or irritated him.

"What do I do?" I asked.

"Can you describe where you are?"

"Just after a sharp curve. That's why I almost hit them," I said. "Well, that and the ridiculously bright sunbeams."

"Yes, right. That turn comes out of nowhere. A design flaw necessary because of the flow of the creek." There was a slight pause before he spoke again. "Hang tight. I'll come get you."

Before I could answer, the line went dead. I glanced at the screen on my phone. The two bars had changed to *No Service.* A wave of homesickness washed over me. I longed for the sanctuary of my apartment in Portland, Oregon. Sure, the hallway smelled of Mrs. Pikes' bean soup, and the lobby of mildew. Outside, the sidewalks were uneven and decorated with urine from the homeless. Millennials with man-buns and kombucha in their coffee mugs marched in the streets. Even so, it was home. I, for better or worse, was a city girl. I liked my restaurants and public transit. I preferred my pathways without elk.

I glanced into the rearview mirror and sighed at the state of my appearance. My brown eyes were bloodshot from getting up so early. I'd chewed off all my lipstick on the way from Boise, becoming increasingly anxious as I climbed to higher and higher elevation with no sign of civilization. Until I reached the town of Peregrine, which consisted of a half-dozen brick buildings, a Victorian house turned inn, and a surrounding population of five hundred people, I'd seen only wildlife. A falcon, presumably of the Peregrine variety, had swooped so low during my visit at a rest stop, I'd spotted his yellow beak.

Where the five hundred residents of Peregrine were hiding was anyone's guess. Thus far, I'd spotted only two humans—a woman working the counter at an empty coffee shop and a clerk sweeping the sidewalk in front of the grocery store.

Elk clearly outnumbered people.

I looked back at my reflection. Was that a pimple on the end of my nose or a dab of strawberry jam from the scone I'd devoured earlier? I rubbed. Off it came. Strawberry jam. I eat when I'm anxious. And happy. Or sad. I love food. Now that I thought about it, I was hungry again. I should have stopped at the coffee shop and gotten something to nibble. No. A second breakfast was not going to conquer the battle with the size of my bottom.

I *was* thankful for the dry air. Any smidge of humidity and my espresso-hued curls sprang from my head like one of those rainbow wigs that clowns wear.

As I sat there, amongst the elk and under the bluest sky I'd ever seen, a hint of worry niggled at me. Had this been a good idea to come to Idaho? Good idea or not, the perfect trifecta had forced my hand.

One, my parents had decided to sell their dental practice and my childhood home to travel across the country in an Airstream, thus freeing me from the guilt that befalls only children. Two, despite modest success with the publication of my first mystery, featuring feisty private investigator Luci Storm, the second in the series had been rejected by my agent as too serious for today's troubled world. "Escape fiction," my chain-smoking, waiflike agent had said during our last conversation. "That's what people want. Can you write a fun, flirty chick-lit book? Maybe toss in a little sexy time? Maybe an experience from your own love life?" If she wanted light, using *my* love life as fodder was not the way to do it. There was no sexy time. No fun. No flirting.

Which brings me to the third reason for *Escape to Idaho*. My small savings was gone, courtesy of my dismal choice of a boyfriend's gambling problem.

Therefore, when my former boss Bliss Heywood called to see if I was interested in coming to the middle of nowhere Idaho to look after her mother-in-law, I didn't hesitate to accept the offer.

Due to macular degeneration, Mrs. Lanigan's eyesight was poor. She'd fallen one night and broken her hip. Now, recuperating at Ardan's house, she had fallen into a depression. According to Bliss, she had no interest in getting out of bed. Could I come and sprinkle some of my magical fairy dust on her and make everything better? Bliss thought a little too highly of my skills, but who was I to argue? I needed the money.

It was quiet, Bliss had explained, as if I needed further convincing. I could write during my free time. Her brother-in-law, Ardan, had a beautiful home. I could stay rent free in one of his guest rooms. He even had a lap pool, so I could do my daily half mile.

I figured looking after a sweet grandmother would seem easy compared to the executive assistant positions I'd had over the years. Besides Bliss, all my jobs had been working for men. All jerks in their own unique ways. The list included: Mr. Grabbyhands, Mr. Over-caffeinated, Mr. Phone-attached-to-ear, Mr. No-deodorant. Good times.

It all came down to one thing. With no rent to pay, I could bank my salary, affording me another year to write without a pesky day job interfering. My writing was all I had left. The rest of my life was in the proverbial toilet.

So, Idaho it is. Elk be damned.

CHAPTER TWO

Ardan

After I hung up with Charlotte, I tossed the phone onto the counter like it was on fire. The dark eyes of my housekeeper, Effie, sparkled with excitement. Moonstone, our local psychic, lover of all things purple, and loyal family friend, crossed her arms over her generous bosom and grinned.

"What?" I asked, as if I didn't know.

"Ardan Lanigan, don't be coy," Moonstone said. "It's elk and a damsel in distress, just as I envisioned, isn't it now?"

"It *is* elk," I said. "And Charlotte Wilde *is* stranded." She also had a pretty voice to go with her pretty face. *If* her author picture on the back cover of her book was accurate and not a work of fiction.

"I don't like to be the type who says 'I told you so,' but I told you so." Moonstone played with one of the peacock earrings that dangled from her left lobe and continued to look smug.

"Mr. Lanigan, this is so exciting," Effie said in her clipped British accent. Everything out of her barely adult mouth sounded better than it was in real life because of that adorable accent. "At last, your soulmate has arrived."

"This whole thing's ridiculous," I said. "Charlotte isn't my soulmate. We haven't even met."

"Don't pretend like you don't understand the concept of soulmates," Moonstone said. "Just because you haven't met doesn't mean you're not soulmates. It simply means that your destiny awaits."

"You of all people should know this," Effie said.

"I should?" I asked.

"You're a deep thinker," Effie said. "Reading all the smart books."

"Yes, and my psychic abilities have been proven more times than any of us want to remember," Moonstone said. "When it comes to predicting the arrival of the Lanigan brothers' soulmates, I'm batting one thousand."

"*A* thousand. And do you even know what that means?" I asked. Moonstone had never watched a baseball game in her life.

"That's not true," Moonstone said. "I've been watching baseball with my husband, Sam." She emphasized the word *husband*. Moonstone was a newlywed. She used the word *husband* as often as she could.

"And yes, I do enjoy saying the word husband," Moonstone said. "For as long as I waited for my soulmate to arrive, I have every right to do so."

She *was* a mind reader. No doubt about it. She *had* predicted the arrival of my brothers' wives, Blythe and Bliss Heywood—sisters who'd married my two remaining brothers. Who could predict that other than a psychic?

The whole idea of Charlotte Wilde had started a week ago when I'd joined Moonstone and Sam for dinner at my brother Ciaran and his wife Bliss's house. We'd met to discuss Mother. As in, *what to do about Mother?*

Ciaran had put it to the song lyric from *Sound of Music,* substituting Mother for Maria. His antics hadn't amused me. I was the one who had taken Mother in after her broken hip. My siblings ran scared the moment the doctors called to tell us she couldn't see well enough to stay alone. I was the one who had hired two perfectly qualified nurses in a row, only to have Mother run them off within one day of their arrival. I was the one who had to console a tearful Effie on a regular basis.

A month ago, Mother was living alone with her loyal staff of two in a penthouse condominium in San Francisco. I was living happily here on the side of a mountain. Between my brothers and their wives, I wasn't lonely. Not exactly lonely. Yes, I would love a woman of my own to share life with, but how could I find one that liked living here? Isolation was not everyone's dream. In fact, most women my age deplored the idea of a life in rugged Idaho.

By dessert, we still didn't have a solution to our big problem called Mother. Bliss had rested her arms on her pregnant belly and looked guilty. She's the type who likes to solve problems with efficient, logical solutions. Mother, however, was a tough case.

With her fork poised over a piece of chocolate cake, Moonstone had stilled as her eyes glazed over like a hazy window. I knew from experience this meant she was having a vision. When she snapped out of it, she looked over at Bliss. "I know what to do. Get Charlotte Wilde."

Charlotte Wilde had been Bliss's executive assistant. She was now the author of a mystery novel which Mother and I had thoroughly enjoyed.

"Charlotte?" Bliss had asked. "My Charlotte?"

Moonstone nodded. "She's the one to look after our large problem with a capital M. She's also Ardan's soulmate."

I'd almost choked on my forkful of cake.

Bliss and Ciaran had stared at Moonstone like she'd just declared the most obvious solution and why hadn't they thought of it?

"I just exchanged emails with her," Bliss had said. "She had a bad breakup six months ago. The jerk stole all her savings and gambled it away in Vegas. She can't find a publisher for her new book."

"That's right," Moonstone had said. "Therefore, it's time."

Time for what?

"She *might* be willing to come," Bliss had said. "But we can't tell her about your premonition. That will scare her off."

Ciaran and Moonstone had nodded like that was a perfectly normal fear. Sam had just shrugged and shot me an apologetic smile. He knew better than to get in the way when Bliss and Moonstone had something on their minds.

Now, Effie waved her hand in front of my face. "Mr. Lanigan stop your daydreaming. You need to get Miss Charlotte. She might be afraid of elk."

"She sounded afraid," I said.

"She's from the city," Moonstone said. "She doesn't know about their spiritual powers."

I grabbed the keys to my truck from the bowl on the counter. "I'll be back shortly."

"Be charming," Moonstone said.

"Don't act shy," Effie said. "Be confident."

"Don't forget to carry her," Moonstone said. "She doesn't want to ruin her shoes in all that mud."

Charming? Not likely. Overcome my shyness? That was impossible. Carrying a pretty girl across the mud? In my wheelhouse. If I didn't have to speak, all would be fine.

As I drove out of my driveway and down the dirt road toward the bend in the road where the elk had trapped Charlotte, I thought about Moonstone's prediction. Was she right? Was Charlotte Wilde my destiny? Would I finally find love after all my attempts with women who clearly were not even close to being my soulmate? I feared that in this instance, Moonstone had her psychic wires twisted. There was no such thing as fate when it came to me and women, unless it was from a dark force. My destiny was to be alone for the rest of my life. Forever a bachelor, never a husband. Only an uncle, never a father.

Moonstone might have a vision, but I had the past as evidence. When it came to romantic love, I was a disaster.

A Peregrine falcon rode the wind above me.

A voice sounded in my head.

Assume the best and it will be.

It was the voice of my father.

What if I did assume Charlotte was for me? How would it change my behavior? What if I assumed my great love had come to me at last?

Assume the best and it will be.

CHAPTER THREE

CHARLOTTE

While I waited for Ardan Lanigan to rescue me, I did a further investigation of my surroundings. Despite the elk and the mud, the view of Blue Mountain against the sky stunned this city girl. Everything seemed brighter and more colorful here. Spring wildflowers in shades of purple and yellow poked their pretty heads up between grasses. Beyond, a thick forest was a mass of greenery.

My thoughts were disrupted by the rumble of an engine. A vehicle resembling a tank bounced down the dirt road. A hundred or so yards from me, the truck veered from the road and into the meadow, dirt and mud flying from its tires. It circled around the herd of elk and stopped several feet from my car. I rolled down the window. There was no way I was getting out until he came for me. What if one of the huge creatures decided to trample me?

Ardan Lanigan jumped from his truck and strode over to my car. What? Holy God. Bliss hadn't mentioned her brother-in-law looked like a BBC miniseries star. Dark blond hair hung over his forehead in perfect dishevelment. He had a square jaw, high cheekbones and one of those mouths that seemed always on the verge of smiling and did just that when I gave him a limp wave. I rolled down my window.

He placed his hands over the open window. "Hello, Charlotte."

My toes inside my pointy pumps curled.

"Um. Hi. Sorry about this," I said.

He wore a black t-shirt and faded jeans over his lean and muscular physique. His brown leather boots had clearly seen their share of mud. Who knew mud could make a man look sexy?

Light blue eyes peered at me through the open window. "No worries. The harem just wanted to welcome you to Peregrine." His hair was damp and unruly, like he hadn't bothered to comb it when he got out of the shower. I caught a whiff of soap and men's cologne. Idaho had just become a lot more interesting. And possibly even more frightening.

"Harem?" I swallowed as a thousand fireflies came to life in my stomach.

"Harem. That's what you call a female herd."

"I never knew that. Not that I would. I don't know anything about elk other than the shedding thing," I said. His eyes were the color of faded blue jeans and fringed in dark lashes. For a breathless moment, I couldn't look away. I forgot the elk and the mud or even why I was here.

"The shedding thing?"

"Never mind." I went hot, embarrassed. Handsome men with radio announcer voices made me nervous. I couldn't stop babbling nonsense.

"I was hoping to make a better first impression." I flushed when he met my smile with one of his own. Nice teeth. My dad would approve.

"You're making a fine impression." His bottom lip was full, almost swollen looking, and pink like the stain from my strawberry jam. I wanted to take it between my own and discover its taste.

"This happens more than I'd like to admit. My brother Kevan is an animal nut. Anyway, that's why I drive this beast around the property." He gestured toward his truck. "Terrible gas mileage, which makes my carbon footprint even larger. In my defense, I never take it out on the highway unless it's snowed. Not that you care about my justifications, really." He laughed in low, staccato bursts of air before opening my door.

A chivalrous, rugged, environmentally conscious man who rescues women from elk. What more could a woman ask for?

"We'll leave your car and come back for it later. Are your things in the trunk?"

"Yes. Just a few bags." I'd sublet my apartment to a friend. Travel light, I'd thought. Free myself of burdens.

I froze midway out of the car, just before my feet touched the muddy ground. My pumps would be ruined. I looked up at him, embarrassed.

His brow wrinkled. "I hope you brought some other shoes."

"I did." All of which were inappropriate. I kept that to myself.

He tapped his bottom lip with his index finger. "You'll ruin your pretty shoes and get mud on your legs unless I carry you."

I gulped. Carry me?

"I'm sure I'll be fine," I said.

"I'm not going to be responsible for ruining a lady's shoes." His precise speech and the low timbre of his voice gave me the sudden urge to close my eyes and curl up in a spot of sun like a spoiled cat. "My mother would never forgive me. Come on now, put your arms around my neck." When I did so, he scooped me up against his chest. Our gazes locked. Another flutter rippled the lining of my stomach.

I should have popped in a breath mint.

"I thought you'd be older." His eyes had flecks of yellow, like fireworks in a blue ink sky. "Your book cover photo makes you look more mature."

"More mature?" I asked.

"Yes, like at least legal."

"I'm older than I look. Thirty, actually."

"I'd have to see your license to believe that."

"It's my Italian heritage," I said. "I look just like my Italian grandmother, Mimi. My dad's mother." She was short and curvy like me. I kept that to myself.

"Can you cook like her?" he asked.

"How do you know if she could cook?"

"An assumption, given no data other than my romantic notions," he said.

"You're right. She could cook. So can my mother. The gene skipped me. I'm only good at eating."

"That's fine. We have Effie."

"What's an Effie?" I asked.

"My live-in housekeeper and cook extraordinaire."

He had his own cook. Right. Millionaires lived this way.

Like I weighed nothing, he crossed over to his tank-like vehicle, opened the door, and set me inside. I realized I hadn't grabbed my purse and would need the keys to open the trunk of my car. "My keys are in my bag."

"No problem." As he sprinted to my car, I took the opportunity to check out his backside. The view of his broad shoulders and a tight rear did not disappoint.

He returned with my bag. "What do you have in there? A cement block?"

"Just the usual." I rummaged through several lipsticks, my writing notepad, phone, mace, flashlight, a package of tissues, and my calendar of daily affirmations before I found my keys. Did he have to stand so close? I could practically bite into his muscular thigh from this angle. "Here you go."

Minutes later, my bags were transferred to the back of his truck, and we were on our way around the elk.

"Will my car be all right?" I asked.

"Sure. We lock the gate at night. I had it open for your arrival."

We bounced in a pothole. My ample chest bounced up and down like water balloons. I crossed my arms over them before one of them smacked me in the face as I silently cursed Mimi for giving me her big bosom and bottom. *May she rest in peace.*

"What about the elk?" I asked. "You don't think one of them will sit on my car, do you?"

"I don't think elk sit on cars." He took his gaze from the road for a split second to look over at me with an amused expression. "Although the image is funny."

The image of an elk smashing in the hood of my little blue Bug was not funny to me. I'd bought that car with my book advance money. It was the symbol of my success and could be wrecked easily. Like my writing career.

Obviously unaware of my misery, he asked how much Bliss had told me about his family and the Lanigan property.

"Just that your father owned this property as a vacation spot when you were kids."

"That's right. When my father died, we all agreed to keep the land and build houses of our own. Bliss calls it *The Compound.*" The corners of his eyes crinkled like rumpled tissue paper when he smiled. I guessed him to be close to forty, although he had a youthful presence. I suspected he was a curious person. My mother always says curiosity keeps a person young.

As we passed a driveway, he explained that it led to Kevan and Blythe's home. "Her ex-husband lives in Seattle, so they have to live there during the school months but spend summers and holidays here." We came upon another driveway. "Ciaran and Bliss's house is in there. Nestled in the trees." I could just spot the outline of a roof. From correspondence with Bliss, I knew that Bliss's sister, Blythe, had also married one of the Lanigan brothers. Ciaran and Bliss had married a year or so ago. Kevan and Blythe had a blended family of her two daughters and his college-aged daughter.

"And you?" I asked. "Any wives or ex-wives? Girlfriends, past or present?"

"No wives, exes or current. A few past girlfriends. None of whom stuck. Currently, *heart open for business*."

My hands fluttered on my lap. *Open for business. Available.*

"Bliss tells me you worked together in Portland," he said.

"Yes, a few years back. She's the best."

"She said the same about you."

"Yeah?" I asked.

"She's one of my favorite people, so I figured it must be true," he said.

"Which is why you hired me sight unseen?"

"Something like that, yes."

I wanted to ask for clarification, but for once my big mouth stayed shut.

We passed a third driveway. "Who lives there?" I asked.

"That was my brother Finn's house."

"Oh, yes, I'm sorry for your loss," I said lamely. Finn had been murdered. I couldn't remember the exact details, but Bliss said it had been a terrible blow to the family. One that had divided the brothers from one another, until the Heywood sisters had brought them together.

"Thank you. We don't know what to do with his house, so it just sits there." His voice had lowered to just above a mumble. I leaned closer to hear him over the roar of the engine. "None of us can bear to go inside now that all Finn's things are gone. My sister, Teagan, plans on building a house at some point, but for right now she's still working in the film industry."

"What does she do?"

"Costume designer."

The fact that she worked surprised me. The Lanigan siblings had inherited fortunes from their late father. Lanigan Trucking had been worth more money than I could imagine. I knew from Bliss that Ardan had started a school for troubled boys and did other similar charity work for kids.

"Bliss told me about your school. Do you still run it?"

"No, I recently hired a headmaster. I wanted to focus on other projects." We turned a corner. A pair of cherry trees in full bloom were so close I could have touched them had I rolled down the window.

"I loved your book," he said. "Bliss gave it to me for Christmas."

"You did?" The thrill of the compliment moved through me in a happy buzz.

"I have a crush on Luci." He smiled without taking his eyes from the road. "Is she like you?"

"I wish." My detective heroine, Luci Storm, was tall, athletic, and brave. "I live vicariously through her."

"Luci reminds Mother of my sister, Teagan. Red hair and all."

We turned down a fourth driveway. I held my breath, astonished by the beauty of the house and grounds. I'd expected a rustic, mountain home built like a ski lodge, but instead grey shingles and white trim gave it a distinctly beachy feel. The grounds were simple, with rolling lawns and a tall oak with a wooden swing hanging from a thick branch. Carefully tended flowers and shrubs were arranged in beds near the house. Buds from the cherry trees that lined the driveway fell from heavy limbs and blanketed the ground.

Ardan pulled into the three-car garage and parked next to a sporty looking black car. "Wait there. I'll help you down."

He jumped from the truck and sprinted around to the passenger side. "Careful now. We don't want you to break your ankle before you have a chance to meet Mother." With one hand holding open the door, he offered the other to me.

I closed my fingers around his. We locked eyes once more. The air between us crackled and lifted the fine hairs on the back of my neck. A million moments not yet lived teased my fanciful mind like photographs fanned out on a dining room table.

He blinked first. I couldn't decide if I was relieved or disappointed to be jerked back into reality.

I allowed him to help me down from the truck. Given the height of the vehicle and my shoes, I'm not sure I could have gotten down on my own. Regardless, I was happy to have his warm hand in mine.

He grabbed my suitcases from the back and set them next to

the steps leading to a door into the house. "I'll come back for those in a minute. We mostly use the entrance just off the kitchen on the other side of the house. Before we go in, I'll show you the back. Bliss said you like to swim."

"I swim a half mile every morning," I said.

"Good for you." He glanced at me. "That's something we have in common."

I followed him through the garage to the backyard. A patio made of grey stone butted up against a lawn that led into a dense forest. Outdoor furniture and a dining table with an umbrella were spots of blue and green against the grey stone. Comfortable looking chairs were arranged around a gas fire pit just outside a set of French doors. To the left of the patio, glass walls from an enclosed lap swimming pool sparkled in the sun.

He pointed to the contraption covering the swimming pool. "That cover opens and closes, depending on the weather. I like to swim year-round. The glass keeps it nice and warm, even in the winter. You're welcome to use the pool whenever you like. I swim in the morning, but there's room for both of us."

"Did you swim competitively?" I asked.

"High school and college. You?"

"Just high school. I was too short to be any good. I loved it anyway."

"I was decent, but not great."

"I have a feeling you're being modest," I said.

He smiled. "Come on inside. I'll introduce you to Effie."

We stepped through the French doors into the kitchen. I halted in the doorway. The kitchen was like something from the movies. White cabinets, black countertops, and chrome appliances screamed wealth. A walnut wood floor gleamed under pendant lighting.

"What a beautiful kitchen." I gestured toward the large island in the middle of the room. "Looks like a great gathering place."

"My family's big, so I need one." He pointed to the breakfast nook nestled next to picture windows. "I love to sit there and read."

I imagined him there with a cup of coffee and a book, the sun bouncing off his blond hair.

The sound of glass shattering broke the tranquility.

"What now?" Ardan muttered under his breath.

A woman's screech echoed through the house. Another crash followed shortly thereafter.

"I'll be right back." He bolted. His boots tracked mud on the clean floor. My mother would be horrified. No shoes were allowed in her house. Boots with caked mud might cause her to hyperventilate. Did she have the same rules for the Airstream?

My chest ached at the thought of my parents. I hoped they were having a wonderful adventure, but I missed them.

I set my purse on the counter and sent them a quick text that I'd arrived safely. My mother wrote back almost immediately that they were in southern Florida at a spot by the ocean. They were planning on spending a few weeks at the campsite before heading to North Carolina. She asked about Ardan. Did he seem nice?

I texted back.

Bliss didn't mention he looks like one of our BBC television heroes in American boots and jeans. Newscaster voice. Old soul. Sensitive blue eyes. Makes my stomach flutter.

`Oh dear. Single?`

Yes. As far as I can tell, he lives out here in the middle of nowhere as chaste as me.

`Be careful. I don't want you hurt again.`

I will be. There's no way he'll be interested in me anyway. I'll be able to crush from afar.

`Why wouldn't he be? You're the best girl in the world.`

I love you, Mom, but you're biased. He's richer than God and super hot. I'm not either of those things.

`Your father says hello and to stop being ridiculous. Any man would be lucky to have you.`

I settled onto a stool at the island, smiling at my phone.

I should go. Love you both. Have so much fun in Florida. Wear your sun hat.

Unlike me, Mom had fair skin and was tall and slender.

I will. Let us know when we can come visit in Idaho. We miss you.

Another crash sounded from the other end of the house. Maybe metal pans smacking onto a marble floor? Dead silence followed. I stared at the granite, looking for a pattern, but it was a haphazard mix of blue, green, and black. The second hand on the clock above the door clicked away, loud in the now silent house. A blue bowl piled with oranges gave off a faint scent of citrus.

A moment later, a woman burst into the kitchen. She carried a tray with several broken dishes. Coffee and egg yolks stained her white cotton dress. Mascara and liner were smeared under eyes the color of shiny brown buttons.

She gasped when she saw me. "Dear me. Did you hear all that?" An English accent and rosy cheeks only added to her attractiveness. "I'm Effie. Effie Smith. The housekeeper." She couldn't be older than twenty. Her face hadn't lost the roundness of youth.

"Nice to meet you. I'm Charlotte Wilde."

Her dark, straight hair was cut in one of those asymmetrical bobs that looked great on women with round, pretty faces like the one standing before me. "Yes, yes. I know you from your book cover. Ardan and I both thought you were terribly pretty, but you're even better in person." As if my appearance made her sad, she set the tray on the counter and started to sob into her hands.

I looked around the kitchen for tissues and found a box on the small desk in the far corner of the kitchen. I ran across the shiny floor, almost slipping in my pumps. "Here, take these," I said when I returned to her with a clump of tissues.

She took them and wiped under her eyes. "I'm sorry to be such a mess upon your arrival, Miss Wilde. I'm usually much more put together and here you are all perfect." She ran her hand over the stains on her dress. "My dress is ruined. I should have known better than to buy anything white. Girls like me should never buy white."

I pointed to my pumps. "There was so much mud Ardan had to carry me to his truck."

She sniffed and gave me a half smile. "How could you know about the elk? This countryside is dodgy. Wild beasts everywhere, including bears. Did he tell you about them? They come right up to the rubbish bins, cheeky as can be."

"Bears?" I coughed. City mouse was about to become country mouse.

"Mountain lions too. And wild turkeys." She shuddered. "Poor things are ugly as can be. It's no wonder you Americans decided to eat them for Thanksgiving."

Bears? Mountain lions? "I'm scared of all those things."

"Don't worry, Mr. Lanigan will keep us safe. He knows this land like his own hand."

"Have you been with him a while?" I asked.

"For a little over a year."

"How in the world did you get to Idaho?"

"I followed a bloke here."

"To Idaho?" I asked.

"No, first to San Francisco, then here. I didn't have anywhere to go after things didn't work out with Charlie, so I answered an ad for a housekeeper as far away from him as I could. Happily, it was a job with Mr. Lanigan. And wouldn't you know, I love it here. There's no man to cause me troubles." Effie dropped her voice to just above a whisper. "At least, I *did* love it here. Until *Mrs.* Lanigan arrived. Mr. Lanigan's no trouble to look after. But her? Well, you heard the noises coming from her room."

"She won't stay forever, though?" I asked. "Bliss told me I'd only be needed for two or three months."

Effie started to cry again. "Two or three months is forever. Did Mr. Lanigan tell you she's already scared away two other companions?"

"No, I hadn't heard that." Two? Obviously, Mrs. Lanigan was

not the sweet grandmother I'd imagined. "What happened just now?" I gestured toward the tray.

"She didn't like her breakfast. I didn't cook the yolks enough." Effie talked through her tears. "And she wanted coffee not tea, even though yesterday she'd asked for tea. She threw her cup and plate at me. Broke these lovely dishes. If she only knew how others live. My poor mum never had a new set of dishes her whole life and here she tosses them at me like they're nothing. You should see the wall. Splattered with blackberry jam and bits of glass everywhere. Mr. Lanigan sent me away, so he could clean up and have a talk with her."

"You poor thing. Here, come sit." I motioned to the breakfast nook. "I'll make you some tea."

"That would be lovely, but there isn't time. Let me show you into the living room."

There wasn't time. Why was that? Were we on a schedule?

We walked out of the kitchen and into the living room. On one end, picture windows displayed a view of Blue Mountain. The other windows looked out to the backyard. Decorated traditionally, with the same walnut wood floors as the kitchen, the room could be featured in one of those architecture and design magazines. The pale blue on the walls, and the white trim and wainscoting were a great complement to the classically designed furniture in dark woods and light fabrics.

"Make yourself comfortable," Effie said. "I'll go change now before Mr. Lanigan needs me to fix her another breakfast."

After she left, I explored the room, looking for details about the man who lived here. A couch the color of butter and a pair of striped blue and white easy chairs faced the window. Landscape paintings of the seaside and a European looking village hung on the walls. Eclectic pieces of pottery and various wood carvings were set about, all of which seemed to have been chosen and collected from a life of travel.

It was as if I'd decorated it myself. In fact, the room was remarkably like a photograph I'd pasted on the vision board I'd made on my laptop. I made a mental note to look at that again tonight.

Bookshelves lined the back wall. I trailed my fingers along the rows of books, curious to see what he read for pleasure and deemed important enough to take up shelving space. He had an assortment, mostly fiction, arranged in categories, with everything from thrillers to classics. An entire section was devoted to spiritual books, a few written by the Dalai Lama and other eastern philosophers, along with Christian thought leaders. Another section was more of the self-help variety, including several books about family dynamics.

If nothing else, this trip would be great fodder for my writing.

CHAPTER FOUR

ARDAN

Mother refused to come out from under her blankets.

"Go away."

"I'm not going anywhere until you explain your behavior," I said. "You've made Effie cry again."

The wall near the doorway was scattered with various breakfast items, including bright purple jam and egg yolks. I pulled the covers back. My anger lessened slightly at the sight of her bony frame and matted hair. "What in God's name are you doing throwing things at poor Effie?"

Mother yanked the blanket back over her head.

I sat in the chair nearest the bed and pressed the palms of my hands into the knees of my jeans. How was a nice woman like Charlotte going to make it here with Mother? I hadn't mentioned it to Charlotte, but Mother had already run off two companions in a matter of days. Both left abruptly in tears. For the past week Effie and I had been trying to manage Mother ourselves. Sadly, we were not very good at the job.

My focus at first had been to get Mother well enough to ship her back from whence she came. This required her to build her strength up by walking and eating, not hiding in this bed. However, it became abundantly clear that her eyesight had degenerated to the point where she saw only shapes and shadows, which was why she'd tripped and fallen in the first place. I'd arranged for a consultant from an organization for the blind to come out to the house and work with her on ways to get more independence back, in the form of a cane and other techniques. Mother had been so stubborn and obstinate the consultant had thrown up her hands in frustration and walked out the door.

Subsequently, I was forced to admit the truth. Mother couldn't live on her own. She needed to be here with her family. I needed to figure out a way for both of us to be happy again.

"Mother, we have to talk."

"Leave me alone." Her voice sounded muffled under the covers, yet still biting. Mother's words were like nails out of nail gun. Fast and fierce. No one was safe from their sharp points.

"I'm not leaving you alone. You're going to talk to me about what's going on with you. Giving up is not like you."

"It is now."

"The doctor said it will take time, but you can expect a full recovery. If you do your exercises and start walking a little every day."

"My eyesight won't recover. It'll only get worse."

"I've hired someone new to help you. Someone interesting."

She went still under the blanket. "Doubtful."

"Do you remember the great detective story we read over Christmas? The one Bliss's friend wrote?" Mother had asked if I'd read it to her as a treat for Christmas. I'd happily obliged. We'd sat on the couch by the fire sipping warm beverages and eating whatever Blythe brought out to us. By early evening, we'd finished the last page and agreed Luci Storm was our new favorite character. "That Charlotte Wilde knows how to tell a good yarn," Mother had said. My hope was that Mother wouldn't be able to resist a writer she admired. She revered artists of any kind. Over her long life, she'd donated a lot of funding to the arts, including writers.

"What about her?" Mother remained under the covers

"I've hired her to hang out with you."

"Hang out? I'm not thirteen."

"Well, whatever you want to call it, Bliss asked her to come spend time with us. She can write between visits with you. She's agreed to help you with your exercises and walks."

Mother drew back the covers to expose her face.

"What do you think?" I asked.

"Why would she come here? Isn't she a famous writer now?"

"Bliss said her first book didn't do as well as hoped and the agent says the new one is too dark."

"How stupid. I love that Luci Storm."

"Well, she needs time to sort out what to do next and here in the quiet is a great place to do it," I said.

"She must be broke." She moved to lay on her back.

"She indicated as much, yes. You know how hard it is to make money in the arts." I leaned closer and deployed my soothing voice. "Mother, she has a sweet nature—down to earth and clever. She has a good sense of humor, given her reaction to the elk."

"The elk?"

"I had to rescue her. They were blocking the road and the fields are all muddy and wet."

"This place is barbaric."

"She's wearing stylish jeans and black pumps. Kind of your style." Jeans that hugged every curve of her tight little body. I kept the image of her round breasts in that pink sweater to myself.

"Piercings? Tattoos, I suppose," Mother said.

"Not that I could see. She looks downright old-fashioned."

Mother brought her hands out from under the covers and clasped them together over her chest. "She sounds a step up from the first two."

"It's also a favor to Bliss. She asked if we could sort of look after Charlotte while she looks after us. Without a job like this she might not write another book." I knew an appeal to Mother's philanthropic side might influence her to give Charlotte a chance.

She did what my brothers and I called her *sniff and shrug,* like the entire subject bored her. "Fine. I'll see her."

"I'm going to give her some coffee and breakfast before bringing her up to meet you. She had a long trip from Boise this morning."

"I thought she lived in Portland?"

I smiled to myself. Mother remembered that detail from Charlotte's back cover biography. This was a positive sign. "She stayed in Boise last night after driving from Portland."

"She's not the snooty kind of writer, is she?" Mother asked as I rose to my feet. "Those are always so disappointing."

"Not a snooty bone in her body. She looks younger and more innocent than I would've thought," I said. "She was honestly scared of the elk."

"They have those eyes," Mother said. "Disconcerting."

"And she's quite small. Like a quarter horse." Compact with just the right curves, like her little blue car. People often looked like their cars or dogs, I'd noticed.

"What's her face like?"

"A young, more modern looking Sophia Loren." Over the past few months, I'd learned to describe people in ways Mother could best relate. "Round eyes the color of English breakfast tea." Her eyes were enough to wreck a man. And that mouth—sensual, full mouth begging for someone to kiss it.

"Is she Italian?" Mother asked.

"On her father's side." I loved her hair with those springy curls. "Her hair is massive. Super curly."

I retrieved a towel from the bathroom to clean up the mess on the wall. When I returned, Mother's mouth was set in a line of disapproval.

"Son, have you developed a crush on Charlotte Wilde already? Don't you dare make a move on her."

"Not that I'm one to *make* moves, but why shouldn't I?"

"Because these things never turn out for you. Do you really want to be responsible for her inability to write after your affair implodes?"

She had a point. Starting with my first unrequited love for Felicity Spinner when I was seventeen, most of my relationships had been disasters. Felicity never had eyes for anyone but Ciaran. Unlike my charming and clever brothers, I was shy and bookish. My father's voice came to me again.

Not with Charlotte.

There was a current that ran between Charlotte and me, connecting us somehow. I felt bold and witty when I was with her.

For now, I needed to concentrate on Mother.

"I'm going to bring Charlotte up in a few minutes. Please, be nice."

"No promises."

I hustled down the hallway toward the front room. Could Charlotte handle Mother? I prayed silently that her kind face hid an inner strength. Because I knew this already. I desperately wanted Charlotte Wilde to stay in Idaho.

CHAPTER FIVE

CHARLOTTE

I was reading the opening passage of a book about former lives when Ardan entered the living room.

"I'm sorry to have left you so abruptly," he said. "Mother was having a tantrum."

"I gathered as much."

He glanced toward the other end of the house as if his mother might hear him. "Let's talk outside."

We went back out to the patio and sat at the dining table under the umbrella. The morning sun shed warmth over the stone patio. Birds chirped from the trees. The scent of lilacs filled the air. I fidgeted, clenching and unclenching my hands under the table. So far everything about Idaho had been unnerving. Not bad, but unexpected, including the man next to me.

I took a good look at him. His hair was even more disheveled than earlier, like he'd tried to tear it from his head.

Effie came out to the patio dressed in a dark blue cotton dress and carrying a tray with a full coffee service. She'd washed and fixed her face.

"You're looking much better," I said.

"Thank you, Miss Wilde." She set the tray on the table and poured two cups of coffee. "Would you like cream and sugar?"

"Just milk, thank you."

"Half-and-half or shall I fetch the milk?"

"Whatever you have is fine." I crossed and uncrossed my legs under the table. No one fetched things for me. I was the fetcher.

Effie poured from the silver pitcher.

"I can add my own cream," I said.

"No, miss. I do that for you." Effie added cream and stirred it with a small spoon. She set the cup and saucer on the table in front of me. "May I get you anything else?"

I shook my head so hard a few of my curls got caught in my sticky lip gloss. "No. Thanks, though."

She did the same for Ardan, adding sugar and cream to his cup. When she left, Ardan turned to me. "Please let Effie know if you need anything. I want you to feel at home here."

"Thank you. I'm not particular. I don't want to cause Effie any trouble. I can take care of myself."

"Good luck with that. Effie's old school—trained in England by a former butler. For the life of me, I can't get her to stop calling me Mr. Lanigan. Every time, I think she's talking to my dad. I'm afraid Mother may run her off, and I'd be lost without her."

A weight of dread landed on my shoulders. Bliss hadn't said much about Riona Lanigan. Now I wondered if that was on purpose?

He spread his hands out on the table. "About Mother. She's always been difficult. Now that her movement and vision have been impaired, she's nearly impossible. I suppose it's obvious what she did to Effie this morning?"

"The stains on her dress and broken dishes were dead give-aways," I said.

"Last night she told me I was keeping her prisoner out here in the middle of nowhere."

Prisoner? Great. I was about to become her guard.

"Bliss said you could tame lions," he said. "Which is what we need. A lioness tamer."

"I've worked for a few tyrants." I had hoped those days were past me, but no such luck. "I've seen some temper tantrums in my time."

"Go in strong. The moment she senses timidity, she strikes. Like with poor Effie."

My teeth stuck to my dry mouth when I tried to smile. "I'll do my best."

"I love Mother. I mean, of course I do. She's my mother. But between you and me, I'm the only one of my siblings who can stand to have her stay for any length of time. She's utterly alienated both Blythe and Bliss. My sister avoids her with excuses about work."

He looked so worried I forgot my own angst. "It'll all be fine. Tell me what you need me to do."

"Keep her company during the day. Encourage her to eat. Make her do her physical therapy exercises. Get her outside for fresh air and short walks. The doctors said she needs to walk a little each day to rebuild her strength."

"I can do that."

"She naps in the afternoons and goes to bed early, so you'll have time to write," he said.

I nodded. If I could find my muse. Lately she seemed to have gone into hibernation. Could I find her in the shadow of Blue Mountain?

"And we've got to get her to eat something. She'll never get stronger if she doesn't have proper nutrition. She refuses to eat most days." He stood and gestured toward the house. "Let's do this."

"Fine. I'm ready." I drew in a deep, calming breath. Nothing to be worried about. I'd worked for some men who could curdle milk with a look.

I followed him down a hallway. "Your room will be upstairs. Mother's is on the first floor because of the stairs." He tapped on the door. A weak voice said to come in for Pete's sake. "You know I'm in here. Why're you knocking?"

He held the door for me to enter before him.

"Mother, I've brought Charlotte."

Mrs. Lanigan winced as she tried to sit up. Ardan went around the bed to slide another pillow behind her back. She was thin and bony. Her hair was dyed blond, but an inch of white roots showed. I had a feeling this was not typical. Was there anyone in town who did hair? I hadn't thought about that until now. Did Peregrine even have a hair salon?

"Hello, Mrs. Lanigan. It's nice to meet you." I stood by the bed and offered my hand.

She gave my fingers a quick squeeze. Not a handshake exactly. I guessed those were reserved for important people. She squinted as she turned her face toward me. "You have a squeaky voice, like a child."

"Squeaky?"

"Quite unpleasant. There's no wonder you became a writer. What else could you do?" Mrs. Lanigan smoothed her ratted hair.

"Mother, be nice," Ardan said as he opened a shade.

I laughed. "It's true. No one ever asked me to be in a movie or even a school play."

Mrs. Lanigan turned toward the light. "Why bother with the shades? It's not like I can see out."

"It'll warm the room," I said. "It's freezing in here."

"Son, you may leave now. Charlotte and I need to have a little chat."

"Do you promise to behave?"

"Get out," Mrs. Lanigan said.

Good luck, he mouthed to me as he left the room.

I glanced around, wondering if I should sit. The room was large for a guest room, with its own bathroom. An easy chair and desk were situated by the window. A wheelchair was parked near the bed. I grabbed the hardback chair from the desk and set it next to the bed.

I put on my invisible warrior armor. Nothing penetrated me when I was in this mode. Years of working for jerks had taught me that.

"Why are you here?" Mrs. Lanigan stared down at her lap.

"I heard Idaho is lovely in the spring."

"Ardan read me your book," she said. "Awful. Written for a third-grade level."

Good one. Go after my writing. Well played.

"I'm sorry you didn't enjoy it," I said.

"Bliss brags about you all the time," Mrs. Lanigan said. "As if knowing an author is like knowing the president."

I smiled. "Not exactly like that, no."

"I'm assuming you're broke, or you would never have agreed to come here," Mrs. Lanigan said.

"Yes, sadly, that's true." I spoke calmly. Teflon. Never let them see you flustered. "Completely my own fault, too."

"Overspending?"

"No, I'm quite frugal. I fell for a man named Zeke. He had a gambling problem and stole my savings, including my book advance money."

"What did you expect from a man named Zeke? I mean, really." There it was. A spark. Not dead yet. There was life in the old goat.

"In hindsight, that and his lack of a job might have been good indicators." A flash of Zeke played before me. His charming smile that first date. The way he'd wrapped himself around me like a snake with its prey. I'd told him every vulnerability within the first weeks. Later, he'd used every single one in mental warfare.

"What would you like to do today?" I made my voice as bright as the sun streaming through the window. "Ardan says you're supposed to take short walks to build up your strength. We could go out on the deck and get a little vitamin D."

She laced her knobby fingers together. "I'm not interested in going outside."

"Would you like me to order you an audible book to listen to? Or we could put on a movie."

"I don't want to do any of those things. I prefer to stay right here and wait to die."

"I don't think you're dying," I said. "You're much too mean to die."

The corners of her mouth twitched. "I ran the others off. I'll do the same to you."

"Not anytime soon."

"Because you're desperate, aren't you? At the end of your rope. Broke. Mediocre talent. No husband."

"I suggest putting your energy into something else because I'm not going anywhere."

A flush had settled on Mrs. Lanigan's cheeks as we talked. She liked sparring with me. Arguing might bring her back to life.

"What about your children?" I asked. "Surely you're interested in them?"

"My children don't come to see me much," Mrs. Lanigan said.

"They're busy?"

"They think I'm critical of them," she said.

"Are you?"

"They do a lot of stupid things," she said.

I stifled a laugh. "They're all grown. Maybe it's too late to help them now. The chance to do that would have been when they were young."

"What about you, Miss Wilde? What kind of mother did you have that raised such an insecure girl as to fall for a man named Zeke? Describe her succinctly. I don't have all day."

"Cashmere and pearls. Peach cobbler and lemon furniture polish. Calls everyone 'darling.' Ran my dad's dental practice with a light touch that hid an iron fist."

"What else?" she asked.

"Wears the words *smitten wife* and *adoring mother* on her forehead." Although not actually written on her forehead, they *were* the description on her Facebook profile. "My parents were college sweethearts." And still acted like it.

"What does she look like?" Mrs. Lanigan asked.

"Tall and reed thin. Curly chestnut hair. Fair skin."

"And your father?"

"The girls who worked for him called him a *Clooney*."

"How disgusting for you."

"Amen."

"Tell me more."

"College track star. Daddy and daughter dances. Generous." I touched the tennis bracelet on my wrist he'd given me when I graduated from college. "Voted best pediatric dentist in Lake Oswego. He has dark skin like mine, with chocolate brown eyes, and salt and pepper hair. Women fell all over themselves the moment he appeared."

"So, there's money," she said.

"Yes. Not Lanigan money, but they did well."

"Are they disappointed in you?"

"No. They're proud. They believe in me. Always have," I said.

"You're overly attached to them." She said this as a definite statement.

"Quite." I smiled, remembering our weekly Thursday dinners. I'd keep that to myself.

"Only children. It happens. How old are you?"

"A bit over thirty," I said. "Too old to be heartbroken that they sold their house and dental practice to travel the country in an Airstream."

"An Airstream? I can imagine nothing worse," she said.

"I'll have to agree with you there. Their house was beautiful. My mother kept it just so." I missed the way it smelled like bacon and maple syrup on Sunday mornings.

"You know, one learns how to negotiate the world by interacting with their siblings. Perhaps this is your trouble. You're strange and needy, thus no luck with men."

"It's a good theory," I said.

"Your lack of self-esteem is curious given your father's obvious devotion."

"My issues can't be blamed on my parents," I said.

"How refreshing. My children love to blame me for all their problems." She drew in a deep breath.

"I have a few fatal flaws for which I have no one to blame but myself," I said.

"Can't you have only one?" she asked.

"In literature, perhaps. But in real life most of us come with at least a half dozen."

"List them, please."

Her expression was almost animated. Mrs. Lanigan was interested in people and what made them tick. This was something we had in common.

"Off the top of my head, I'd have to say foremost is bad judgment when it comes to men. I always choose the wrong ones. I'm in love with love which makes me blind to their faults until it's too late."

She tilted her head to the side. "If you know this about yourself, then why do you keep doing it?"

"That's why it's a fatal flaw."

"Or is it that you don't feel you deserve someone good?" she asked. "Blind as I am, I can see you wear your insecurity like a crown of thorns."

"I'm not the type who gets asked to the dance," I said.

"You need to wait for the right one to ask. Don't give yourself to an unworthy man. You haven't been patient enough."

"I'm not sure that's it. Have you ever thought maybe some people are meant to be alone? Like there's just no one right for them?"

I surprised myself with how vulnerable I was with Mrs. Lanigan. Despite her bite, I liked her. She was strong and insightful under her fear.

"Don't be morose," she said, gentler than previously. I'd gotten to her. She liked me too. "You're young. My son told me you're beautiful. You'll find the right one."

Ardan had said I was beautiful. Angels sang in my ears.

"You're pleased by that?" she asked.

"Who wouldn't be?"

"Tell me who you look like. Someone I know from my era"

"I look like my father's Italian mother," I said.

"Do I know your grandmother? Honestly, you can't follow a direction to save your life."

"Right. Someone you know." Who were movie stars from her era? "A friend of my father's once told me I looked like a fat Audrey Hepburn. He could make a compliment into an insult like no one's business."

Mrs. Lanigan sniffed. "Bliss and Blythe are always talking about that waif."

"Audrey Hepburn?"

"Yes. They love her for some reason. I always thought she looked like an elf."

I laughed. "I would love to look like her."

"My son said you look like a modern Sophia Loren. *She* was a great beauty."

"I'm no Sophia Loren," I said. "Trust me." My insides hummed with a thousand happy bees. Ardan thought I looked like Sophia Loren? How was that possible? Who cared? He thought I was pretty.

"It's unbecoming to be so insecure," Mrs. Lanigan said. "Let me tell you about my friend Sky. She wore these awful socks instead of stockings because she thought her ankles were too big. They *made* her ankles look big by drawing attention to them. Don't point out your flaws. Most people are too stupid to see them anyway."

"Maybe they're just too polite to point them out," I said.

"Either way, keep them to yourself."

"I'll try and remember that."

"Ardan's also had disastrous love affairs. Like you, he isn't able to discern a woman's true nature."

"Until it's too late," I said.

"Exactly." Her skin was remarkably smooth for a woman in her eighties. Too smooth. Taut. She'd had work done. Good for her.

"It's perfectly obvious what one of your other fatal flaws is," she said. "You're remarkably frank without any sense that you should hide your vulnerabilities. You shouldn't tell people things they can use against you."

I laughed. "It takes too much energy to be fake. Plus, I only do that when I really like someone."

She played with the edge of a blanket with her fingertips. "Whether you like me or not means nothing to me."

"Excellent. I feel the same way about you."

"Good. We can agree this is a relationship of captor and guard."

I laughed. "That works. As much fun as this has been, it's time to get you up and into the fresh air."

She crossed her arms over her chest and shook her head. "No thank you."

"You can't stay in this bed all day."

"I told you. I'm waiting to die. Nothing else." She lifted her chin to the ceiling like a stubborn child.

"You've plenty of life left," I said.

"Trite, Miss Wilde. You can do better."

I took a moment to think through my strategy. "Ardan said you see only shadows and shapes?" I asked.

A curt nod.

"How long?" I asked.

"It's been deteriorating for a year. That's why I fell. I hadn't told any of the children, but now the cat's out of the bag." She set her mouth in a firm line.

"But why would you keep it from your family?" I asked.

"I'm afraid they'll put me in a home."

"Not Ardan. You're here at his home, aren't you?"

"Because he thinks he can get rid of me soon. If they could, they'd ship me off to one of those places that smells of urine."

"I don't think so." I studied her. What would it take to get her out of this bed? "What do you like to do? I mean, when you're not recovering from a hip fracture?"

"Shopping. Lunching with my friends. Hosting parties. Art openings. The opera. All the usual things. Now, I'm useless."

"We could choose a classic novel. I could read to you."

"With your squeaky voice? Dreadful."

"Television? Do you like to binge watch series?"

"Pedestrian," she said. "Plus, I can't see the screen."

"Music?"

"Miss Wilde, you're boring me now. I preferred when you were spilling your guts."

I looked around the room, hoping to find inspiration. Decorated in sage green and black, the room was tidy but without much life. A guest room, not a home. A shipping box on the table by the window drew my attention. "What's in that box?" I asked.

"There's a box?"

I crossed over to the table. "It's addressed to you."

"From who?"

"Carly Cooper."

"I don't know her."

"Would you like me to open it?"

"Suit yourself."

I found a letter opener on the desk and used it to cut open the box. A card addressed to Mrs. Lanigan lay on top of tissue paper. "It's a card."

"Read it to me," she said.

"In my squeaky voice?"

"Beggars can't be choosers."

I slid the notecard from the envelope and read to her from the thick card stock.

Dear Mrs. Lanigan,

My husband and I bought the home once occupied by your parents. We recently did a renovation that required structural changes in the attic. We were surprised to find a box of letters tucked behind an eave, making them impossible to see without proper light. Given the dates on some of the envelopes, they've been hidden away up there for many, many years. As you'll see when you open the box, they are a jumbled mess.

I thought to ask around the neighborhood if anyone recalled the previous owners. Our next-door neighbors are in their eighties and remembered you from school. They said they lost touch with you after your parents' death the summer after you all graduated from high school. They knew only that Augie and Nicholas's daughter had married the famous Edward Lanigan of Lanigan Trucking. Because of that, I was able to locate your sons and daughter on Facebook. Your son, Ciaran, and his wife, Bliss, are easy to find, given their philanthropic work. Ciaran was kind enough to answer my email message and asked that I send the box, thinking you might be interested in the contents of the letters.

Wishing you a wonderful trip down memory lane. I'd give so much to have a glimpse into my mother's young adulthood. I wouldn't have been able to live with myself had I not made sure you received them.

Sincerely,

Carly Cooper

I set aside the card and investigated further. There were at least a hundred letters strewn about the box. I rummaged around until I found one in an envelope with a date stamp. "This is addressed to Augusta Devin from Nicholas Garfield. The date stamp says January 1938." I glanced over at Mrs. Lanigan, expecting her to be as excited as I. "Are they your parents?"

"Quite the curious cat, aren't you?"

"I'm a writer," I said. "I can't help myself."

"Yes, those are my parents. 1938 is the year they met. I was born two years later."

"Do you think they're love letters?" I asked.

"I remember Mother saying they'd written letters when they were courting because she lived in a chaperoned house and wasn't allowed out at night very often. Don't expect anything riveting. My parents were middle class country people." She sniffed and gestured toward the box. "But still, I might like you to read one or two."

"So, you *are* curious? Dare I say interested?"

"Yes, I'm curious. Are you happy?" She tugged at the blanket in a gesture of impatience.

"As a matter of fact, I am."

"Voyeurism is a very unattractive quality," she said.

I laughed, which made her mouth twitch again. There was something so familiar about Mrs. Lanigan that made me more comfortable than I should be. I picked up another envelope. "Some are from him to her. They're all mixed up though. Most aren't even in envelopes."

"My mother probably thought she'd go through them at some point and put them in order. They didn't expect to die in their early forties."

"How did they die?"

"They were killed in a car accident on the way home from dropping me at the train station. I was leaving for college in California. We lived out in the country in Indiana. Long country roads. People drove too fast."

"I'm sorry. That must have been hard."

"The only comfort is they went together. I couldn't imagine either of them wanting to live without the other. They were fiercely loyal and madly in love. Other than my father's time overseas for WWII, they spent every evening of their marriage holding hands on the porch swing or the couch."

"I want that with someone someday," I said dreamily.

"Charlotte Wilde, no good ever came from being a romantic. You must be realistic. Fairy tales aren't real."

I blinked, yanked from my dream world into the real one.

She clasped her hands together. "Are they all typewritten?"

"No, the ones from Augusta are handwritten."

"What's the writing like?"

"Loopy and round," I said.

"That's her writing, yes." She clapped her hands like I was a misbehaving pet. "Open one and read it to me."

I tried to remain calm, but I was practically twitching. I

unfolded the one in my hand. "There's no date or envelope," I said before reading out loud.

Dear Augie,

My brother is dead. The doctor and police said Boyce drank poison. They think it was suicide. He would never take his own life. He loved Mother and me too much to leave this way. I am certain he was murdered. You and I both know by whom and why. There's no way I'll ever prove it.

I love you, my dearest Augie. I won't be able to come for you tomorrow as planned. I must stay and bury him. I'll send this note over with Fred. Wait for further news. I'll come get you as soon as I can. Keep your bags packed.

Yours,

Nicholas

Mrs. Lanigan's hands shook. "My father always told me he was an orphan, which I took to mean his family died when he was young. He never mentioned a brother."

"He said he knows who killed him. Do you think the answers are in these letters?"

"How many are there?"

"Probably a hundred." I explained how they looked like they'd just been tossed into the box. "Most aren't dated and have no envelopes, like they were hand delivered by this Fred. I'd have to read them all to try and piece together the order."

"Would you?"

"It'll take a while, but yes. I'd be happy to."

She touched her trembling fingers to her temple. "I don't know what to think."

It occurred to me these letters could be used as bargaining chips to coax Mrs. Lanigan back into life. "Let's make a deal. One letter in exchange for a walk and a meal that you actually eat instead of throw at the wall?"

"For the record, I was frustrated because I burned my mouth."

"I can see how that would frustrate you." How terrifying it must be to face this without any tools. I added that to my list of items to conquer. Mrs. Lanigan must learn how to navigate the world without her sight. "Next meal, I'll be here to describe where everything is and to make sure nothing's too hot."

"This is extortion," she said. "Using the letters to make me do your bidding."

"It's for your own good."

She released a shaky breath. "How fitting that you're bribing me with the past. I have no future, I may as well go back."

I moved from the chair to perch on the edge of the bed. "I know you're frightened. Who wouldn't be?"

"I'd be better off dead."

"Your children don't think so," I said.

"You sure about that?"

"Is that your fear or the truth?"

"It's the truth." She sighed. "Believe me, I know my own children."

My mother always told me the way to get people to open up to you was to be vulnerable about your own fears and worries. "I'm scared too."

"Of what? Not me, apparently."

I smiled. "Not you, no. But most other things. Failure. Loneliness. Dying alone with a cat who eats me before anyone discovers my body."

Mrs. Lanigan shook her head and smiled. Not just a twitch, but a full smile. "That's a bit far-fetched."

"I was afraid to come here. Just driving here was scary. Then, the elk were there, which made it even worse."

"You have your whole life ahead of you. Mine is over." A lone tear leaked from one eye and rolled down her cheek. "I don't know how to live this way."

"I'll help you. We'll figure it out together." I took one of her hands. "You won't be alone."

"We're always alone. We come in alone and go out alone."

"But there's all that time in between where we can be together."

"You may go now, Miss Wilde."

"Please, call me Charlotte."

"Very well. I'll remain Mrs. Lanigan."

"Yes ma'am."

* * *

Ardan was coming in from the patio when I walked into the main living room carrying the box of letters. "How did it go?" he asked.

"Quite well."

"Really?" He raised an eyebrow.

"I made some inroads." I set the box of letters on the coffee table.

"What did you do? And what's in the box?"

I quickly told him about the contents and how the letters arrived here. "Read this." I handed him the letter I'd read to Mrs. Lanigan and waited while he read.

"This is astonishing on many levels," Ardan said.

"Your mother thought so too. Her father told her he had no family."

"That's what we've always believed."

"We know he had a brother," I said. "Who was murdered in 1938. I plan on sorting through the box to see if I can get more information."

"Isn't it odd you happened to pick this one?" he asked as he peered into the box. "I mean, this is a mess in here."

"That's exactly what I thought. Like it was meant to be. Your mother needs something to interest her, to motivate her to start living again. And bam, I pull out this letter. It's like magic."

"Or a higher power," Ardan said. "I *have* been praying for a miracle."

"We might just have found one." I shared with him my strategy to motivate Mrs. Lanigan with the letters. "She called it extortion but agreed to it anyway."

"A mystery writer unfolds a mystery right here in my own house," he said.

"I can't wait to sort through these letters. It's going to take a while."

"I'll help," he said. "We can use my study. There's a table in there. We can spread them all out and see if we can put them in chronological order."

A project. Time with Ardan. Sign me up.

He smiled. "I'm glad you're here. The tightness in my chest has lessened."

"It's good to feel useful." I smiled back at him. The current buzzed between us.

"Come on, I'll show you to your room. I already took your suitcases up." He grabbed the box of letters and asked me to follow. "We'll get your car tomorrow, if that's okay?"

"Fine with me," I said.

We walked up a two-level staircase to the second floor. He chatted about the house along the way, telling me he'd had it built just after his brother Finn died to busy himself in the details of the construction. "I found it easier to cope with my grief when surrounded by minutiae."

"I remember how that is," I said.

He shot me a quizzical look.

"When I was fourteen, my best friend was murdered." I didn't usually talk about Roberta. People always wanted to know more, and I didn't enjoy reliving that awful time. Ardan, however, was not like other people. If he asked questions, I wouldn't mind. "I buried myself in schoolwork and swimming. But the grief's still there anyway. There's not a day I don't think about Roberta."

"Is that why you decided to become a mystery novelist?"

No one had ever asked me that before. My parents knew this to be true, but it was an unspoken understanding between us that almost every aspect of my life had been shaped by Roberta's death. "I think so. My friend Susan's a romance writer. She hasn't yet found her Prince Charming, but she believes if she keeps writing about love eventually it will come to her real life. I like that I can always solve the crime, unlike real life."

We arrived at the end of the hallway. "This is your room," he said.

He held the door open for me. I passed by him, inhaling his spicy scent. The smell of Ardan. Like nothing else. It was already familiar to me, as was the curve of his jawline and the particular blue of his eyes.

My suitcases were tucked beside a dresser. I thanked him for bringing them upstairs.

"You're welcome. Will this do?" he asked.

"Sure. It's fantastic." The room was larger than I'd expected and decorated in pink and white accessories. The furniture was wood with a black finish, including a queen bed, dresser, and desk.

"Will the pink bother you? I had this room decorated for my smallest niece, Clementine—Blythe's daughter. The girls stay with me sometimes in the summer when their parents want privacy. I asked Clemmie what she wanted, and she said pink. Her sister picked turquoise and black."

"I love pink. How sweet of you to give them their own rooms."

"They've wrapped me around their pretty little fingers. I love being an uncle."

"I'd like to be your niece." I blurted it out before thinking. My cheeks burned. "Sorry, that sounded dirty." Yet another inappropriate sentence out of my mouth before I could stop it.

The corners of his eyes crinkled. "It *did* sound a little dirty."

"I'm sorry. The altitude's making me loopy." It wasn't the altitude unless its name was Ardan Lanigan.

"I hope that's not all it is," he said.

"What else could it be?" I flashed him a flirtatious smile. What was happening to me? I did not flirt with men I'd just met, especially ones who were technically my boss. Ardan was different. I knew him already. There was a connection, like a current of electricity that no one could see or feel but us.

"Maybe you have a little crush on me?" he asked. "Could that be it?"

"Maybe." We smiled like goons at each other for a moment before he crossed over to the windows and opened the curtains.

"You have a view of Blue Mountain from the desk." He opened the window a few inches. "I thought you'd like that for writing."

I went to the window to get a better view. The top of the mountain was still covered in snow, stark white against the cobalt blue sky. A shaft of sunlight kissed my skin. I caught a whiff of fir trees. "I feel alive here."

A muscle in his jaw twitched. He turned slightly to gaze down at me. "I do too. More than anywhere in the world."

"Have you been a lot of places?"

"I have, yes."

"I've never been out of the country," I said. "I'd like to travel but haven't had the funds so far."

I'll take you everywhere you want to go.

I started. Had he said that aloud? His face was impassive. I'd imagined the words, perhaps because I wanted to hear them.

"Why is it named Blue Mountain?" I asked.

"At twilight it looks blue," he said. "That's my guess. No one knows for sure."

"I'll love writing in here. I'll never want to leave."

"You can stay as long as you like."

Stay forever.

That time I knew I was imagining it.

"I'm relieved Mother didn't make you cry. The other two cried within the first hour."

"I'm tougher than I look," I said.

"I noticed."

"I find her funny."

"Funny?"

"She makes grumpiness an art form. Plus, I know just where I stand with her. I find it refreshing."

"Refreshing's one way to put it."

"She's surprisingly perceptive." I rubbed the window with my sleeve, pretending there was a spot, to distract myself from the urge to lean against him. "She was right about my luck with men."

"Bliss told me what happened," he said.

I turned to him, surprised. "She told you about Zeke?"

"No. I meant about the guy who harassed you at the company party."

"Oh, right. *That* thing."

"Sadly, it seems most women have a similar story," Ardan said.

"I'm fine. It's not like what's happened to so many others. He tried to put his hand up my skirt, but he didn't get very far. I was too fast for him. The second I felt him go for it, I stabbed his hand with a fork." I'd been about to stab a brownie when I'd felt his greasy breath on my neck.

"Did you hurt him?"

I grimaced. "Not any permanent damage. Barely punctured the skin. I did negotiate a nice settlement though. It was the first brave thing I've ever done. I walked into the Human Resources office and told them what happened and what I wanted. I'd calculated it out that if I lived frugally, the money would give me five years to write before I'd have to get a real job again. I made a bargain with myself. Choose myself for once. That's how I got the first book written and published. Then I messed it up by getting involved with Zeke."

He sat down in the cozy white chair in the corner. "Zeke?"

I crossed the room and sat on the bed. "He's my ex-boyfriend. We broke up after he threatened to kill me, drained my savings account, and took off with my nubile neighbor for a gambling binge in Vegas."

His eyes widened. "No!"

"Yes. I didn't know everything about him. Obviously." At the time, he'd seemed like the perfect man. Medical student. Wealthy family.

"I'd say. Did you get your money back?" he asked.

"No. It was lost on the ponies, so to speak." The entire advance from my book and the settlement, gone in a weekend. I didn't know if it was ponies or casino tables. In the end, it didn't matter. Nothing was left. "That money was supposed to keep me from a day job, so I could keep writing."

"Is he dangerous?" he asked.

"Not anymore. He's dead."

"Dead?"

"Yes, it really takes the sting out of hating his guts," I said.

"What happened to him?"

"Someone shot him. The authorities suspect it was gambling related. Fortunately, I had a rock-solid alibi or they might have suspected me." I smiled to let him know I was joking. "I was at the gym swimming my half mile, like every morning. The staff vouched for me."

"They say exercise helps all areas of one's life."

I laughed. "This was certainly a good example."

"How long ago did this happen?"

"Ten months ago. Honestly, this job was like a lifesaver. I didn't want to go back to a corporate job. Bliss said the Idaho air would be good for my creativity."

"Are you angry?" he asked.

"It's over now. I mean, I *was* angry. Absolutely furious, especially because I couldn't do anything about it. Then the asshole ends up dead, so I couldn't even have my day in court."

"It's not as satisfying as you might think." His voice deepened a register. "Your person's still gone."

"Yes. And this was just money. Not the life of someone I loved. That's something you can never forgive."

"Did they ever find Roberta's killer?" he asked.

"Yes, they did." I loved that he said her name. "He was someone we knew. They say that's usually the case."

"It was for us."

"I knew the minute I heard the news. I'd been home sick from school that day. Normally, Roberta and I walked to and from school together. Her house was two doors down from mine." I gritted my teeth to stop the tremor in my voice before continuing. "All year I'd noticed one of the janitors at school staring at her in the hallways and the lunchroom. When we left school in the afternoons, he was always over by the dumpsters, watching us. We talked about it many times. I realized too late we should have told an adult, but we thought he was just a creepy guy. Roberta was beautiful. A lot of guys stared at her."

"Did you speak up right away?"

"Yes. The minute my parents told me the news, I knew with complete certainty. Have you ever had that feeling? Like you know something deep in your bones?"

"Once or twice."

"He'd been waiting for a time when she was alone. When the police came to our house to question me, I told them my suspicion. They brought him in for questioning and matched the DNA evidence he'd left. He raped her before he choked her to death." I bit the inside of my mouth to keep from crying. The thought of what she endured in her last minutes of life was a black, helpless rage that closed around my heart, even after all these years. "They convicted him. He was sentenced to life in prison without parole." I blinked back tears. "When I think of how...of what he did...and that they were her last moments on earth, I just can't understand why."

"I wish I didn't get it, but I do."

He did, of course, only too well. The shared language of grief did not need words or even descriptions. From one battered heart to another, we understood.

Ardan tilted his head, studying me. "Talking to you it's as if we've known each other—"

I finished the sentence for him. "Forever." The sensation of belonging to him, of being understood by him in ways no one else ever could, washed over me in warm waves.

He shoved his hands in the pockets of his jeans. "You'll need a pair of boots if you stay past the summer."

"What?"

"I don't know why I said that—it just slipped out." It was his turn to blush.

I grinned at his discomfort. "We're even then. One inappropriate comment about being your niece. One outlandish comment about how long I'll be here. Check and check."

He laughed. "After you unpack, come down for lunch. Effie's making chopped salads."

"With garbanzo beans and salami?" My mouth watered. "That's my favorite."

"I believe so." I watched as he crossed to the doorway and into the hallway. Could his backside look any better in those jeans?

He turned back to me. "I'm sorry the elk scared you, but I'm glad Mother didn't."

"It was an inauspicious start to my time here. However, the ensuing rescue made it all worth it."

"What kind of host would I be if I let you ruin your pretty shoes upon your arrival?" He winked and left.

I unpack faster than I'd ever unpacked in my life. All I wanted was to be near him. And that salad sounded darn good. Effie was going to make me fatter.

As I hung clothes and organized my toiletries in the bathroom, I thought over the morning's events. It was as if my life before was a distant dream. I loved this new world of elk, Effie, and Mrs. Lanigan. And Ardan Lanigan. Especially him.

Ardan wasn't like the men I knew in Portland. They were hipsters with beards and tattoos who lacked any sense of chivalry, perhaps in the name of feminism, but it was more likely laziness mixed with improper etiquette training. Men no longer opened doors or held the elevator, perhaps too busy looking at memes on their phones. Ardan was like a man from another era. Polite and just on the edge of shy, he had an old school formality about him, yet was approachable and seemingly without affect.

After I finished unpacking, I freshened my makeup and changed into a cotton skirt and t-shirt. I looked at myself in the full-length mirror. Was I losing my mind, or did I look better in Idaho? Or maybe it was just the glow of Ardan Lanigan?

* * *

Ardan wasn't in the living room when I returned downstairs. A shrill scream came from the kitchen. Alarmed, I ran into the room. Ardan and Effie stood together at the island looking at an upside-down glass on the counter.

"I heard a scream. Is everything all right?" I crossed over to the island.

"It was me, miss. I saw a spider," Effie said.

"We've trapped it." Ardan pointed at the glass. "And now we're wondering what to do with it."

"What to do with it?" I asked, unsure how to read the situation.

Effie shook her head. Her finely trimmed hair swung from side to side. "We're afraid this might be a brown recluse."

I stepped backward, knocking a stool with my hip. "Why do you think so?"

Ardan held up his phone. "We looked it up. And it matches the picture we found."

"Can you squash it?" I shivered. "I hate spiders."

"We do too, miss," Effie said. "But not enough to kill them. Mr. Lanigan prefers they be taken outside."

"Unless they're venomous. In which case, we've no choice but to kill them. Right?" He looked over at me as if I were the spider-killing-decision-maker.

"I kill them no matter if they're venomous or not," I said.

"Mr. Lanigan's too kind-hearted for that, miss," Effie said. "He can't bear to hurt any living creature."

"Even spiders?"

She nodded solemnly.

"They're helpless," Ardan said. "We're so powerful. It's not really fair."

"Regardless, they're creepy," I said. "Venom or not. You've got to squash them with your shoe."

"You're ruthless," Ardan said. "I didn't see that coming."

I looked over at him. He watched me with a slight smile. If I hadn't been so concerned that a venomous spider was trying to crawl up the side of a glass feet from me, I might have gotten lost in our little world again. However, a potentially life-snatching spider took precedence. I scratched the base of my skull. Were they crawling everywhere? Idaho must be full of spiders, given the number of trees. Was it a common occurrence that they entered the house? I would have assumed a new house would be tight as a drum. No open spaces for a spider to crawl into and make their way to my bedroom.

"How did it get in the house?" I had to ask. "Do you have a lot of spiders?"

Effie pointed toward a box on the table. "It came in there." The side of the box was labeled "Carver Farms."

"Local fresh produce," Ardan said. "The box comes once a week."

"It was on the lettuce bunch," Effie said. "Thankfully, Mr. Lanigan was here and acted quickly."

"I had to sacrifice my water," he said.

"All right. We have to take this situation in hand," I said. "The spider has to go." We all stood there looking at one another. "Well, I'm not going to do it. I'm the new girl. The city mouse."

I heard the clicking of heels on the hardwood floors and turned to see Bliss in the doorway. The spider flew from my mind at the sight of her. She was as gorgeous as always, tall and athletic looking, with dewy skin and lustrous honey-hued hair, but there was something distinctly different about her since the last time I'd seen her. She was pregnant. Quite pregnant, if the size of her belly was any clue.

"Bliss, I had no idea," I said as we wrapped our arms around each other.

"I wanted to surprise you. I'm due next month," Bliss said. "Can you believe I'm going to be a mother?"

"You'll be a great one," I said. "But I *am* surprised." When I worked for her, Bliss was the most driven woman I'd ever met. She did little else but work in those days. In fact, I'd never seen her without a phone or a laptop in her hands. Idaho and a Lanigan man had obviously changed her.

"Charlotte, you look wonderful." She looked over at Ardan. "Did she meet Mrs. Lanigan yet? Has she agreed to stay?" She turned back to me. "Have you agreed to stay?"

"Yes, Mrs. Lanigan will be just fine," I said. "I've dealt with more difficult bosses. Not to worry."

Bliss seemed to notice the spider under the glass for the first time. "What's that?"

"We think it's a brown recluse," Ardan said. "We're about to draw straws to see who has to kill it."

"For heaven's sake." Bliss removed her ballerina flat and flew around the corner of the island. Like a superhero, she lifted the glass and smashed the spider with her shoe.

Effie screamed. I gasped. Ardan's eyes widened as he stumbled back from the counter. Bliss held up her shoe. The spider's remains were stuck to the bottom in a gooey mess. I shivered again.

"Get rid of it," Effie said to Bliss. "You can't have it on your shoe and walk on my clean floors. I just cleaned up from Mr. Lanigan's boots."

"Effie, you're such a stickler for rules." Bliss tore a paper towel from the dispenser and wiped the bottom of her shoe.

"Outside with that please, Mrs. Lanigan." Effie already had a can of sanitizing cleaner aimed at the counter where the spider had been. "Put it in the rubbish bin in the garage. I can't have it anywhere near me."

Bliss tossed her hair behind her shoulders and laughed. "You should all be ashamed the pregnant lady had to kill the spider."

She was already across the room and yanking open the door to the garage.

Effie exhaled and picked up the glass with the tips of her fingers. "We'll just put this in the dishwasher and be done with it."

Bliss returned with the same satisfied smile she'd left with. "Now, where were we?"

"I was about to make Mr. Lanigan and Miss Wilde lunch. Would you care for a bite, Mrs. Lanigan?" Effie wiped the counter with a paper towel like she wanted to punish the granite.

"No, thanks Effie. I only came by to say hello to Charlotte. I have to drive to Hailey to pick up the last few items for the baby."

We chatted for a few minutes before Bliss headed out the door, promising to visit again soon.

After she left, I turned to Effie and Ardan. "Tell me the truth. How many spiders are in this house?"

Ardan shook his head and laughed. "None. Effie keeps it too clean."

"It was the box, miss. I swear."

"Okay, because when I get into bed tonight, I don't want to worry about one crawling in there with me. This city girl does not do spiders."

"I swear you're safe," Ardan said.

"From spiders anyway," Effie said with a mischievous glint in her eyes.

"If I get eaten by a bear, you'll have my mother to deal with," I said. "And you don't want that."

* * *

After lunch, Ardan and I talked in his study. I'd come up with a few ideas for Mrs. Lanigan that I wanted to run by him. One was to load her phone with audiobooks. He agreed, but said he'd already suggested it to her and she'd flatly turned him down. "She said she won't be able to operate the device to play them. Which is a good point," he said.

"I'll find a way. Do you have a pair of headphones I could give her?"

He reached into a drawer in his desk and pulled out a high-end pair with soft cushions. "She broke her phone when she dropped it. I tried to get her another one, but she refused." He pushed a tablet across the desk. "We can load them onto this."

"What type of books does she enjoy?" I asked.

"Mysteries, historical fiction. No romance. She says romances are for dreamers."

"Romances it is, then."

He laughed. "You have a wicked streak."

I fluttered my eyelashes. "Not me."

We chose a dozen audiobooks we thought she'd enjoy and downloaded them onto the tablet.

I suggested we have another consultant come out to teach Mrs. Lanigan techniques for independent living.

"I know it would change so much for her, but I'm not holding my breath," he said. "You underestimate the Lanigan stubbornness."

"I'll work on her. One day at a time."

For the next hour, we stood side by side to sort through the letters, grouping all the ones with dates or date stamps in one pile on the table and the ones without in another. Letters in envelopes with just a handwritten name and no address were put in a third stack. Next, we put the thirty or so dated envelopes, all with letters inside, into chronological order. After that was done, we both read through the first several letters. "I can't wait to read these to your mother," I said.

Ardan stared at the wall. A flush had risen to his cheeks.

"What is it?" I asked.

"Nothing. Or, I'm not sure if it's something. After you read these to Mother, please tell me what she says."

The sound of the bell interrupted further conversation. Mrs. Lanigan was awake from her nap. "I'll bring her a snack and the promise to read the first two letters out loud if she'll eat. What's something she can't resist?"

"Sharp cheddar cheese and Honeycrisp apples," he said. "But you won't get her to eat them."

"Is that a challenge, Mr. Lanigan?"

His eyes twinkled at me. "Maybe."

"What do I get if I win?"

He stuttered an answer. "I'll...I'll have to think about that."

"Don't think too hard. I wouldn't want you to waste energy that could be used for other activities."

I didn't wait for a response. As I crossed to the doorway, I felt his gaze following me. I smiled all the way to the kitchen.

I asked Effie if she would cut some cheese and apples slices for Mrs. Lanigan. "Please arrange her food like the hands of a clock. That way she'll know what's where."

"Will do, miss." Effie practically danced toward the refrigerator. "You're a clever one."

Effie's hands flew as she cut perfectly even slices of both cheese and apples. "I got these especially for her at the store yesterday." She made a row of apples near the top of the plate and cheese on the bottom. "Mr. Lanigan told me she liked them, but I was too afraid to try again after the breakfast incident."

I explained about Mrs. Lanigan's frustration over burning herself. "Everything's foreign to her and scary. Not that it's any excuse for throwing dishes at you." Then, I told a small fib. "She feels terrible and asked me to tell you how sorry she is."

Effie's eyes shone with compassion. "It must be awful. Tell her I accept her apology."

"Until I get her sorted out, please let me bring all her meals. There's no reason for you to fall victim to her moods."

"That would be a great relief," Effie said. "Thank you."

"It's going to all work out," I said. "Don't worry."

Armed with the snack, headphones, and tablet, I made my way to Mrs. Lanigan's room. "May I come in?" I asked at the door.

"I called for you, didn't I?"

She was in bed, leaning against a stack of pillows.

"Did you have a good rest?" I asked.

"Not really. It's hotter than Hades in here."

"It *is* warm." I glanced around the room. There was a ceiling vent near the window that would be for air conditioning or heat, depending on the season. I set the tray on the end of the bed and went to inspect. "Ah, here's the trouble. The vent was closed. Ardan might have worried you would get cold."

"He thinks all old ladies are chronically cold."

"My mother's always cold. Not that she's an old lady. I think it's because she's so skinny." I stood on the hardback chair to open the vent. Immediately, air came through, rustling my curls. "That should do it."

"It won't help. It's like a prison camp in Africa in here." She raised her chin and sniffed the air. "What's that stink?"

"I've brought a snack. Apples and cheese."

She licked her lips. I got her. She *was* hungry, and I'd brought just the snack to tempt her.

"Doesn't that sound great?" I asked.

She scowled. "What kind?"

"Sharp cheddar and Honeycrisp. Effie got them especially for you."

"I don't care for that combination."

"Ardan said it was your favorite."

"It was at one time."

"Good, because you're going to eat them."

"I'm not a child." She crossed her arms over her chest.

"Then stop acting like one." I sat on the side of the bed. "I'm putting a rectangular tray on your lap." I snapped the legs of the tray open and placed it carefully around her thighs. "The plate's in the middle of the tray. From now on, food will be arranged like the hands of a clock. That way you'll know what to look for. Apples at twelve and cheese at six."

She touched the edge of the tray, then ran her fingers all around the circumference of the plate.

"Good," I said. "It's best to understand the size and shape of things. Now, eat up and I'll read you the first two letters."

Her eyelids fluttered. She sat up straighter. "You found them?"

"Yes, and you'll want to hear them."

"This is blackmail."

"Technically, it's bribery," I said.

"You're a bad person."

"It's true." I sat in my usual chair and pulled the two letters out of my pocket. "Go ahead. I'm waiting."

"Fine." She felt with her fingers until she found the apples and the cheese, then popped one of each in her mouth and chewed dramatically. "Happy now?"

"I am. Keep eating."

She gobbled another. I was right. She was half-starved.

"I'm the only one who needs to be on a hunger strike," I said.

"Are you fat?" She ate another.

"Chubby."

"Give me your arm. I want to feel."

I put my arm out in front of her. She gave my upper arm a good squeeze.

"Muscle," she said. "Not fat."

"I swim a lot. But I'm wide. Everywhere."

"All the girls want to look like twigs now. It's not attractive."

"I want to look like one, but it's not going to happen." I described my height and measurements. "My D cups and big butt were given to me from my grandmother. My mother's a tall twig. So unfair." I smiled, thinking of my pretty mother and her pearls and dresses. She would think Mrs. Lanigan was hilarious too. My mother was also a lion tamer, only her forte was little children. She could wrestle a child into the dentist's chair and get him settled in for an exam with one hand tied behind her back and not even break a sweat.

"I can hear you smiling," she said.

"I was thinking about my mother."

"What about her?"

"She was very good with the children at my father's office. The kids loved coming there, once they met my mom. She could win over even the most reluctant visitors."

"Are you suggesting I'm like your father's patients?" she asked with a huff.

"If the shoe fits."

"You have an annoying quality of sounding perpetually cheerful. My mother was like that," Mrs. Lanigan said.

"I do?" I *wasn't* cheerful all the time. Not at all. Most of the time I was a hot mess. "Maybe it's because I like it here so far."

"What do you like about no-man's-land?" She munched on another combination of cheese and apple.

"I like this house. It's exactly what I would've built if I'd had a choice. I have a thing for Cape Cod. I like Effie and her cute accent and big heart. I like you because you make me laugh. And the color of the sky here. Oh, and Blue Mountain and Ardan's pool with that glass contraption over it. I mean, seriously, being rich must be awesome." *And Ardan. Mostly Ardan.*

"It is. But none of it matters one fig if you don't have your health," Mrs. Lanigan said.

"My mother always says that."

"Why didn't they have more than one of you?"

"They tried, but Mom couldn't get pregnant again."

"How sad."

"She never talked about it much," I said. "Talk about perpetually cheerful."

"How nauseating."

I laughed. "Not on her. She wears it well."

"It's offensive that I make you laugh. I haven't said one funny thing since I met you. Which means you're laughing *at* me not *with* me."

"True."

Her plate was empty. I wanted to fist bump something, but it would have to wait. Lion taming was a lonely job.

"Would you like me to get you something else to eat?" I asked.

"No. I'd like my letter now."

"You got it."

I pulled the letter from the faded envelope.

January 2, 1938

Dear Augusta,

I hope this letter finds you well and with your scarf back on the neck of its beautiful owner. Your landlady, Mrs. Purdy, was unmoved by my heartfelt plea to deliver it to you myself. She cast cold eyes upon me with such ferocity I quickly abandoned my plan to plow through her in a brave attempt to rescue your cold neck.

Your description of her looking like Groucho Marx was frighteningly accurate. I knew her right away. Her eyebrows are like one long caterpillar. From this day forward, I'll not question your descriptions.

How lucky I am you dropped your scarf as you ran to catch the train. It's given me an excuse to see you right away. Not that I needed one. I would gladly embarrass myself in front of Mrs. Purdy a thousand times if I thought I could spend time with you.

I've not stopped thinking of you since our chance encounter on New Year's Eve. I never thought a snowstorm shutting down the trains would bring such a gift. The gift of you. How fortuitous that I happened to be in Indiana for business just as you were coming back to Chicago from a visit with your parents. I've never been one to think much of destiny or fate, believing that much of what happens to us is because of our own actions or reactions. After our time together, I might have to rethink my stance on this subject. The first time I looked into your eyes, I felt a softening of my heart and a feeling of inevitability.

You said the other night it was impossible for two people from such different circumstances as ours to be friends. I didn't say so at the time, but I wholeheartedly disagree. This is America. We don't have classes here as they do in England, for example. A man can choose whomever he wants as his companion. Even, as you described yourself, a maid from a little farm town in Indiana. Until I told you who I was, you appeared as smitten as I. If I hadn't opened my big mouth, perhaps you still would be? Yes, it's true that if we hadn't been stranded at the train station in the middle of the night waiting for the same delayed train we might not have spoken. Perhaps, also, we would not have agreed to sit together in the dining car and talk until dawn broke over the horizon. However, we were. Fate brought us to that same station at the same time.

After I told you I was the great-grandson of William Garfield, you tucked your feet under the chair and hid your chapped hands in your lap. I'd seen your shoes and your hands all night by then. Your worn shoes and chapped hands told me the story of who you are just as clearly as your words. Being the daughter of Irish immigrants who works hard to make something of her life here in America is nothing to be ashamed of. Indeed, a young woman who moves to Chicago to find work and then sends most of her wages home to her ailing parents is a person I want to know. A woman I would be proud to have by my side.

All this to say, would you allow me the pleasure of escorting you to dinner out?

Please write back to me with a date and time before I die of a broken heart.

Yours truly,

Nicholas Garfield

I carefully folded the thin paper back into its faded envelope. An image of Mrs. Purdy's face flashed before me. Merely an imagination, I figured, given my writer's mind. She'd looked like a potato left too long in the cellar, all lumpy and creviced. Those caterpillar eyebrows had wriggled when she laughed.

"Do you have the answer to his first letter?" Mrs. Lanigan sounded small and scared, all pretenses of the severe woman I'd met earlier vanished.

"I do."

She closed her eyes. "Please, read."

Dear Nicholas,

Thank you for returning the scarf. My neck is much warmer now. I didn't expect to see it again. There's no money for a new one. Even yarn is scarce in my world. I'm grateful for your kindness.

I've given your request much thought and concluded that I cannot go to dinner with you. I'll not know the right fork to use. I have nothing nice to wear. My hands are red and chapped. There's a new hole in my shoes. I'll embarrass you.

While I have to admit how much I enjoyed getting to know you, our worlds are too far apart for this to ever go anywhere. You said yourself that your father has high expectations of you. The description of the type of work you do and the society in which you exist tells me there is no place for a girl like me. I could never be the wife of a Garfield. I'm uneducated and coarse. You know this to be true. It's best for both of us if we never start what can only finish badly.

Thank you for asking me. In our brief time together, you have made me feel beautiful and special.

Sincerely,

Augusta

Mrs. Lanigan's hands trembled. "If I'm understanding this correctly, my father was the great-grandson of William Garfield. Do you know who that is?"

"The name sounds familiar," I said. "But I can't place it."

"William Garfield was one of the founders of the railroad system. At one time, he was the richest man in America."

I remembered studying about him in school. "They were ruthless, isn't that right?"

"I believe so," she said.

I leapt up from the bed and grabbed my phone from the table. "I'm looking him up." The search pulled up an article about William Garfield and his contribution to the railway system in the middle part of the nineteenth century. I summarized the content of the article for Mrs. Lanigan.

He and the other tycoons of the first railroad systems were known for ruthless business practices, many of which put passengers of their trains in great danger. Before the train industry was regulated, the founding men cared little about safety and a lot about amassing great amounts of wealth. He and his wife, Rose, had a son and daughter, Randolph and Ivy. Randolph inherited the family fortune. There was no mention of Ivy. Of course. They never told the story of the sister. Randolph had two sons: Nicholas Garfield and Boyce Garfield.

"It says here that Boyce died from suicide in 1938. Shortly thereafter Nicholas was disowned from the family. From that point on, Randolph said both of his sons were dead."

"Does it say why they argued?" she asked.

"No. There's no mention of him other than one sentence. Hang on, I'll search for Nicholas." I typed into the phone and waited as it pulled up several articles about him. I scanned them as quickly as I could. "There's not much. No one knows what happened to him after he was kicked out of the family."

Her complexion had paled to the color of her white sheets. "But why wouldn't they have told me who he really was? He never talked much about his past, other than he grew up in Chicago. He told me he didn't have any family. They were all deceased."

"Maybe he thought it would be better if you didn't know, since there was no chance of reconciliation?"

"Or it was too painful to talk about," Mrs. Lanigan said. "Maybe he thought I'd want him to go after the money."

"Or they thought they'd tell you when you were grown but didn't have the chance because they died when you were so young."

"They were protective of me," she said. "Overly protective. They might have worried his family would try and take me."

"What did your father do for a living?"

"He ran a magazine and smoke shop in our town in Indiana. There aren't many places like this left, but when I was a child, they were the heart of the town. People of all ages would spend time together, talking or reading. In addition to newspapers, magazines, and tobacco, he sold popcorn, candy, and ice cream. My mother did the books and he took care of the customers. Like I told you, they were always together. Home and work."

"May I hold the letters?" she asked.

I placed them in her lap. With her fingers she stroked one then the other. "One is thick, like card stock."

"That's Nicholas."

"The other's as fine as rice paper." She brought the envelope addressed by her mother to her nose and sniffed. "It doesn't smell like her."

"I wouldn't think so. Not after being in an attic for sixty years."

"Do you have another?" she asked.

"I do."

January 4, 1938

Dear Augie,

I don't care what you're wearing or what fork you use. I want to spend time with you, not your dress. I don't care two figs about anything but what is below the surface. That which we cannot see with eyes alone, one's essence, one's soul, is what matters to me. Your essence makes you as rich as any man or woman on this earth.

You're the opposite of coarse. You're gentle and compassionate, yet strong and smart. All the rest of your worries of forks and manners and society are easily learned.

You could never embarrass me. Furthermore, the finest dress from Paris does not make a woman beautiful. A dress is only as pretty as the woman wearing it. In a room full of women, you will always be the most beautiful to me, regardless if you're wearing men's trousers or a gunny sack.

Please, I'm asking again. May I take you to dinner?

Sincerely,

Nicholas

I didn't waste time asking if she wanted me to read the next one.

. . .

January 5, 1938

Dear Nicholas,

Yesterday, after I finished my duties at the Perry's, I walked home in the newly fallen snow. There's a hole in my right shoe and snow gets in there and the cold comes through my thin coat. I shivered all the way home, thus I walked fast and touched my scarf wrapped around my neck from time to time, marveling that just a day ago it had been in your hands and in your home.

As I walked, I thought about the story you told me about your father. The image of the burn mark on your shoulder will not leave me anytime soon. There's never a reason to physically harm a person, especially your own son. I don't care what you did or didn't do. Taking a hot poker to an innocent boy's skin is unconscionable.

This will seem strange to you, I suppose, but when you're poor, there's a feeling that rich people are somehow better than you. I can see now that although my father is poor, he is a fine man. He would never take his hand to my mother or me.

My parents came to America from Ireland to have a better life, only to find the same poverty waiting for them in this world as the one they left. All I want is to give them the life they dreamed of when they left everyone they loved behind. Today, as I walked past the men lined up for a cup of soup, I wondered if the promise of America is false. These times are hard for so many. Will it ever be different?

By the time I arrived at the boarding house, my left toes were wet and numb with cold. When I was a child, I dropped a heavy piece of firewood on them. Ever since then, they hurt when I'm cold. All I could think of was warming them under the stove in Mrs. Purdy's parlor.

Those thoughts vanished the moment I arrived inside the house. All day I'd thought of you as I scrubbed and polished floors, hoping there might be a letter waiting even though I'd rejected your invitation. I was feeling quite sorry for myself until I saw my wish had come true. Your letter was on the table. No one was in the parlor, so I ran up the stairs to the sleeping room to read it in private. The other girls would hound me for details if they knew mail had come from a man.

I leaned against the door, still wearing my coat and hat, to read your letter. I didn't even take off my wet shoe, though my left toes ached. As I read your words, I smiled, no longer cold. Just as quickly, though, I remembered who I am and who you are and that we're from disparate worlds. I had myself a little cry and then went down to join the others for dinner.

At dinner, Mrs. Purdy asked me why my eyes were red. I told her and the girls about meeting you and your invitation to dinner. Like women do, they wanted to know every detail: how we met, and what we talked about, and what you looked like. When I told them who you are, everyone went silent, even Gladys.

I started to cry again when I told them I couldn't accept because I didn't have a nice dress and there were holes in my shoes, and I wouldn't know how to behave, and the whole idea was ridiculous because I was nothing but a scullery maid.

Mrs. Purdy became cross with me. She said she would teach me about forks and glasses, for all that's holy, and what kind of imbecile turns down the offer of a good meal from a rich man? She gestured toward our dinner of thin potato soup. "If for no other reason than to get something to stick to your bones, you must say yes."

The girls all chimed in at once. Glamour puss Gladys said she'd cut her heel off like the ugly stepsister in Cinderella for a date with someone like you. Shy Millie said she understood perfectly. She wouldn't be able to go either for fear she'd make a fool of herself. Hedda just shook her head like I was soft in the head and spoke to me sternly in her deep voice. "No more crying, you little idiot. If you're too stupid to see when something wonderful is about to happen to you, then you deserve to be stuck here with the rest of us."

Gertie's eyes filled with tears and said I had to go for all of us. "When was the last time something good happened to any of us? You have to go for all the working girls."

Lucinda said that I'm beautiful no matter how shabby my clothes, but that if it was a new dress I needed, she would make sure I have one. If you recall, Lucinda is a seamstress. She said she'd been sewing a new dress from scraps she'd gathered at the shop to give me for my birthday. If she worked hard on it all week, she could have it done by the weekend.

Gladys said she'd help me with my hair and let me borrow her lipstick. She works at the department store and knows all the latest fashions.

Mrs. Purdy looked around the table at each one of us and tapped the table with her fingers for emphasis. "Listen to me, young ladies. I don't want to ever hear again that one of you turns down an opportunity because you're ashamed of being poor. You're all hardworking girls and in America we all have the chance for a better life. That a rich boy like Nicholas Garfield noticed our girl Augusta isn't proof of that, I don't know what is."

Right then and there, she gave us all an etiquette lesson. After she'd worked with us for an hour, she said to march right up to my room and write back that I would gladly accept your invitation.

All that to say, despite my better judgment, I accept your dinner invitation. The only evening I'm allowed out past six p.m. is Saturday. Mrs. Purdy said you would have to come in for a visit first. "I made a promise to your parents to keep you safe and I intend to make good on it." She went on to say it's her responsibility to make sure you're a decent young man who won't chop me up into a million pieces like Jack the Ripper.

Yes, she really said that.

She added that you'll have to have me back no later than nine or I'd have to sleep on the porch. She and her caterpillar have strict rules.

I'll count the moments until we meet again.

Sincerely,

Augie

"How remarkable," she said.

"Which part?"

"The girls. Mrs. Purdy. All of it." She pushed both envelopes toward me. "Put them away. I don't want anything to spill on them."

"I do have another surprise for you." I slipped the letter back in its envelope and set it on the table.

I explained to her about the audiobooks and headphones. "Before you say no, you have to let me read you the descriptions of the books Ardan and I picked out."

"I won't be able to push the right buttons."

"I'll start it for you. When you're done reading, you can just ring your bell and I'll come turn it off."

"Fine."

Fine. I needed to start counting how often she used that same word to admit defeat.

* * *

When I brought Mrs. Lanigan her dinner, she was huddled under the covers and didn't answer when I called out to her. I set the tray with the bowl of clam chowder on the dresser. I sat on the side of the bed and placed my hand on her shoulder. "What's going on?"

"I don't feel like eating. Leave me alone."

"Did something happen?" I pulled back the covers. Her pillow was soaked with tears.

"I'm alone and useless," she said. "I wish I would just die and get it over with."

I brushed her hair off her damp cheeks. "I'm sorry you're feeling like this. Do you want to talk about it?"

"Not really."

"I want you to eat. It's clam chowder." Ardan had told us it was one of her favorites.

"Fine. Help me up."

I helped her to a sitting position and put the pillows behind her back.

"Tell me what prompted this," I said.

"It's Finn's birthday tomorrow and I forgot because I don't even know what blasted day it is."

"Oh, I'm sorry. I didn't know."

"How is he gone when I'm still here? It should be Finn that lived, not me."

I had no idea the answer to that question or to the one that haunted me. Why had I lived when Roberta had died?

I set the napkin in her hand. She wiped her eyes. "He was everyone's favorite. All the kids loved their brother Finn. They adored their dad. Yet, I'm the one still around."

Roberta's laughing face flashed before my eyes. Years and years after she died, I woke to the same question. Why was I alive when perfect Roberta was dead?

I set the tray over Mrs. Lanigan's legs. Steam rose from the bowl of chowder.

"It's hot, so let me help you," I said.

"I can feed myself," she said.

"The chowder's right in the middle of the tray." I put a spoon in her right hand and led her to the side of the bowl. "A piece of bread is to the left."

She tapped the bowl with her spoon, then dipped it into the soup and brought it up to her mouth, missing it by centimeters so that it spilled out of the spoon and onto her chin. "Blast it all." She dropped the spoon into the chowder. "I told you I'm not hungry."

"It'll just take a little time to adjust," I said as I wiped her chin. "You've got to eat. You'll never gain your strength back without the proper nutrition."

She set her mouth in the thin line that was supposed to deter me from further pursuit. I didn't back down that easily.

"How about if I help just this once?" I asked. "Tomorrow, if it's not something hot and runny, you can practice with your fork."

Mrs. Lanigan's eyes filled with tears. Her bottom lip trembled. "I hate being like a child."

My heart ached in sympathy. "I get that it's hard. But it's just you and me. You don't have to pretend. You know *I'm* a mess."

"That's obvious to everyone."

"It's going to be all right." I much preferred her feisty and sharp-tongued to this.

"People always say that when the exact opposite is true. With your perfect mother and Pollyanna attitude, you couldn't possibly understand."

I picked up the spoon and wiped the handle clean with a second napkin. "I have more insight into how you're feeling than you might think. When I was fourteen, my best friend was murdered while walking home from school. Normally we walked together, but I had the flu that day and stayed home in bed. I don't know why it was her and not me. I wish I had the answers, but I don't. She was pretty and popular. It should've been me."

"Nonsense," Mrs. Lanigan said. "No one should have to die at fourteen."

"You know what I mean."

Her fingers searched until she found my wrist. "I *do* know what you mean. But that doesn't make it true."

"She was destined for greatness. I'm just plain old Charlotte Wilde. Moderate talent, below average courage and above average disappointment."

"Poppycock. You're hardly a failure. How many people can write a book?"

"A book no one reads but my parents?"

"Ardan and I read it."

I scooped some soup onto the spoon and placed the utensil in her hand. "Yes, what did you call it? Drivel?"

"Fine, if you're going to make a federal case over it, I lied. I loved your book. As a matter of fact, I'd like the second one. When's that idiot agent going to sell it?" She brought the spoon to her mouth. This time without spilling.

"She can't seem to get any nibbles," I said.

"What a twit," she said. "We'll publish it ourselves. People do that now. Ardan's friend from college just published his first novel. Most dreadful thing you ever read."

"Maybe I should." I took the spoon from her and filled it again.

"You will. I'll help you figure out a marketing strategy. Edward always said it was because of my clever mind that he was able to build his empire." Her cheeks had flushed as she spoke. I saw a glimpse of what she must have been like as a young woman, full of fire and ambition. She ate from the spoon but instead of giving it back to me, she scooped it into the chowder herself.

"Eat the whole bowl or you'll never get rid of me."

"Will you stay with me until I finish?" she asked. "Tell me more about your new book?"

"It's another Luci book," I said. "This time she's at a vineyard and the winemaker is murdered."

* * *

After wishing Mrs. Lanigan goodnight, I went back to my room to find a sweater. Outside, twilight presented in rich pinks and oranges across the sky. In contrast, Blue Mountain, majestic and rugged, showed me how it earned its name. At home I would be curled up in front of the television with a glass of wine. What did Ardan do this time of night? Effie had promised to leave dinner for me after I had Mrs. Lanigan settled. I hadn't seen Ardan since that afternoon. He'd gone into Hailey for a few errands. I hoped he was home by now.

To my delight, I didn't have to search for him. He was on the couch in the living room, with his long legs stretched out on the coffee table. Lights were dimmed. The gas fireplace cast a warm glow about the room. Dressed in sweats and an Oregon Ducks sweatshirt, he looked better than a man should in slouchy clothes. A paperback was open on his lap, but he stared into the fireplace, seemingly lost in thought. He looked up at the sound of my footsteps.

"Hey." On the table next to him was a glass of red wine.

"Hi. Your mother's all tucked in for the night," I said.

"Great. Effie has dinner for us in the kitchen. I thought we could eat together. If you'd like?"

"Sure."

"I'm having a glass of wine first. Would you like one?"

"This is the best job ever," I said.

He got up and went to the buffet where he kept wine and other liquor.

It was my novel he'd been reading. "Haven't you read this already?"

"I'm reading it again. It's different now that I know you. I can hear your voice in my head."

"Your mother says I have a squeaky voice."

"You do *not* have a squeaky voice. Sweet is a better description."

I picked up my book. Flipping through, I saw that many passages were underlined.

He handed me the glass and gave me a sheepish grin. "I highlighted passages I particularly liked. I do that with writers that are better than me."

I flushed at the compliment, hiding my embarrassment by taking a sip of wine. The taste of the bold, fruity wine almost knocked me over. "Holy crap, this is good."

"Mark Ryan's Dissident." He sat back in his place on the couch.

"Mark Ryan?"

"He's a winemaker out of Walla Walla. They're one of my favorites. I go every October to buy wine. This year Kevan and Blythe went with me. We had a lot of fun."

"I don't know anything about wine. I'm more of a food person."

"Wine and food go together," he said.

Like you and me.

I stared at him. But no, he'd not said it out loud. It was his voice in my head again. Was it my imagination or wishful thinking? I shifted, pulling my legs under me.

He turned to face me. "If you can make this much progress

with Mother in less than twenty-four hours, I don't know what to expect next."

"I think you both need to accept she may be here to stay."

He closed his eyes and sighed. "I wish she liked it here better."

"Give it some time. She's still adjusting to a new reality."

We talked for a few minutes about different ideas for equipping her room and bathroom with tools to help. We both finished our glasses of wine. He poured us another.

"What were you thinking about before I came down," I asked, emboldened by the wine.

"Something strange happened today. Last year I went to my house in Italy to write—"

"Wait. You have a house in Italy?"

"Yes, in Tuscany, to be exact."

"Go on."

"I had been working on a book for years that I chucked because I started having vivid dreams about a young couple. Images mostly. It felt like I was meant to write their story, even though I didn't fully know what it was. You know how it is—ideas just come to you out of nowhere. When I sat down to write, the story—their story—poured out of me."

"Their love story?" I asked.

"Yes. He's rich and she's poor. His father doesn't approve and threatens to cut him off if he marries her, but he does it anyway. He gives up everything to be with her. They moved to a small town somewhere and he opens a store."

"What are you saying?"

"I'm saying that the story is a lot like Nicholas and Augie. Mother told me stories about them sometimes. I figured the idea that my characters move to a small midwestern town was borrowed from their story. But I had no idea who Nicholas really was until today. When I read those letters today, I completely freaked out. Coincidence? Maybe. But don't you think it's odd?"

I had goosebumps up and down my arms. "Have you ever seen pictures of them?"

"No. My mother didn't have any."

"But you could describe the people in your dream to her?"

"I describe them in my book, yes."

"What about the brother? Is he in your book?" I asked.

"No. In my story, the hero is an only child."

"Do you think they're sending you the story from wherever they are?"

"It's possible. I mean, I believe in heaven or a life after this one. I've always wondered where writers get their ideas. Maybe there's more to it than mere talent."

"I've always thought creativity came from a mystical place. The mysteries of the universe and God are both powerful and elusive." I'd always believe this to be true. Since coming here, I felt it even more so.

"You're so damn pretty and smart." His neck flushed pink. "I'm sorry. I can't believe I just said that."

"It's okay. You're pretty too." I flashed him my best flirtatious smile, reckless and wild like the beasts of Idaho. Here I was drinking wine with a man I'd met less than twelve hours ago, sitting in front of a romantic fireplace wishing he would take me in his arms and kiss me. The entire thing was ludicrous. I didn't care. Nothing but this moment mattered. Not my past mistakes with men, so numerous they were laughable. Especially the latest one who sucked the life out of me down to my bone marrow.

Only days ago, I was a dried-up sack of nothingness. Desolate, lonely, ashamed of myself and the ways in which I'd allowed my life to implode. But here? I was reborn in this land of dry air and elk and blue-eyed Ardan Lanigan.

He set aside his empty glass and inched closer until he was next to me. I smelled the sweet scent of wine on his breath. Stubble showed on his chin. His lashes lowered as his gaze traveled down my body and back up. Holding my gaze, his voice lowered in both pitch and tone. "You make plain cotton t-shirts look ridiculously sexy."

Normally I would have made some self-effacing comment, but

not here in Idaho. Here I was self-confident and brash. I shivered with desire. "And you with sweatpants."

He stared at my mouth and bit his bottom lip. Wasn't that my job? To either bite my own or his? Either way worked for me.

"I can't kiss you yet," he said. "It's too soon."

"Right. Kissing me would be shameful."

"I've known you for less than twenty-four hours," he said.

"I couldn't agree more."

He leaned in and kissed me anyway. That kiss! I'm a writer, prone to romantic notions, so it should be assumed I exaggerate certain moments of my life, both good and bad. I add color or emphasize certain details for dramatic purposes. But not this. The heat of his mouth against mine obliterated every kiss that had come before.

His kiss pushed aside the past and altered the course of my future. From that moment on, I belonged to Ardan Lanigan.

I'd always belonged to him. I just hadn't met him yet.

When he pulled away from me, he tucked a mass of curls behind my left ear. "I can't resist a girl with curls. I can't resist you."

"Is that right?" The thrill that came from the first heady nudge of intimacy coursed through me.

"Yeah." The corners of his mouth lifted in a smile both charming and genuine. His eyes danced with the joy of being right there next to me. "That's the last kiss I'll steal. You can give me the rest, as I earn them. And, let me tell you, I plan on earning every single one of them."

Gulp.

CHAPTER SIX

ARDAN

My brothers both told me they fell in love with their wives at first sight. Being a romantic, I believed it to be true. My novel of Augie and Nicholas was based on this belief. However, I never thought it could happen to me.

Until today.

The moment I saw Charlotte I knew there was something between us I'd never experienced with anyone else. It was not simply her physical beauty, which was limitless. There was a quality about her both familiar and fascinating.

Whether or not I believed in love at first sight, I hadn't planned on kissing her on the first day I'd ever met her. I was possessed by a power larger than myself. Charlotte was my destiny. That's the only explanation. Or perhaps it was as simple as Moonstone's vision. Her sureness that Charlotte was my soulmate gave me a confidence I'd never had before. I would never in a million years have been so bold—so alpha male—without the confidence that Moonstone's prediction was true. She'd been right about everything else, including my brothers and their wives.

After I kissed her, we ate dinner in the kitchen and talked of benign subjects, having both agreed that any further time together on the couch would lead to a lot more than a first kiss. After we ate, we both went to our rooms.

I tried to sleep, but tossed and turned, my mind churning between images of Charlotte and the strange discovery about Nicholas and Augie. Was it possible that divine intervention had whispered the story to me? Had the same power brought Charlotte to me?

All my life I'd believed that more existed than we can see with our mortal eyes. Here it was again. Evidence that the mysteries of the universe and God were not easily understood by an ordinary man. An unknown force had brought Charlotte and that box of letters here at the same time. Was it to solve an eighty-year-old mystery, or heal Mother, or bring Charlotte and I together? Perhaps a combination of all three?

Around midnight, my phone buzzed. I jumped up. For a mad second, I believed the call would be from Charlotte.

It wasn't Charlotte.

The call was from Felicity Spinner.

Dammit, the woman had impeccable timing. She knew exactly when to reappear just in time to ruin anything promising in my life.

I let it buzz and stared at the wall. Two years had passed since I'd last heard from her. Here she was again. The moment Charlotte enters my life, she suddenly appears.

I drifted back in time, remembering what havoc she'd caused the last time I'd seen her. She'd arrived drunk on the doorstep of my condominium in San Francisco, wrecked over another bout of sex with my brother, Ciaran.

This was their pattern. Ciaran came to town. They hooked up. She was his San Francisco hook up. There was a woman in every city. When he left in the morning, as he always did, she came to me. Usually, I'd fix her up with a grilled cheese sandwich, tomato soup, and a romantic comedy on television. After a good cry on my shoulder, she'd swear this was the last time. No more Ciaran. I suspected she truly believed it at the time, but I didn't. I knew there would always be one more encounter with my brother. Each time, she would think this would be the time he'd see she was the one.

For weeks after, she would come by my place every night. We'd have dinner and watch movies. There was never anything physical between us, but we were close. Too close.

But then something altered the pattern. My brother, the ultimate playboy, met Bliss Heywood. Bliss was his one and only. He knew it the moment he met her. When Felicity contacted him, he told her he was officially committed. Devastated, she came to me.

I recalled the moments in perfect detail.

I was on the couch watching a soccer game. Melanie, my girlfriend, was on her way over with Chinese food. When the doorbell rang, I figured Melanie had forgotten her key. I rose from the couch and sprinted to the front door. Felicity stood there with makeup smeared down her cheeks and whiskey on her breath.

"He blocked me," she said. "From his phone and email. Everything."

I knew she meant Ciaran. There was no reason to pretend otherwise.

"He's met someone," I said.

"The one. He said she was *the* one. I just wanted to talk to him. I needed to talk to him one more time." Felicity sobbed and threw herself into my arms.

She weighed just over a hundred pounds, despite her height. Embracing her was like hugging a bag of bones. She sagged against me. I lifted her into my arms and over to the couch. As I gently set her down, she threw her arms around my neck and pulled me to her mouth.

"Don't. I have someone," I said. "She's important to me."

"Please, Ardan, just this once. Take me to bed."

"I'm not your pain killer," I said.

The front door opened. I looked up to see Melanie drop the bag of Chinese takeout. Noodles and fried rice spilled out of the cartons. Sweet and sour sauce smeared the carpet.

I leapt to my feet. "It's not how it looks," I said.

"That's all you've got? I trusted you," Melanie said. "Screw you." She leaned over and picked up the carton of cashew chicken and hurled it at my head. I ducked. The carton smacked right into the middle of my flat screen television. A second later, the door slammed behind her.

I knew better than to go after her. Melanie thought I had a weakness when it came to Felicity. She knew I'd been in love with her when I was a kid. She might have been able to listen to my explanation, except for her own damaged past. Melanie's husband had cheated on her. She would never trust me again.

I turned to the pitiful, rumpled mess on my couch. Felicity had curled into the fetal position. "I'm sorry, Ardan."

For the first time in the history of our friendship I understood the truth. We were in a toxic, unhealthy relationship. Several of my past girlfriends were threatened by our intimate friendship. One accused me of being in love with her. Another said I would never have a relationship with the right woman if I continued to drop everything when Felicity needed me. I had to end this pattern.

"We need to take a break," I said. "I can't do this any longer."

"But Ardan, I need you."

"Seriously. We're done. Go home."

We hadn't spoken since.

Now, the phone buzzed again. *Felicity Spinner.*

I switched my phone to silent. My thoughts returned to Charlotte. I couldn't allow anyone to interfere or come between us. Especially not Felicity. Not this time. Whatever she wanted, I couldn't give her.

* * *

The next morning, I dressed in my swim trunks and a sweatshirt and went downstairs. Effie usually fixed my coffee and a light breakfast whatever time I wandered into the kitchen. Today was no exception. She was already hard at work stirring batter in a large mixing bowl.

"Good morning, Mr. Lanigan."

"Morning, Effie."

"I'm making your favorite coffee cake." She set aside the wooden spoon and poured me a cup of coffee, handing it to me as I sat at the breakfast nook.

"I slept terribly last night." I said.

"Why is that?" She returned to her mixing bowl.

"Overstimulated."

"By one Charlotte Wilde?"

"Don't be silly," I said. "I hardly noticed her."

"Don't you give me that cheeky smile. I know a smitten man when I see one."

I drank the cup of coffee while reading the New York Times on my tablet. "It's the same terrible news as yesterday."

"Out there, maybe. In here, life is better than it was yesterday. I'm not touched with the gift like Moonstone, but the vibration in this house changed the moment Charlotte walked through the door."

"I kissed her. Last night."

Effie dropped the wooden spoon into the batter. A few drops landed on her nose. "You did?"

"Yes. I'm a bolder version of myself when I'm with her. She makes me feel confident and clever like my brother, Ciaran."

"Mr. Lanigan, I'm pleased for you." She bounced on her feet and let out a happy sigh that made her seem like a little girl. I often forgot she was barely twenty, younger than my niece Rori. "Maybe there will be a wedding and babies."

The wistful tone of her voice made me wonder if she was as lonely as I had been. "Do you ever regret coming here? There's nothing for you here, other than taking care of a boring, middle-aged man. There's no night life, or young people. Nothing really, other than a ski area." Which was thirty minutes away.

Effie poured batter into a cake pan. "I won't be getting on two wooden sticks to slide down a mountain and break my head. No sir. And you know I'm through with love. I can't go home with my tail tucked between my legs and face my father. He was sure I'd gone daft when I followed an American man half way round the world. Turns out he was right, now wasn't he? I couldn't stay in San Francisco unless I wanted to live on the streets. Coming here was a blessing from God."

I'd known from the first interview that San Francisco was no place for a girl with no money or family. The city would eat her alive.

"I worry you're lonely for people your own age," I said.

Most nights, after she served my dinner and cleaned up, she went off to her room to watch television or read. Sometimes, I heard her crying.

"I've my nights out with Moonstone and Sam," she said.

"Moonstone told me a young man asked you to dance last week, but you said no."

"That wanker?" She shook her head with such force that her hair swung back and forth. "He's the son of a rancher. Do I look like a nutter? Getting involved with a bloke like my father? I've had enough of that, thank you very much. You know what farm life is, Mr. Lanigan?" She didn't wait for an answer. "Mud, dung, and afterbirth."

I winced and laughed. "When you put it that way."

"My mother had nine babies. Nine. Being oldest, I've changed enough nappies for five women. If I never hear another wobbly, I'll die happy."

"Wobbly?" Often, I had to have Effie translate her slang.

"A toddler's fit. Like your mother had yesterday."

"Ah, yes. A wobbly. Do you miss your family, though?" I asked. "Aside from the mud, dung, and afterbirth?"

"I miss them. However, I've become myself here. I can think here without the voices of the little ones drowning every coherent thought from my daft head. Would I like to meet a man and fall in love? Yes, but I don't want to leave here and lose myself again. Do you see the problem?"

"I do. I have the same one. I could live anywhere in the world, but I want to be here. What woman would want to live here? I mean besides you."

"You mean Charlotte?"

"She was afraid of the elk. I might have to make a grand gesture."

"A grand gesture?"

"In books, when people fall in love, one has to offer something really big in order to have that person. Leaving here to live in the city would be about as grand as it gets for me."

"She might learn to love the elk," Effie said.

"I have to meet her where she is. Trying to change someone never works out."

"Sometimes we overcomplicate things that are actually quite simple." Effie smoothed her hand over the front of her apron. "You know what my mother used to ask me when I'd come home all moony faced? 'Is the sound of two hands clapping still a noise if no one is there to hear it?' "

Effie often said things that made no sense. This was a good example.

"What I mean, Mr. Lanigan, is if she's your soulmate, you won't care where you live."

CHAPTER SEVEN

CHARLOTTE

I woke to the sound of birds chirping outside the window. When I opened my eyes, I expected to be at home in my apartment. Instead I was in the pink and black bedroom. I burrowed deeper under the comforter and stretched my bare legs against the softness of the five-million-thread-count sheets that cradled me in softness. I sniffed the air and smelled coffee and maybe a cinnamon cake. Was I in heaven?

Images from yesterday flooded my consciousness. Blue Mountain at twilight. Mrs. Lanigan's trembling hands. The letters. Effie's tears. Elk. Then, Ardan's face just before he kissed me. Would today bring another kiss? He said he had to earn them. How exactly would he do so? Whatever it was, I hoped it would be accomplished today. I wanted another kiss.

I sat up and rubbed my eyes. My laptop was closed on the bedside table. After Ardan had left me last night, I'd written for a solid hour until my eyes stung with fatigue. The words came easily in the quiet house. Before I fell into a sound sleep, I'd decided I would swim first thing in the morning before Mrs. Lanigan woke. After I cleaned up, I'd bring Mrs. Lanigan her breakfast.

I padded over to my bathroom in bare feet and brushed my teeth. The tile on the floor was warm. A heated floor? I *was* in heaven.

After tying my hair into a ponytail, I pulled on my bathing suit and robe, then grabbed my goggles and swim cap. I followed the scent of coffee to the kitchen. When I arrived, Effie was taking a cake out of the oven. The scent of cinnamon and butter made my stomach growl. "Do you ever sleep?" I asked as I helped myself to coffee from the pot on the counter.

"I could ask the same of you," she said. "I heard you typing away as I passed your room."

I poured cream into my coffee and smiled. "The muse was good to me last night."

"Pardon me?"

"I mean, I was on a roll, in the flow—whatever you want to call it. The Idaho air must be good for my brain."

"Earnest Hemingway must have thought so." I turned to see Ardan slouched in the doorway dressed in swimming trunks and nothing else. I swallowed and avoided eye contact. My cheeks burned hot. There was no need for a second look. The image of his practically naked body was now seared into my memory. He had the torso of a swimmer, with wide shoulders and a tapered waist. I'd love to explore the sprinkling of hair on his chest with my fingers, then dip under the elastic of his trunks to see what prizes waited for me there.

I leaned against the counter for support. I hadn't known it was possible for one's legs to go completely numb in a matter of seconds.

"Hemingway?" I asked, sounding as breathless as I felt.

"He lived in this area for part of his life," Ardan said.

"Yes, of course." I'd temporarily forgotten due to the naked man in front of me. "He liked cats."

A puzzled look crossed his face, like I was either amusing or strange. Maybe both.

"Or was that just his Florida period?" I asked.

"No, I think he liked cats here too," he said.

"Great. I'm off for my swim," I said, anxious to leave before I made a complete fool of myself.

"Without breakfast?" Effie sprinkled powdered sugar over the cake.

"She'd sink with a piece of your coffee cake in her stomach. But I'll take one."

"Maybe later, Effie," I said. "Now I need to get to it before Mrs. Lanigan needs me."

"I took the cover off the pool," Ardan said. "It's time to enjoy some warmer weather."

I said my farewells and escaped to the patio. My bare feet grew cold as I walked across the stone patio. Idaho spring mornings were brisk, despite the sun that rose from the east. When I reached the pool, I dipped a toe in. Nice and warm. Maybe too warm. Like me. Ardan's hotness must warm up the water.

After I'd secured my swim cap and slipped out of my robe, I swam a half mile, my mind numbed into silence by the rote exercise. When I was done, I hopped out of the water. The sun had risen above Blue Mountain and shed light over the yard and patio. Steam rose from the pool. I shivered, suddenly cold in the crisp morning air.

"Hey, Charlotte. Come join me?" Ardan grinned at me from the hot tub.

Into the hot tub—with him? That would be way too close to his mostly naked body. But, I mean, he offered. I couldn't be rude and say no.

I ambled across the patio. My bare thighs rubbed against each other. My thighs would jiggle all over the place when I stepped into the tub. "I thought you'd be showered and dressed by now." I paused at the bottom of the tub's steps and looked up at him.

"I love to watch the sun come up over the mountain from here."

I shrugged out of my robe. How could I walk up the stairs with the least jiggle? I sucked in my stomach and wished I could do the same with my boobs. Why had I eaten that bread last night? Or the bread of the last twenty years?

There was no choice. I had to walk up the steps and get in the water. *Don't be ridiculous. You want to spend time with him. Now's your chance.*

I took one step and then another and I was in. Nothing like parading around in a bathing suit to trigger every insecurity.

Ardan hadn't turned on the jets. Without having to ask, I knew he liked to enjoy the sounds of the morning. A bird chirped from one of the pines just outside the confines of the yard. Several branches of a tall pine shook, but I couldn't spot a bird.

"The bird's song is the sound of spring," I said, forgetting my self-consciousness. "When I was a kid, the first morning I woke to the sound of birds chirping, I knew it was spring."

"For me, freshly cut grass is the *smell* of spring," he said.

"What about taste?" I asked.

"Strawberries. Your turn."

"Touch? That's a hard one." I thought for a moment. "Morning sun on my face."

"Good one. What do we have left?" he asked.

"Sight?"

"Right. Let's see." Using his index finger and thumb, he flicked water at me. "I've got it. Wild flowers in the meadow."

"After my initial fear of being killed by a herd of elk, I *did* notice them," I said.

"Elk would not kill you. Some believe they're a spiritual animal."

"I'll take that under advisement, Mr. Lanigan," I said. "Do you think there's a sixth sense?"

"I do. I know someone who sees things before they happen."

"Really? Like a psychic?"

He nodded. "Her abilities are just one example of how there's so much more than what we experience through our five senses."

We quieted and listened to the love languages of birds.

"You swim well," he said.

"You watched?" Which meant he'd seen me get out of the pool too. Every part of me exposed in the bright morning sun. Great.

"I could spend every last moment of my life watching you do just about anything." The tone of his voice was tender, teasing. Utterly sexy.

I was stunned into silence. A drop of water raced down the muscle that ran down the side of his neck.

"Did I embarrass you? I can't seem to keep my mouth from misbehaving when I'm around you."

"You didn't embarrass me. I'm flattered. I'm not really the type of woman a man would watch walk out of the ocean." I surprised myself with my honesty.

His brow furrowed. "Like a Bond girl, you mean?"

I smiled. *He gets me*. "Yes, like a Bond girl."

"You're wrong. Come here." He put out his hands. When I gave him mine, he pulled me toward him. "I can't keep my eyes off you. Here, there, anywhere you go, I'll follow." Our knees came together like magnets. A current of electricity so intense passed between us I feared the water might electrocute us. "And last time I checked I'm all male."

"Yes, you are." I breathed in just as he yanked me onto his lap and captured my mouth with his. I wrapped my legs around his waist. From what I could feel, his maleness was on full alert. Our mouths crashed against each other, hard and intense.

His hands explored my legs. Those thighs I'd hated just minutes before turned into silk under his touch.

"You're beautiful. Everything about you is perfect." He trailed kisses from my ear to my collarbone.

"To you, maybe."

"Not to be arrogant, but I'd like to be the only opinion that matters."

If I could have wriggled out of my swimsuit, I would have in a second. Instead, I placed my hands in his damp hair. "This is not like me."

"Me either. I've never been this way with anyone, ever."

"Like what?" I traced his bottom lip with my thumb.

"Bold. Flirtatious. Alpha."

"What's happening to us?" I asked.

"Everything good." He put a finger in one of my ringlets. "These curls. They never give in, do they?"

"They're resilient, like me. Always spring right back up."

"An excellent quality in a curl and a girl." He removed his finger from my hair and grinned. "I promised no more kissing until I earned it. I've already broken my promise."

"What do you have to do to earn more kisses?" I asked.

"Take you to dinner tomorrow night?"

"If that's a question, then the answer is yes."

He groaned. "Is it tomorrow yet?"

"It's not even breakfast." Like pulling apart the aforementioned magnets, I unwrapped my legs and stood. "I have to go check on your mother."

With a hand on each side of my hips, he gazed up at me. "For our first date, it should be low key, like the bar and grill in town. If that goes well, we'll fly into the city for dinner."

"How rich are you?"

He smiled. "You'll still like me even if I'm part of the one percent?"

"I'd like you if you were the ninety-ninth percent. But it's nice you're not."

"So shallow, Charlotte Wilde."

I tossed my curls. "I can't be perfectly virtuous all the time."

* * *

Mrs. Lanigan was awake and sitting up in bed when I arrived with her breakfast tray. Effie had put together a slice of coffee cake, a boiled egg, and a half-dozen strawberries. We went over where everything was on the plate, then I fixed her a cup of coffee with cream and a little sugar, per her request. She successfully brought the cup to her mouth and sipped without spilling.

"How about a few bites of coffee cake?" I asked. "Effie made it this morning."

"Terribly fattening. I hope you didn't have any."

"I didn't." I went to the windows and lifted the shades. "Not that it's any of your business."

"You're the one who said you were fat. I'm simply looking out for you." She took another sip from her coffee cup.

"Eat your breakfast, you mean old thing," I said.

"This is what happens when you try and help a person. They don't listen."

I laughed as I put away newly washed laundry Effie had left in a basket outside the door.

"What are you doing?" She brought a strawberry up to her mouth and took a bite.

"I'm putting away your clean laundry."

"You don't know where things go."

"It's not that hard to figure out." Effie had obviously organized the drawers by types of clothing. "Would you like me to tell you where everything is?"

"Not now. I'm eating."

"You need to learn how to get around your room by yourself. Ardan told me you sent the consultant away."

"That person was an imbecile."

"Why do you say that?"

"She spoke to me like I was a child," Mrs. Lanigan said.

"Were you misbehaving?"

"I most certainly was not. It's just her methods were ridiculous. She wanted me to use a cane."

"Wouldn't a cane be helpful?" I asked. "The sight impaired have used them for a long time."

"If I use a cane, everyone will know I can't see."

"Who are you trying to hide it from?"

"Never mind. You wouldn't understand."

Ardan showed up in the doorway. He'd showered and dressed since I'd left him in the hot tub. Now, he wore loose-fitting jeans and a striped t-shirt.

"May I come in?" he asked.

"What do you want?" Mrs. Lanigan asked.

"Morning, Mother." He leaned down to kiss her on the cheek.

"Are you checking up to see that I'm eating?"

"Yes. Are you?" he asked. "I don't see much eating."

She sniffed. "It's coffee cake. How am I supposed to stay slim if Effie keeps making this nonsense?"

"Mother, you don't need to worry about calories right now. You're too thin."

"One can never be too rich or too thin," she said.

"Weren't you just telling me young ladies are too thin these days?" I asked.

"I was saying that to make you feel better," Mrs. Lanigan said with a wicked smile.

"You really are a mean thing," I said.

"Mother, I have something I wanted to run by you."

"Don't tell me. You're in cahoots with Pollyanna here and want me to use a cane."

"I am indeed in cahoots with Charlotte, aka Pollyanna, about the cane and many other things." He winked at me.

I blushed and stifled a nervous laugh.

"She and I both agree that having someone come out and help you get accustomed to things here at my house would be a good thing, especially since you're going to be here a while."

"The more independent you are, the sooner you can get rid of me," I said.

"Yet another reason to live," she said. "Fine. I'm a prisoner here, so I might as well learn how to stumble around using a cane."

"As luck would have it, Miranda from the association for the blind had a cancellation and said she could come out later," Ardan said. "This is a different person than before. She refused to come out again."

"What did I tell you, Charlotte? The woman was a twit."

"She's probably in some facility for post-traumatic stress disorder," Ardan said.

Mrs. Lanigan rolled her eyes. "Everyone's so sensitive these days."

Ardan and I exchanged a triumphant smile. Moving Mrs. Lanigan toward acceptance and independence was an inch by inch kind of job. We'd just moved her another inch in the right direction.

* * *

That afternoon, while Mrs. Lanigan worked with Miranda, I went out to the patio with the stacks of letters to search for ones that would tell us more of the story of Nicholas and Augie. I'd read through a few that were sweet but not informative. I kept on, hoping to find one that would reward Mrs. Lanigan for her cooperation with Miranda. A few minutes later, I hit the jackpot.

I heard footsteps and looked up to see Ardan, dressed in cargo shorts, a t-shirt, and hiking boots. He carried a fishing pole and had a backpack slung over his shoulder.

My stomach did the flipflop dance. I greeted him with a wave.

"Have I interrupted you from sleuthing?"

"Yes. But look what I found." I handed him the letters.

Like me, he was a fast reader. In a few minutes, he was done. "Mother's going to freak out."

"I'm freaking out."

"Do you have time to take a break and come with me down to the creek?"

"Are you fishing for our dinner?"

He laughed. "Unlikely."

"Do I have to put a worm on a hook?" I asked.

"I fly fish. No worms."

"Like Norman Maclean?"

"Kind of," he said.

"I loved that book. Not that I'm keen to touch a slimy fish."

"I promise not to make you kiss it," he said.

"I won't even pretend to know what that means."

"Kiss them and throw them back in. That's how we fly fish in Idaho."

"As much as I love your kisses, I would not enjoy one after you've kissed a fish."

"You better hope I don't catch anything then," he said. "Because I would really like to kiss you by the creek. It's one of my favorite places on the property."

I glanced down at my feet. Would tennis shoes work or did I need boots?

"Tennis shoes are fine," he said.

"Did I just ask that out loud?"

"No. But I could tell from the way you glanced at your feet."

"You're way too observant."

"You're my favorite subject," he said.

I put the letters back inside the house and followed him across the yard to a trail that led into the woods. Too narrow to walk side by side, I let him take the lead, enjoying the view of the man in front of me. Damp and cool in the woods, it smelled of fir trees and dirt. Roots and rocks made the path uneven. I concentrated on staying on my feet. Falling would be the opposite of sexy. Several times we had to jump over puddles that looked like they were filled with chocolate milk. New growth on the firs and pines were a shade lighter than their friends from previous years.

We passed through the wooded area to a meadow. Purple, yellow, and red wildflowers were scattered amongst tall grasses. He stopped abruptly in front of me. I put my hands out to stop myself and smacked into his cute backside. The momentum knocked him a few paces into the tall grass. A flock of birds rose from the grasses and fluttered into the sky. A green snake slithered out from under a rock.

I screamed. "Snake. Ardan, there's a snake."

Ardan turned around to look at me and laughed.

"You really are a city girl."

"That's a…a snake. Right there by your foot." I pointed to where the snake had frozen, like he thought he was invisible if he didn't move.

The horrible reptile started toward me. I shrieked and leapt onto Ardan's back. I tangled my arms around his neck and wrapped my legs around his waist. I hid my face in his shoulder. "Don't let it get me."

He was laughing so hard his whole body shook.

"It's not funny." I lifted my face to see where the snake was now. Nowhere to be seen. Did it go back into the woods or the grasses? There was no way I was heading into that grass now. Not after what had just crawled out of them.

The muscles of his back rippled under my hands as I slid down him and onto the ground. I kept a hold of his arm as I looked around.

He finally stopped laughing and wiped his eyes with the back of his hand. "That might be the funniest thing I've ever seen."

I crossed my arms over my chest. "Not funny. At all."

"You're cute when you're scared."

"I am not cute," I said. "I'm terrified."

That gave him another fit of laughter.

"Are you done?" I asked.

He pressed his fingers against his mouth, obviously trying to get control of himself. "I'm sorry. I don't mean to laugh at you."

"*At* me. Exactly. Not nice."

"You're not really mad, are you?" he asked.

"I might be." I heard a rustle behind me and whipped around to see a squirrel running up a tree.

"You're not afraid of squirrels, are you?"

"Very funny."

He gestured across the meadow. "Come on, I want to show you my special place."

"I'm not going through that grass. No way."

"I'll go first. Once I trample it down, you'll see there's nothing to be afraid of."

"If we see another snake, you're toast. I mean it," I said.

"It's either this or climb back up onto me."

"Don't tempt me."

I followed him. My eyes darted back and forth as we crossed the meadow. He was right. The grasses bowed under his feet, creating a nice path for me. Finally, we arrived on the other side of the meadow where the terrain took a steep dive. Below, a creek wound through the cavern. We eased our way down, using rocks and roots for footholds until we arrived at a large pool of green water.

"This is Lanigan creek. We named it ourselves," he said.

"It looks more like a river." I walked closer. "How deep is it?"

"About eight feet." He gestured toward a wall of rocks that helped dam the pool. "See those? We put them there years ago to create a deep area for us to swim in. Kevan thought of it. He was always the brains of our endeavors."

Further up, the creek narrowed. Water burbled over rocks. "Do you ever catch anything?"

"Not often in this creek. April's a little early. June is when it gets good."

"Then why today?"

"Practice."

I wiped my sweaty forehead with the back of my hand. Between the hike and snake scare, I was hot. "I want to dive in there."

"During the summer, it's a fantastic swimming hole." He pointed to an oak with a rope tied to a thick branch. "We used to come here as kids."

"Does it stay this deep all summer?"

"Yes, it's fed by melting snow at the peak of Blue Mountain."

I perched on a fallen tree and took off my shoes. "I'm putting my feet in."

The corners of his mouth lifted in a half smile, like he was trying not to laugh again. "You are?"

I walked to the edge of the water, yelping as sharp pebbles pierced my tender feet.

"City feet," he said.

"Well, obviously. I don't run around the streets of Portland in bare feet except on special occasions." I plunged my manicured toes into the water and yelped. I jumped out as fast as I'd jumped in. "It's so cold. Why didn't you tell me?"

He doubled over, laughing his silly head off at my obvious naïveté about all things Idaho. "I said it was melted snow. What did you think?" he asked between bursts of laughter.

"I'm delighted to provide entertainment, Idaho."

"Thank you, City Feet." He perched on a large rock and tossed a pebble into the water. "I come here all the time, to read or think or fish. It's my special place."

I sat back on my log bench and rubbed my feet. "I might have frostbite."

He laughed some more.

"You done?" I asked.

"Until you do something else funny."

I tossed a small stick at him.

He caught it and tossed it back. I tried to catch the damn thing, but it landed in my bushy hair instead. I yanked it from my head and threw it on the ground. "Do you think that had any bugs on it?"

"You're hilarious." He tilted his head to the side. "And adorable."

"Don't try and butter me up with that kind of talk," I said.

He jumped up and pulled a small plastic square from a pocket on the backpack. "This is a portable tarp. I wouldn't want you to get your gorgeous booty dirty." He gave it a strong shake and placed it over a grassy area. "You can sit and read while I fish."

"I didn't bring a book."

"He pulled out his phone and handed it to me. "My manuscript is on here. I would like you to read it."

"You'll let me read your baby?"

"You're the first person who will ever have read it. Be kind, please. I'm not as good as you are."

"Are you kidding? I know how hard it is to give someone your work."

"You'll see how similar it is to our Augie and Nicholas. The more I read of the letters, the stranger it becomes."

A few minutes later, he'd pulled on plastic pants called waders and trudged upstream, casting the line in a circular motion so the fly skimmed the surface of the water. I settled in a spot in the sun and opened the document on his phone.

Nicholas Garfield fell in love with Augusta Devin the instant he saw her huddled in the corner of a bench at the train station in Benton, Indiana. She was no bigger than a half-grown boy and wore a coat thin from wear and shoes with a hole by the left toe. Her dark eyes took up most of her heart-shaped face. Unlike most of the young women he knew, she had long hair coiled at the nape of her neck.

The station was mostly empty. They were the only two people in the station, other than the man in the booth, who was now asleep sitting up, his snores the only evidence he was still amongst the living.

"May I sit with you?" he asked.

She raised giant, round eyes up to look at him. "If it pleases you." She gestured with a narrow, chapped hand toward the platform. "From what they said, we're most likely here until the storm's over." She tucked her hands inside the sleeves of her jacket.

Nicholas looked outside where the blizzard raged and made the terrain nothing but a sheet of white. No train would come tonight.

"We're lucky to be inside and not stuck out there," she said. "My parents will have barely made it home."

"The snow came suddenly," he said.

He detected the slight hint of an Irish brogue. "Are you Irish?"

"My parents came here when I was five years old."

"Are you hungry?" He patted the bag in his arms. "I have some cheese, bread, and a jug of wine. I'd be happy to share."

"You speak like an American but have the supper of a French peasant." She narrowed her eyes and looked at the gold watch on his wrist. "What's a boy like you doing here?"

"I've come from a visit with my university friend, Billy Walcott. Do you know him?"

"He was above me in school, but I know who he is. He had a scholarship to Northwestern. Talk of the town a few years ago. Is he back here now?"

"He came back to use what he learned at university on his family's farm. I spent the week after Christmas with them. Mrs. Wilcox insisted I take food with me because of the weather. She was afraid I'd be stuck."

"I wouldn't mind some bread and cheese," she said. "My mother wanted me to take some bread with me, but they have so little, I left it on the table."

I continued to read, astounded by the similarities to Augie and Nicholas. The chapter went on to describe their night together and subsequent journey home to Chicago when the storm cleared the next day.

By the time Ardan returned to me, I'd finished the first chapter.

"I don't understand how this is possible," I said.

Ardan stepped out of his waders and put aside his fishing gear. "Me either." He plopped next to me. "Do you think it matters that we understand?"

I looked out on the water where the sun made diamonds of the ripples. "I don't suppose it does. Sometimes we have to accept that there are occurrences of the divine all around us. We don't see them or understand them, and maybe we're not meant to. It is possible God whispered this story in your ear while you were sleeping."

"But for what purpose?"

"Because the world needs more love stories. Especially now when hatred wants to kill love in all its forms. Stories like Augie and Nicholas are important in the continued quest to heal the world of sin and hatred."

He stared at me. "Where did you come from? And why did it take you so long to get here?"

I looked back at him, lost in his eyes. "I've been looking for you. In all the wrong places. But I'm here now."

"I'm going to kiss you now."

"Did you kiss any fish? I was too distracted by your great writing to notice."

"No fish. Only a beautiful angel named Charlotte."

* * *

Later, I knocked on Mrs. Lanigan's door and waited for her growl of permission to enter. "Come in. I'm awake."

She was sitting up in bed. The tray with her lunch was on the bed next to her, most of which had been eaten.

"You ate?" I asked.

"You made such a fuss about it yesterday."

"Yes, I did, but I didn't think you would actually listen to me."

The corners of her mouth twitched.

"No wonder you're tired," I said. "It takes a lot more energy to frown than smile."

"For God's sake, I'm not a kindergartener." She let out a harrumph without nearly the venom I had already come to expect from her. "Did you have an opportunity to sort through the box of letters? Because I ate my lunch, so you owe me."

"I did. I have two that are dated right after the first ones we read. Would you like me to read them to you now?"

"What do you think?"

I read out loud.

January 7, 1938

Dear Augie,

I've just returned home from our dinner. As I walked into the house, I wanted to dance down the street like that showy Fred Astaire.

The dress Lucinda made you brought out your eyes. Please tell her for me that it was as fine as any dress my mother or her friends would wear. I would never have known it was made from scraps.

When I came into the house, Mother was in the parlor with my brother, Boyce. The two of them enjoy playing cards together in front of the fire. I believe I told you he just turned sixteen, but he doesn't act like most boys his age. Meaning, he isn't loud and obnoxious like many of the boys I've known over the years. Boyce is quiet and painfully shy. He only has one friend, Martin, who he spends time with after school. Other than that, he prefers the company of Mother or me. He tries to avoid Father, which isn't difficult, given how little time he spends here at the house. Father spends most evenings at his club and doesn't return until we're all in bed. I think Mother's lonely, but she never says so. She often says how lucky she is to have two such devoted boys.

They asked where I had been, and I told them I finally convinced my New Year's Eve girl to go out with me. Once Mother heard that, she wanted to know all about you and our evening. I told her I took you to the Wescott and how pretty you looked. I described how hard you work and that you send most of your wages home to your parents. Mother thinks this shows remarkable character. She asked if you might come for a visit one of these days soon. I told her I'd like to keep you to myself for a while longer. The truth is, I'm afraid of what you might think of our family. Mother rarely leaves the house. Father rarely sets foot in the house. Boyce cannot wait to leave the house.

My family is like a cracked mirror, together but broken.

I asked her what it was like when Father was courting her. She seemed to struggle to find the right words. Finally, she said he was charming, with impeccable manners.

Out of nowhere, Boyce asked why Father wasn't home more. "Martin's father spends most evenings at home," he said. "Is it because he dislikes me so?"

"No, dearest. Not you. He finds me tedious."

Tedious. Have you ever heard such an awful word?

"He thinks I'm soft," Boyce said.

"Don't worry about what he thinks," I said. "He doesn't understand anyone who isn't just like him."

Boyce is sensitive and artistic. It's like he has fewer layers of skin than the rest of us, so he feels everything more deeply, both good and bad. I worry sometimes he's too good for this hard world.

I must close. The hour is late, and my eyes are tired.

Until next week.

With affection,

Nicholas

I barely looked up before opening the next envelope. Mrs. Lanigan didn't move a muscle other than to make an impatient cluck with her tongue. "This one isn't dated, but I feel certain it's in reply to the one I just read."

Dear Nicholas,

I, too, enjoyed our dinner, other than the time went too quickly. Although my room was its usual frigid temperature upon my return, my stomach was full, a rarity these days. Mrs. Purdy and the girls all wanted to know about dinner. What dresses were the ladies wearing? What did we eat? Was I nervous about which fork to use? Mrs. Purdy was pleased when I told her I didn't make any mistakes with the silverware or glasses. She's proud to have taught me so much in such a short time.

The restaurant was too nice. All those black suits and crisp aprons and me with my ratty shoes and inability to open the clams with that tiny fork. Why would they serve something in a shell and expect a person to open it right there in front of everyone?

Do you think the waiter noticed my shoes?

I'm sorry if I appeared terse when you asked about my parents. I find it difficult to talk about them without crying like a little girl. I didn't want to cry at the restaurant and embarrass you. I miss them so. I've been in Chicago nine months and my homesickness has only faded a little. I wake up some mornings and think I'm back in my little room at home, but then I hear Mrs. Purdy lighting the stove downstairs and I remember where I am. I love the girls and strict Mrs. Purdy, but living here isn't the same as being with Mam and Pa.

I would love to meet your mother and Boyce. However, I agree it's too soon. One more date and you'll see what an oaf I am and go off to find a girl who knows how to get a clam out of a shell with a miniature fork.

Yours truly,

Augie

I folded the paper back into thirds and put it carefully back in the envelope.

"Please tell me you have one more," Mrs. Lanigan said.

"Not yet." I explained how many of the letters were nothing more than sweet nothings and that I'd read them to her after we'd solved our mystery. "I'll read some more tonight and find some to read you tomorrow."

Mrs. Lanigan felt for her cane. "I need to use the ladies' room. I *do not* need your help." She clasped her fingers around the handle and gingerly got out of bed. "Watch this, smarty pants." She counted out loud as she headed toward the bathroom, feeling in front of her with the cane. "I'll be a minute or two."

I tidied up the room, fluffing pillows and remaking the bed. I lifted the shades and opened several windows. Right outside, a lilac tree burst with fragrant clusters. A fat jay hopped around the lawn, looking for worms. I breathed in the scent of the lilacs. They were my mother's favorite. I took out my phone and snapped a picture and sent it to her with a text.

The view from Mrs. Lanigan's room.

Immediately, I received one in return.

Oh, that poor dear. How horrible to know they're there but not be able to see them. No wonder she's grouchy.

Mrs. Lanigan coughed, announcing her return. She stood in the bathroom doorway, blinking into the light and leaning on her cane. "Are you on your phone? I hear clicking."

"I was texting with my mother."

"I suppose you were complaining about me."

"How did you know?" I asked.

"Let me guess. 'Dreadful old woman—blind as a bat—send help.' "

I laughed. "Why didn't I think of that? Instead, I sent her a photo of the lilacs."

"I smell them." Mrs. Lanigan crossed over to the chair by the window, muttering the steps under her breath.

"I opened the windows. They're blooming right outside. Sit in the chair here. The sun is shining right in through the window. The vitamin D will do you good."

With her fingertips she brushed the edge of the chair before sitting. "What do you want me to do, just stick my bare arm out the window in the pursuit of vitamin D?"

"Great idea," I said.

She closed her eyes and drew in a deep breath through her nose. "I've always loved lilacs."

"My mother too."

She frowned. "Am I supposed to marvel at the odds of both of us loving lilacs? Everyone loves lilacs."

"Maybe not everyone. You don't know. Right now, there could be a woman telling her husband how the pungent scent of lilacs makes her feel imprisoned."

"You must've been an exhausting child."

"I was an angel."

"I highly doubt it." She opened her mouth then closed it.

"What?" I asked.

"I wondered if you might fix my hair for me."

"I'd love to."

"How bad is it?" She tugged on a tuft of her hair and grimaced.

"Not *too* bad. Hang on. I'll get a brush." I sprinted into the bathroom, afraid she'd change her mind if I took too long. A soft bristle brush lay on the counter by the sink.

Back with her, I ran the brush down the mass of tangles from the back of her head.

She yowled. "That hurts."

"Stay still."

"I want to know about my roots. Give it to me straight."

"A good trip to the salon wouldn't hurt," I said.

"That's not straight. That's beating around the bush. Finally, we've discovered your talent."

"Ouch." She yelped again as I tugged on the last tangle. "You did that on purpose."

"I did no such thing."

I ignored her and continued to brush out the last of the tangles. A few minutes later, I had it mostly cooperating. I smoothed her bangs to the side and stood back to look at my progress. "You're officially ready for town," I said.

"I can't go to town. Not in this state. The townspeople would love to see how snooty old Mrs. Lanigan has fallen into disgrace."

I clucked my tongue, like my mother used to do to me when she thought I said something ridiculous. "You've hardly fallen into disgrace."

"Look at me."

"Would you like *me* to touch up your roots?" I asked, hoping this would entice her to agree to a trip to town and the salon. "I always did my mother's hair."

"I'm used to the finest salon in San Francisco, Charlotte. I doubt you could replicate it with a box from the drugstore." She said 'drugstore' like I might say meth house. "I used to be perfectly turned out at all times."

My heart ached when her eyes glistened with tears. Growing old was not for sissies. Someday it would be me. I hoped someone would be kind to me when the time came.

I knelt next to her. "Let's go into town and have your hair and nails done."

"Fine."

Fine!

"I can't go without cleaning up. Since you're here to help, you may as well actually do something useful."

I wanted to jump up and down with happiness, but I remained calm. "Great. Would you like me to run you a bath?"

"No, I'd like a shower, so I can wash my hair." She clasped her hands together so tightly her knuckles turned white. "But I'll need you to help me get situated. I'm afraid I might fall."

How it cost her to ask for help.

"Not a problem."

In the bathroom, I found a nonslip pad in the bathtub and moved it into the shower. The entrance into the shower was flat, so nothing would trip her. The doors were made of glass so I could keep an eye on her. "Mrs. Lanigan, there is a shelf to the right with shampoo and conditioner."

"Yes, I remember this shower," she said.

I explained they were both pumps and that the shampoo was closest to her. "Soap is a bar on the other shelf."

She nodded. "If I drop the soap, you'll have to get it for me."

"I'm happy to."

"You'll get all wet."

"Nothing can make my hair worse than it is," I said. "So, don't worry about it."

I turned on the water and we waited for it to get hot.

"My son likes curly hair."

"Not this curly." I felt the water with my fingertips. "Good. Nice and warm."

"You'll avert your eyes?" she asked. "I don't want you to see what I look like."

"No peeking, I promise."

She unbuttoned her nightgown and removed her underwear. "I suppose I look like a plucked chicken," she said.

"I'm not looking, so I wouldn't know." I had her hold on to my arm and guided her inside the shower. "I'm going to sit right here. Call out to me if you need anything."

She knocked over the shampoo twice before successfully getting it into her hair. Same went for the conditioner. Each time I picked them up and put them back in place. When she scrubbed her body with a bar of soap that smelled of honeysuckle and vanilla, she seemed more comfortable.

"I'm done now," she said.

I reached in and turned off the water. Tomorrow I would help her shower with my bathing suit on. I was soaked.

"I'm a tad damp," I said as I wrapped her in a towel. "I'll have to change before we go."

"I'm sorry."

"Don't be. I'm proud of you for doing something so scary."

She sniffed.

"Come sit at the vanity. I'll comb your hair. Would you like me to put a little makeup on you?"

I was surprised when she agreed without a fight. She sat on the padded stool while I combed out her hair.

"I used to wear it in a straight bob," she said. "My housekeeper, Gabriella, fixed it for me at home, after I started getting bad. She was the only one who knew how..." She trailed off.

"How bad your sight had become?"

"Yes."

"How come she didn't come here with you?"

"She has children. A family to take care of." Her voice sounded wistful.

"Were you close to her?"

"She'd been with me for twenty years."

That didn't exactly answer my question, but I let it go. With Mrs. Lanigan, one had to read between the lines.

"My makeup's in the drawer there," she said.

I found a neatly organized bag with the basics, including a matte foundation. "I'm very good at makeup," I said.

"Of course you are. Insecure girls always are."

Progress.

* * *

I helped her dress in a pair of attractive designer jeans and a cotton sweater, then helped her back to the chair by the window. "I'll be right back to get you, but I have to go change."

"Don't take forever."

"I won't."

"Charlotte?"

"Yes?" I asked from the doorway.

"I might like to join you and Ardan for dinner tonight. Downstairs."

"Fantastic," I said.

"With my hair fixed and a shower, I'll feel a little like my old self."

"I won't be a minute. Hang tight."

I hustled down the hall to the living room. Ardan sat in a chair by the window, reading. He looked up when I came in. "What happened to you? You look like you were caught in a rainstorm."

I did a curtsy, Effie style. "You are looking at the woman who successfully got Mrs. Lanigan showered and dressed to go to town. She wants to have her hair done." I bounced on my toes. "And she wants to join us for dinner tonight downstairs. The price of which is that I am soaking wet and need to change."

His mouth hung open for a good second. "No way."

"Her idea. I believe she's embarrassed about her appearance, which is part of the reason she's been hiding out in her room."

"She always insisted we dress for dinner and eat in the formal dining room. Losing control has been hard for her."

I shared with him that before she came here, Gabriella had helped her with her hair and getting dressed. "That's how she was able to hide it for so long."

Before I realized what was happening, he had scooped me off my feet and into an embrace. "Thank you, Charlotte Wilde."

His muscular arms tightened around my waist as I wrapped my arms around his neck and breathed in the scent of him. No man had ever smelled this good in the history of the world. My heart beat so fast I thought I might faint when he kissed me.

When he set me down, my legs shook like I'd had to give a presentation in front of the class. I stumbled backward, almost tripping on a table before miraculously righting myself. "I, um, need to go get changed."

"We'll eat in the dining room. In honor of Mother's reappearance."

"Should I wear high heels?"

"By all means."

And nothing else.

My eyes widened. No, he had not said that out loud. My mind was on overactive imagination mode. Had to be the altitude.

"There will be no mud or elk during this evening's festivities," he said. "You're safe. I'll drive you both into town."

My hands flew to my mouth. "I've been so wrapped up, I totally forgot about my car. Has it been rescued?"

"Yes, I got her. She's tucked into the garage next to my car."

"That sounds nice."

"It's almost like she belongs there."

Like me.

* * *

The little shop in Peregrine was run by an adorable lady in her fifties named Heather Roberts. She was trim and lively, with a cap of wavy dark hair and a round face.

"Ardan Lanigan, I just cut your hair last week," Heather said. "I take it these lovely ladies here with you are the ones in need of pampering?"

"That's right. Mother would like to have her hair and nails done." He glanced at me. "This is Charlotte, our friend from Oregon."

I smiled and held up my hands. "I'd love a manicure and pedicure if you have time."

"Ah, so *this* is Charlotte," Heather said. "Moonstone was in yesterday to tell me all about you." She hugged me. "Welcome to Peregrine. Ardan is one of our favorite people. We're downright pleased as punch you're here."

I looked over her shoulder at Ardan. What was a Moonstone and why was she talking about me?

He shrugged.

I'll explain later.

There it was. Ardan's voice in my head.

"Mrs. Lanigan, you probably don't remember me, but I used to babysit your boys a million years ago." Heather took both her hands.

"Little Heather Roberts? Of course I remember you. I thought you moved away years ago and married a pilot."

"I did. My husband helped himself to a few too many flight attendants, so I divorced him, took half his money, and came home. My dad left me his house when he passed and thank God I'd never sold it. I'd always worked at the salon even when my kids were little, so I opened this shop to keep doing what I love and boom, here I am."

"Good for you," Mrs. Lanigan said. "Act II."

"Yes ma'am," Heather said.

"I'll leave you ladies to it," Ardan said.

"Don't hurry back," Heather said. "We'll need a few hours."

"The mystery of women and their hair," Ardan said. "Slaves to time and money."

"Be off with you, young man," Heather said.

Ardan handed her a credit card. "Whatever they want." He smiled and waved and was gone.

"Your sons are always the talk of the town, Mrs. Lanigan. I overheard two of my young clients talking about them as snacks."

"What's a snack?" Mrs. Lanigan asked.

"Like a hottie," I said.

"Hottie? That sounds like a drink."

I laughed. "That's a hot toddy."

"We used to say foxy back in my day," Heather said.

"Finally, a word I can understand," Mrs. Lanigan said.

Heather helped Mrs. Lanigan into her chair. "Now tell me, how do you like your hair done?"

Surprisingly, Mrs. Lanigan answered without her usual sharpness. She was acting downright gracious and well-mannered. "I like it straight and sleek with an ash blond color. My Gabriella used to smooth it for me with a flatiron, but I'm unable to do so by myself."

"I have just the solution," Heather said. "There's a new product that will make it shine and lay flat with or without a hairdryer or iron. I have the perfect color for you as well."

Mrs. Lanigan sighed. "I'd be most grateful."

Heather waved me over to the pedicure chair. "Have a seat, Charlotte. Relax for a bit while I work on Mrs. Lanigan." She turned on the water and added some bath salts.

I put my feet in the warm water and closed my eyes. This really was the best job ever.

* * *

That evening, I walked into the dining room. Ardan and Mrs. Lanigan were already seated at the rectangular mahogany table.

Place settings for three were on one end, with Mrs. Lanigan and Ardan sitting across from each other.

Ardan started and drew in a quick breath at the sight of me. His gaze traveled from my face to my chest to my legs and back up again. "Well, that's what I call dressing for dinner."

"This old thing?" I wore a dark blue dress with white polka dots. The A-line skirt and sweetheart neckline gave it a retro vibe that flattered my hourglass figure. Instead of my black pumps, I wore strappy, four-inch sandals. My hair liked the dry air, curling cooperatively around my face. Subtle makeup expertly applied emphasized my eyes. After I'd dressed, I'd twirled before the full-length mirror in my room, imagining myself a film star from the forties. I'd *almost* admired myself.

No reflection from a mirror could ever convey what I perceived in Ardan's gaze. From his viewpoint I was glorious, spectacular, the most exquisite, sexiest woman in the world.

He stood and pulled out the chair at the head of the table. "Please, sit."

I did so, smiling up at him as he scooted my chair closer to the table.

"Mother, you look beautiful," Ardan said as he returned to his seat. "Heather did a great job on your hair."

"Charlotte picked out my dress," she said.

I'd chosen a pink sheath to match her lipstick. "You look ten years younger," I said. "Heather's suggestion of the side bangs are like a facelift."

"I'll have to take your word for it. I take it you look nice as well," Mrs. Lanigan said with a droll lilt to her voice.

"Yes," he said. "She does."

Ardan looked good enough to eat in his black jeans and a button down, untucked shirt.

"What are you wearing that made my son gasp?"

"A blue dress with polka dots," I said. "Kind of old-fashioned and modest. Nothing special."

"It's not the dress that's special," Ardan said.

I flushed. Happy bees buzzed in my chest.

"What did my father say in his letter to Augie about her dress?" Mrs. Lanigan asked. "Do you remember?"

" 'A dress is only as pretty as the woman wearing it,' " Ardan said. "I couldn't agree more."

"Oh, brother," Mrs. Lanigan said. "Is this what I can expect all evening?"

Ardan and I laughed as our gazes locked. It was probably best Mrs. Lanigan couldn't see us. She'd be even more disgusted.

Effie arrived with plates of food. She served Ardan and me first, then quickly returned with Mrs. Lanigan's plate.

The dinner consisted of marinated flank steak, scalloped potatoes, and asparagus spears that had been sautéed in butter and garlic.

"Mrs. Lanigan, steak at twelve, potatoes at three, and asparagus at nine," Effie said. "I took the liberty of cutting the steak into small pieces."

"Thank you, Effie."

"You're welcome, Mrs. Lanigan."

"Also, Effie, I'm sorry for what happened earlier. I lost my temper and took it out on you. I'm sorry."

"Charlotte already told me you apologized and explained about the food being too hot."

Busted. This was the perfect example of why people like me should never lie.

"Did she now?" Mrs. Lanigan asked.

"Yes, Mrs. Lanigan." Effie did a little half-curtsy and exited the room.

"Charlotte, that was quite interfering of you," Mrs. Lanigan said. "And manipulative."

I darted a glance at Ardan. He was smiling as he cut his steak, obviously amused by my predicament.

"I wanted to smooth things over between you," I said. "It was wrong of me."

"You didn't trust me to apologize on my own." The corners of

Mrs. Lanigan's mouth twitched. She was messing with me. "I'm deeply hurt."

"In her defense, Mother, you haven't exactly demonstrated your humanitarian side since Charlotte's arrival."

"There's no need to lie on my behalf," Mrs. Lanigan said. "I'm fully capable of a mea culpa when necessary."

"Duly noted," I said.

"It was sweet of you to look after my best interests," Mrs. Lanigan said. "Loyalty is a good quality in a friend. Even when we act badly."

A friend. Was she referring to me as a friend?

I took a bite of the potatoes. They melted in my mouth. I groaned with pure pleasure. "God, these are good."

"Effie spoils us," Ardan said.

I had a bite of the juicy, peppery steak. "She's a genius."

Mrs. Lanigan brought a piece of steak to her mouth and chewed. "It's not the best I've ever had."

"I love it," I said.

"Your obvious enthusiasm about food is quite apparent," she said.

"I *do* love food," I said. "Especially when someone else makes it. At home I usually just warm up a frozen dinner."

"How sad," Mrs. Lanigan said.

"And lonely." I looked over at Ardan. "This is much better."

"I agree," he said.

Mrs. Lanigan cleared her throat. "Ardan, are you aware of who William Garfield was and what it means?"

"That your father was an heir to a fortune?"

"Yes. The Garfield fortune," she said.

"What I want to know," I said, "is what happened to the money with no heirs to leave it to?"

"He must have left it to someone or something," Ardan said.

"Randolph Garfield died in 1950, according to what I found with a quick search this afternoon," I said. "There might be a newspaper article about his death and who he left the money to in archived Chicago papers."

"Randolph had a sister, Ivy," I said. "Maybe she had family."

"We might have long lost cousins somewhere," Ardan said. "That's an odd thing to contemplate."

"There are answers in the letters themselves," I said. "There have to be."

"Like who murdered Boyce," Mrs. Lanigan said.

"I'm dying of curiosity," I said.

Ardan looked over at me and smiled. "With a mystery writer on our team, I have a feeling we'll figure it out."

CHAPTER EIGHT

ARDAN

The evening after Mother joined us for dinner, I waited in the living room for Charlotte to come down for our dinner date. She was five minutes late when I heard footsteps coming down the stairs. My breath caught when I saw her. That glorious head of hair was piled on top of her head with a few tendrils cascading around her face. A pair of earrings sparkled against her soft neck. Her skin glowed. She'd done something with her eye makeup that made them seem even larger. I loved the way she looked all rosy in the hot tub with no makeup and her hair sleeked back. I loved her in jeans and flat sandals. I loved her this way.

I was a goner.

"You're breathtaking," I said.

She flushed and let out one of her throaty laughs that made the room tilt like I'd had too much to drink.

I offered her my arm and led her out the front door where I had the sedan waiting. As I helped her into the car, I enjoyed a nice glimpse of her supple calves. Gorgeous legs, from ankle to thigh. I shut the door and hurried around to the other side feeling like a sixteen-year-old kid on a date with the prettiest princess ever born.

I pulled out of my circular driveway to head down our dirt road. A pair of deer grazed on the wild grasses that grew alongside my fence.

She leaned forward in her seat. "Oh, look at them. Aren't they beautiful?"

The deer raised their heads, then leapt into the woods. "Do you see how they run?" Her voice took on a wistful quality. "So graceful and elegant on those slender legs." She smoothed her skirt over her thighs. "I'd gladly come back as a deer."

This was new information. She was insecure about her body. *Okay, God, challenge accepted.* It would be my job to make sure she knew I adored every inch of her luscious body. I knew just the way to do it, too. Actions would speak louder than words. I'd start by caressing her…focus now. With that kind of thinking, I might swerve off the road and never have the chance to please her with my tongue or any other body part.

We were at the corner where the elk had stalled her journey to my house. The first time I'd laid eyes on her seemed far away now, like she'd been here for years already.

"No elk tonight," I said.

She pointed to the left where the herd hovered at the far corner of the meadow. "There they are. I was mortified to have to call you."

"You were so pretty in the middle of all that mud."

"I wanted to die when you said you'd carry me."

"I was serious. Mother would never have forgiven me had I let you ruin those shoes."

She laughed as we approached town. The sun set behind us in streaks of pink.

I passed Moonstone's inn and parked on the street in front of the bar and grill. "Stay put. I'll get your door."

I ran around to her side and offered my hand, pleased she allowed me to help her from the car. I shoved the door closed with my hip and took her other hand. "Have I earned another kiss yet?"

She stared up at me, her brown eyes shimmering in the last light of the day. "You held my door and helped me to and from the car, so I'd say yes."

I tipped her chin before lowering my mouth to hers. She drew in a breath as I kissed her. With a super human effort, I managed to remain gentle, brushing my lips against hers. She wrapped her arms around my neck and kissed me back, less gently.

To the left of us, a man said: "Get a room."

I jerked away from Charlotte's mouth. That voice belonged to my brother, Kevan.

I looked over Charlotte's head. My brother Kevan stood in front of the bar and grill, wearing cowboy boots, faded jeans, a flannel shirt, and a goofy grin. He carried a bag of groceries.

"Kevan, what're you doing in town?" My face burned like a kid caught stealing candy.

"Spring break for the girls. We decided to come out with the hope that Bliss will have her baby while we're here. Blythe's beside herself." He turned to Charlotte. "And who is this beautiful young lady you coerced into kissing you in the middle of the sidewalk?"

I glanced at Charlotte. She flashed Kevan one of her brilliant smiles. "This is Charlotte Wilde," I said. "Charlotte, this is my brother, Kevan."

"Charlotte, of course." Kevan said. They shook hands.

Kevan shot me a questioning look, his dark blue eyes shining with curiosity. He and Blythe were both privy to Moonstone's wild prediction. I could almost hear him congratulating me on wasting no time.

"It's nice to meet you," Charlotte said. "I love putting a face to the name."

"We're all big fans of your book," Kevan said. "How's it going with Mother?"

"Charlotte's a miracle worker," I said. "She's tamed her from a lioness to a purring kitten."

"I'd say she's doing the same for you," Kevan said. "Except you don't need taming."

Change the subject pronto. "Where are Blythe and the girls?"

"I left them at the house, so I could get supplies," Kevan said. "Blythe's making dinner as soon as I get home."

"Well, great. Tell them hi for me. We should probably get on our way," I said. *As in, shove off.*

Kevan adjusted the grocery bags in his arms. "I'll be sure to tell Blythe I saw you. She'll want you to come over tomorrow to catch up."

Catch up. Code for grilling me for every detail.

"Will do," I said.

"I'll look forward to meeting Blythe," Charlotte said.

"She'll be anxious to get to know you better." Kevan nodded and was on his way down the street to his car.

I took Charlotte's hand and escorted her over to the front door of the grill. The moment we were inside, she tucked her head into my shoulder. "How embarrassing. What will he think of me?"

"He'll think I'm damn lucky," I said.

"He didn't seem surprised. Or bothered that you were kissing the help."

"You're hardly the help."

The waitress on duty greeted us with a weary grimace and showed us to a table by the window. Even with live music promised later, there were only two other tables occupied. The old place was looking more ragged than usual. Red and white vinyl tablecloths older than me covered the tables. Stuffing peeked out from the benches of the booth tables. Various decades of ketchup decorated the faded paint. On the other side, the bar with its ornate but weathered wood counter looked like something from a bad western movie, other than there were no ladies of the evening sitting at the counter.

"I love this place," Charlotte said.

"You do?"

"It's perfect in every way. I mean, look at the bar. It's the type of place you meet friends and have too many beers and dance your heart out. This is America."

I smiled. "If you say so. I've always been partial to it myself, but I wasn't sure a city girl would see the charm."

"Maybe I'm a country mouse after all." She grabbed the plastic menu and slapped it onto the tabletop in front of her. "I can't wait to eat." She ran her finger down the menu items. "What's good here?"

I walked her through the choices, such as they were. "Burgers are decent. Salads are hit or miss, depending on the time of year and how Mrs. Pocket's garden's performing. Stay clear of the chipped beef."

"No need to convince me of that." She tugged on an earring and grimaced. "Chipped and beef should never be beside each other in a sentence or otherwise."

When the waitress came, Charlotte ordered a grilled chicken burger. She tapped her fingers over the side offerings. "I *should* get a salad, but I want fries." She glanced at the waitress's name tag before looking up at her. "Sally, are they worth the calories?"

Sally shrugged. "They're the thick wedge kind."

"With skins?" Charlotte's eyes widened.

"Some of them have skins, yes." Sally's gaze skirted toward the kitchen. "What's it going to be? I've got orders up."

"Fries," Charlotte said. "Greasy, salty fries."

I ordered the mushroom cheeseburger. "Do you want a beer?" I asked Charlotte.

"Yes. More than life itself. You have an IPA?" Charlotte asked.

Sally sighed. "Yep."

"Just one?"

"I believe so," Sally said

"Do you have pints?" Charlotte smiled up at her. "I'd like it in a pint glass rather than a schooner."

"We have glasses," Sally said.

"Big ones?" Charlotte asked.

"I'll bring it out in the glass we have."

"Awesome. Thank you," Charlotte said. "Is it a local beer? I love trying local beers."

"It's American. Is that local enough for you?" Sally asked.

Charlotte flushed. "Sure. That'll be fine. I'm excited."

"Obviously." Sally said raised one eyebrow as she wrote down the order on her pad. The excitement was clearly getting to Sally too.

"Make that two," I said.

Sally left, muttering something under her breath.

"I don't think Sally likes me." Charlotte grinned. "Next time, I'll keep my questions to myself."

"That's probably best."

We chatted for a few minutes about Charlotte's favorite places to eat in Portland. Her eyes lit up whenever she talked about food, which amused me. How could I not fall for this woman?

Sally came with our beers. They were served in mason jars. *Pint* mason jars. I glanced at Charlotte to see if she'd noticed. Her eyes twinkled at me as she placed a finger over her mouth.

When Sally left, I picked up my jar. Foam ran down the sides and dampened my fingers. "To us."

"To our first date."

Our first date? Already it felt like we'd known each other a lifetime.

Charlotte told me more about her life in Portland. Mrs. Cline, her elderly neighbor, made bean soup every Wednesday afternoon and always brought Charlotte a jar. The soup was awful, goopy, and tasting of burned cabbage.

"Burned cabbage?" I asked. "How can that be?"

"I don't know. Maybe it's the pan she uses."

Charlotte always pretended she loved the horrid soup. "She shows up every Wednesday night with the soup and her cat on a leash and these sad eyes that practically beg me to invite her in for wine and a game of cards."

"Every Wednesday?"

"Don't look at me like that. I can't send her away. She's lonely.

All she has is that mangy cat, who was sent by Satan to torture any human he comes in contact with unless you give him a can of tuna."

"Let me guess? You buy tuna in bulk?"

"What choice do I have? I don't want that thing sneaking into my apartment and killing me in the middle of the night." She laughed at my expression. "It's not a joke. It's only because of my wits that I'm here to tell the story. I figured out right away how to get Mooky to purr happily under the table. Give him tuna and don't make eye contact. All of which is how I ended up tipsy with an apartment that reeked of canned tuna and burned cabbage and a blocked garbage disposal on yet another Wednesday night."

"From the soup?" I asked.

"Exactly." Her eyes widened. "I swear, that stuff's like tar when it goes down. For the sixth time, I had to call the grumpy janitor, Rufus, to fix it. He showed up madder than a hornet because I'd interrupted his night watching the Seahawks playing the Rams. Shouldn't a young lady such as myself be out at a bar doing the same? When I confessed it was Mrs. Cline's soup that did it, he let out a series of expletives about that crazy old lady and her furball cat clogging up drains and suggested I grow a backbone and tell her I hated the stuff. Like everyone else in the building."

"Wait? Everyone else? Does that mean you weren't the only recipient of soup?"

"Oh, no. I was the only recipient because I was the only one who accepted the offer. The rest of the building simply said no thank you."

I was laughing so hard I didn't notice Sally bring the food. She dropped the plates onto the table. Several fries plopped onto the table.

"Anything else?" Sally asked.

Charlotte picked up one of the fallen fries and licked her lips. "Do you have ketchup?" she asked Sally.

Sally pointed the bottle on the table.

"Sorry, didn't notice that," Charlotte said. "These look great."

"If you say so," Sally said.

Charlotte squirted a generous amount of ketchup onto her plate. "I really shouldn't eat these."

"You sound like Mother," I said. "She would never eat fries."

"That's the difference between her and me," Charlotte said. "I eat them but regret it later."

"No wonder you're so much more pleasant than Mother."

"You think she's cranky because she's hungry?" Charlotte asked. "Because I've long suspected that about skinny people."

I laughed. "Mother's crankiness goes deeper than hunger." I bit into my burger. Mushrooms covered with swiss cheese oozed out and onto my plate.

"I hate mushrooms," she said.

I pretended to write a list on the palm of my hand. "No mushrooms or bean soup for Charlotte. Got it. What else don't you like?"

"Chicken livers."

"Does anyone like those?" I scrunched up my face in mock horror.

"They have them in Vegas, so apparently, yes."

Charlotte scooped her fry into the pile of ketchup like it was a delivery mechanism for condiments rather than food. "Too slimy." She took a bite of potato, then made an appreciative groan. Good God, this girl and her throaty noises were killing me.

"What else makes you groan like that?"

Her eyes flew open. The fry in her hand hovered in the air between her plate and mouth. "Ardan Lanigan!"

I laughed. "I'm sorry. You bring it out in me."

"Eat your dinner. You'll need your strength later."

It was my turn to stare at her. "Charlotte Wilde!"

"Maybe we should change the subject," she said, "Before I have to rip off a layer of clothes or risk bursting into flames."

"Please, don't stay dressed on my account."

"What's your opinion of Vegas?"

"Too many people. I'm more of the monastery retreat type."

Her eyebrows raised in perfect symmetry. "Really?"

"A couple years ago, I went to a retreat held at an old monastery. We were forbidden to talk."

"What made you decide to go there?" she asked.

"It was supposed to provide an opportunity to write without distractions."

"Did it work?" Charlotte asked.

"Kind of." I played with the cross I wore on a chain around my neck. "With the noise of the world shut out, I felt a deeper connection to my unique voice."

I pointed at her dinner. "Eat up. We want to finish before it's time to dance."

"We're dancing?"

"Would you like to?" I asked.

"Depends on the song. I refuse to dance to disco."

"I'm fairly certain you won't have to worry about that in Peregrine, Idaho." My phone buzzed inside my jacket. "Let me just make sure this isn't Mother calling."

"Yes, please."

I took my phone out of the inner pocket of my jacket. The call had not come from my mother or anyone in my family. It was yet another call from Felicity.

"What is it?" Charlotte asked. "Is she all right?"

"No, it's not Mother." I clicked the phone off and put it back into my jacket pocket. "It was no one important."

"From the look on your face, it seems like someone important."

The waitress came with another round of beers. "Did we order another round?" I asked Sally.

"You will." Sally set them on the table and left without further explanation.

"Would you care to share who interrupted our date?" Charlotte scrunched the earlier straw cover into a small ball. My reaction to the phone call had triggered her distrust. Who could blame her after the last man in her life? She was worried that a red flag would suddenly blow up into a disaster.

She tucked her chin against her neck and watched me like I might make a sudden move. I reached across the table and touched her arm with my fingertips. "Charlotte, I'll never lie to you. I don't have a gambling problem or a drinking problem or a secret baby tucked away in the attic."

The last one evoked a burst of laughter.

I continued. "I don't have a girlfriend, or a wife stashed in another one of my homes."

"How many homes do you have?"

"A few. Three, to be exact. That phone call was from an old friend I haven't heard from in a few years. In the spirit of full disclosure, she was the first girl I ever loved. The first of several unrequited loves."

"How could anyone not love you?" she asked.

"I believe there are many reasons, but my mother says to never point out flaws, especially during dates."

"She told me that very thing today," she said.

"In this case, we were teenagers and she loved my brother, Ciaran, as did most females under the age of nineteen in the state of Idaho."

"Why did your face change when you saw it was her?" Her gaze narrowed. I was being watched, picked apart and analyzed.

"Because she has this way of showing up in my life at just the wrong time. For example, she's now hijacked our dinner and she's not even here."

"Not hijacked, just provided an opportunity for deeper conversation," she said. "Do you know why she's calling you?"

"No idea. Felicity appears in my life at the worst moments. I haven't heard from her in two years and all of the sudden I'm spending time with the girl of my dreams and, boom, my phone rings. I can guarantee you she's calling because she needs something." I hesitated. Should I tell her the whole sordid story? Would she think less of me?

Tell her everything. Tell her your soul.

"We had a fight the last time I saw her. I told her to get out of my life." I explained to her about the dynamic with Ciaran and how I fit into the disfunction. "This last time, she showed up at my condo in the city, drunk and crying about Ciaran. He'd told her he met someone and to stop texting and calling. I was waiting for my girlfriend to arrive with dinner. When Melanie came in, she got the wrong impression of what was going on between us."

"Why?"

"Felicity had thrown herself on me. It looked like we were kissing. We weren't. Melanie never spoke to me again. That's the last serious girlfriend I had. I swore that was the last time I'd let her ruin something in my life."

"And you haven't heard from her since?"

"That's right."

"How weird that she's calling now," she said. "Did she know how you felt about her back when you were kids?"

"We've never really talked about it, but she knew," I said. "I was pretty obvious."

"Maybe she's seen what a mistake she made," she said.

"No, she wants something. That's the only reason she's calling."

"Please, don't blindside me. That's all I ask."

"I'll never blindside you. It's me who should worry. You're too young for me, too smart, and my mother likes you better."

"None of those things are true." Her eyes returned to their usual soft brown, all glimmer and steel vanished. I breathed a sigh of relief. Charlotte was sensitive, and she noticed every small detail of every situation. I had to be careful with her heart. In that way, it was like looking in a mirror.

"I almost want to thank her," Charlotte said. "You could be married to this Melanie right now and I'd never stand a chance."

"I don't think we would've gotten married. She wasn't the right one."

The air turned dense, like just before a thunderstorm. I looked up to see Moonstone and Sam entering the bar. When she spotted me, she let out a whoop and charged our direction. Why had I thought bringing Charlotte out was a good idea? In the course of thirty minutes we'd run into my brother and now Moonstone.

She headed toward us with a determined gait, carrying a floppy cloth, tie-dyed bag against her ample chest. A pleated, velvet, purple skirt squished about her legs. Sam, her husband, followed closely behind. I glanced out the window to see Sweetheart, their three-legged dog, curled up near the lamppost.

"How groovy is this?" Moonstone set her bag on the table, almost knocking over my water glass, before planting both hands on her round hips.

"Hi Moonstone. Sam." I nodded at him. He nodded back. Sam couldn't speak. No one knew why, including him, as amnesia had wiped him of all memories less than five years old. Bliss had rescued Sam and Sweetheart from living on the streets of Portland and brought them to Idaho. After a good scrubbing, some new clothes, and a decent haircut, I would never have known he'd ever been homeless. In mere months, Moonstone had captured the lonely man's heart. Now they lived together with Sweetheart at Moonstone's inn here in town. Sam took care of our homes and properties when my brothers or I were out of town. There wasn't much he couldn't do, including repairing fences, weeding gardens, and keeping pipes from freezing.

I introduced them both to Charlotte.

"Nice to meet you," Moonstone said as she studied Charlotte. "Sam can't speak, but he says it's nice to see you again."

Sam gave a shy smile to Charlotte and waved.

Charlotte stood and gave Sam a brief hug. "You remember me?"

Sam nodded and touched his hand to his head.

"That's right. I was there the day Bliss hit her head," Charlotte said.

Sam moved his arms like he was running.

"Yes, I remember you chased the ambulance," Charlotte said. "It seems as though a lot has happened to you since then."

He nodded and smiled.

"What are you two up to?" Moonstone asked. As if she didn't know.

"I'm showing Charlotte the wild side of Peregrine," I said.

"Charlotte has no need for a wild life," Moonstone said. "She's a family-oriented girl."

Charlotte had moved her attention back to Moonstone. "I am?"

"Obviously," Moonstone said.

Charlotte glanced at me, a question mark etched across her forehead as she sat back in her chair.

"Remember when I told you I had a psychic friend?"

She nodded. "This is her?"

"Meet Moonstone," I said.

"That's what Heather was talking about?" Charlotte asked.

"Correct. I have visons. I had one about you, for example," Moonstone said. "Your arrival was greatly anticipated. You're the woman Ardan's been waiting for."

Charlotte coughed. "Waiting for?"

"You're soulmates. Isn't that obvious to you yet?" Moonstone asked.

"Oh." Charlotte cheeks flamed bright red.

"We're on our first date," I said with a not-so-subtle undertone of *get lost*.

Sam tugged on Moonstone's sleeve.

"You're right, honey," Moonstone said to Sam. "I'm being rude. We should let them eat in peace. But Ardan, I have something I need to discuss with you. It's urgent."

"Now?" I couldn't keep the irritation from my voice.

"Two minutes of your time. Outside." Moonstone pointed to the sidewalk outside the window.

I looked over at Charlotte. "I'm sorry. Do you mind?"

"Not at all," she said. "I'll visit with Sam for a few minutes."

Sam nodded and smiled.

"Would you like to sit?" she asked Sam.

Sam nodded and took the seat next to mine. I followed Moonstone out to the sidewalk.

"What's up? You realize you're interrupting our date," I said.

"I'm very sorry, but Ardan, I had the most disturbing dream today during my afternoon nap."

"Go on."

"There was a blond woman in it, fragile and beautiful. She's going to be trouble to you, but you must not let it ruin your courtship of Charlotte. You *are* soulmates, but dark forces can tear even soulmates apart. Do you understand?"

I didn't understand. At all. But I nodded so I could get rid of her. Inside, Charlotte was talking to Sam, seemingly comfortable, even though he couldn't answer her back.

"You have to get back now," Moonstone said. "It's rude to be outside with another woman on your first date."

"You think?" I asked.

"No need for sarcasm," she said.

Once inside, Moonstone turned to Charlotte. "It's nice to meet you. Come by and see me at the inn sometime. I'd love to have tea and a snickerdoodle."

"Sure. I'll do that," Charlotte said. "Nice to see you doing so well, Sam."

He patted her shoulder before he and Moonstone ambled off to sit at a table on the other side of the restaurant.

"Sam is with your psychic friend," Charlotte whispered. "Do you think she can really read his thoughts?"

"I do."

"How romantic."

"There have been a few times that her abilities have helped our family." I told her about the crimes she'd helped solve. "Without her, my brothers might still be at odds. She was a big part of our coming back together."

"Do you guys always have that much excitement in your family?" she asked.

"I think we've had more than enough for a lifetime."

"Okay, good. Just making sure a crime isn't headed our way."

Later, when the band started playing, Charlotte and I danced for the first time. As I held her in my arms, I thought about what Moonstone had said about the woman in her dream being blonde and fragile. Could it be a coincidence that Felicity had called? Was Moonstone picking up on something? Would it be wrong to ignore her call? I wanted a chance to be happy. That was all. I knew without a doubt that the minute Felicity rolled into town there would be trouble.

A little before closing time, we walked to the car. The moon was a sliver in the sky, not even big enough to count as a crescent. Billions of stars lit the black night.

She waited as I unlocked the car door, shivering in the chilly spring night. I grabbed my phone from my jacket and slipped it into my back pocket, then draped my jacket around her shoulders. "Better?" I asked.

"Yes." She pulled the jacked tight against her chest as she looked up at the sky. "The stars. Oh, how are there so many?"

"They're always there. You just can't see them in the city."

Her words seemed to stretch with wonder. "I've never seen a sky like this, yet the whole time it existed, hidden from me. How do the stars shine this brightly? And why? Why are they here?"

"They light the sky to remind us that love exists even in the darkest of times. You need only look up to the heavens to remember why we're here—to love."

She inhaled a sharp breath. "Yes."

"Do you think you could be happy here?" I asked.

"I already am." She answered fast, like she didn't even have to think about it.

"Life is quiet here."

"You said it's easier to connect to your spirit in the quiet." She wriggled her way under my arm. I held her tightly against my side. "I can think here."

"That's what Effie says too."

"I've been able to write here. I feel useful."

"Is that the place or the people?" I asked.

"Maybe there's no difference. When it's where you're meant to be, the place and the people come together at the same time."

I squeezed her tighter. She fit effortlessly under the crook of my arm. I would tell her some other time that God had made her to fit perfectly against my side.

"This jacket smells like you." Her words were more an exhalation of breath than a sentence. She tilted her face to look up at me. "It's the best thing I've ever smelled. I never want to take it off."

"Keep it. Forever, if you want."

"Ardan?"

"Yes?"

"Did you really say I was the girl of your dreams? Or did I imagine it?" The sparkle from her eyes mimicked the stars.

"I said it. I'll say it the rest of my life if you'll let me."

"How can you be sure?"

"Our brains, our conscious selves can never be sure. But our souls? They know."

Our gazes locked and held. I fell into the warmth of her brown eyes, oblivious to anything but her. This was a world that belonged only to us, undefined by time or space or even memory. The world of us.

"Kiss me?" she asked. "So the stars can see why they shine?"

I held her precious face in my hands and kissed her gently. *I've done this before. I've kissed her before under this same sky.* Our bodies may have changed. But the sky and our souls remained the same.

"I've known from the first moment," I said. "It's you. It was you all along. I didn't know where you were."

"Like this sky," she said. "I couldn't see you, but you were here just the same."

CHAPTER NINE

CHARLOTTE

It was nearing eleven when we returned to the house. The moment we were in the kitchen, we started kissing. He lifted me onto the island. My skirt hiked up around my hips as I wrapped my legs around his waist.

"Take me upstairs," I whispered.

"Are you sure?"

"Since the first time you carried me to your truck, I've been sure."

With my body wrapped around him, he carried me upstairs to his bedroom. As swept away as I was with him, I couldn't help but admire the bedroom. Bay windows looked out to Blue Mountain. The same dark wood floor and white trim as the first floor were accented with gray furniture. A ceiling fan turned lazily above the bed.

I forgot all about everything but Ardan the moment he set me on the fluffy white comforter. For the next hour we explored every inch of each other. His touch was familiar, like home, yet made me new again. I was reborn under the strokes of his hands and nibbles from his mouth. I was no longer self-conscious or worried that he would find me fat or lacking in any way. That Charlotte died under the weight of his body. I was melted caramel and fearless tigress and wanton seductress. His love led me to my true self. I'd been waiting to be released from stone, like a Michelangelo sculpture.

After we were spent and satiated, we lay side by side in his big bed, holding hands. I suspected it was nearing midnight, but I wasn't tired yet. My mind and body buzzed with life. The ceiling fan cooled my overheated skin.

I turned on my side to look at him. "Do you know what you've done to me?"

He brushed a curl from my forehead. "No. I only know what you've done to me."

"You uncovered me."

"Uncovered?"

"Michelangelo believed his subjects were trapped in the stone. He had to chip away until he found them. You chipped away and found me. I didn't even know I was hidden. With you, I'm uncovered. I'm this version of myself I didn't think existed."

"I understand exactly." He smiled. "Do you have any secrets?"

"Yes. One."

I looked into his eyes. It would be easy to say to him the words I had never uttered to another living soul. Not even my parents knew.

"The day Roberta was killed, I pretended to be sick. There was a dance that night, and Roberta and I had dresses and permission to attend together. We were not allowed to date yet. I'd already played the entire night out in my mind. Roberta would shine so brightly that no one would see me. All the boys would ask her to dance and I would be alone, stuffing my face with cupcakes and punch. So, I faked an illness. I knew Mom wouldn't let me go if I'd stayed home from school. She was killed on the way home from school because I wasn't there with her. Because of my petty jealousy and low self-esteem, I let my friend die."

"You didn't kill her. A monster did that."

"There are shades of guilt," I said.

"You've carried that around with you all these years. My little Charlotte with the heart too big for your body."

I flickered my eyelids, unable to speak.

"You had a very human response," he said. "It's hard to be always in someone's shadow. It was that way for me with Ciaran. Some lights are brighter than others."

"To me, you shine the brightest of all."

"I see no other light but you." He swiped a tear that slid from my eye. "Let me shoulder some of your burdens. Lay them on me. I'm strong."

"What about you? Do you have any secrets?"

"No, only sins. I despaired, gave up hope that God would send me a woman to love. He had His plan."

"Here I am."

He brushed his lips to mine. "Tell me your dreams. What's something you want that I could give you."

"I'd like to travel the world. Like you've already done."

"Not with you. Traveling with you would make everything new. I'll take you wherever you want to go. As long as it's safe. I don't want anything to happen to you."

"Deal."

He pulled me to his chest and stroked my hair. "Now, sleep."

I snuggled closer and shut my eyes. *This is where I will sleep from now on. Next to this man.*

* * *

I opened the blinds in Mrs. Lanigan's room to let the late afternoon sun warm the room. She had just woken from her nap and I had an agenda.

"We have to take a walk outside. Doctor's orders," I said.

"What if I don't want to?"

"I'm going to have to play hardball, Mrs. Lanigan. You have to go outside with me or I'm cutting you off from the letters."

"Bribery? How barbaric."

I laughed as I crossed over to the closet. Dozens of dresses draped from hangers. "I'm pulling a dress out for you. Something cheery to go with your attitude." I chose a knit dress with a pattern of yellow flowers that looked easy to get on and off. "We'll walk before dinner."

"I'll be cold."

"You can wear a sweater." I helped her to her feet. "Now unbutton that nightgown."

"Awfully forward of you." Mrs. Lanigan undid the first few buttons.

I helped her shrug out of the nightgown.

"Which dress is it?" she asked.

"The one with yellow flowers. It looks comfortable."

She sniffed but didn't comment further, allowing me to slip the dress over her head.

"I suppose you're going to make me wear those compression socks." This was said as a statement of fact with a disgruntled set of her mouth.

"Doctor's orders."

"I hate him."

"I let you out of the house without them yesterday." I found some flat sandals in the closet and held her steady while she slipped her feet into them.

"You're an annoying person," she said. "No wonder you're single."

I'm no longer single. I blushed thinking of all the very unsingle things Ardan and I did to each other the night before.

"I want you to loop one arm through mine and use your cane with the other."

"Fine."

Fine.

A short time later, we stepped out to the patio. The sun was high in the western sky, pelting the yard with light. Temperatures were in the upper sixties. I breathed in the dry, fresh air. We ambled with an unsteady gait across the stone toward the swimming pool. "Let's make it our goal to walk five times around the circumference of the swimming pool."

"You'll need to be more entertaining than this," she said.

"What's Blythe like?" I asked.

"She's a good mother and a remarkable stepmother to our Rori. She turned that girl's life around."

"She sounds nice."

"Nice, Charlotte, is a terrible word."

"It is?"

"My God, yes. What good does nice get you? You've got to take the world by its tail or it eats you up." The fresh air was doing her good.

"Bliss always takes the world by its tail," I said.

"Bliss is like a strong wind that blows into town and knocks over a hundred-year-old oak."

"And playboys named Ciaran?"

She chuckled. "Indeed. I find it ludicrous that two of my boys married sisters. It's not 1848 on the homestead."

"I wish I could be more like her," I said.

"She's got nothing on you. The world needs gentle people with good senses of humor. Not everyone has to be loud and bossy to make a difference."

"It's not a competition," I said, warming at the compliment. The old battle axe liked me as much as I liked her.

"You're obviously an only child," Mrs. Lanigan said. "Or you'd know everything's a competition."

I tucked that away to think about later. We started our second lap around the pool. "What about your daughter? Does she have anyone special?"

"Teagan. No, she works too much. Travels around the world for work with my poor grandson along for the ride."

"How old is he?"

"Six. She had him out of wedlock. Terribly embarrassing for us."

"Do people still care about that?"

"Her father cared. He cared a great deal." Her voice changed from its usual biting tones to a slight shake. "I believe it killed him in the end. They had a huge fight—both said things they shouldn't have. The girl's so stubborn she wouldn't forgive him. She was our youngest—his little princess."

"Did they make up before he died?"

Mrs. Lanigan shook her head. "No. She and I don't talk much."

"I'm sorry." I couldn't imagine not speaking to my mother for more than a week at a time. Up until the big announcement about their Airstream, I'd had dinner with them every Thursday night and spoken to her over the phone every day.

Mrs. Lanigan sniffed. "She has red hair, so you know what that means."

"What?"

"It's God's way of making sure we see them coming."

"Was your hair red?" I smiled to myself.

"Amusing, Charlotte. Perhaps you should give up writing and focus on your comedic career." She sagged slightly against me.

"Are you getting tired?" I asked. "We could rest for a moment."

"Maybe, although I have to admit, it feels good to be in the fresh air."

"Should I feel victorious?"

"Did you make the air?" she asked.

"Come on, let's sit under the shade. You've earned a rest." I led her over to the covered table and eased her into the chair. "What would you like to drink?"

"I would like a vodka soda with a twist."

"Vodka?" I looked at her with genuine surprise. "Is that allowed?"

"Allowed? I'm a million years old. It's late afternoon, which means its cocktail hour."

"Are you on pain meds?"

"I stopped taking those. They made me sleepy. Don't let it go to your head, but this is the best I've felt in ages."

"I *do* feel victorious. Regardless who made the air."

"Until you, I didn't know you could actually hear someone grin. It's a very masculine way to smile." She crossed her arms over her chest and looked in my general direction. "Stop gloating and tell Effie to make my drink. She knows the exact amount of lime to squeeze in it."

"Will you be okay out here alone?"

"As long as a bear doesn't eat me," she said.

I glanced nervously toward the thick forest to the left of the house. "Should I be worried about that for real?"

"Not here at the house."

I scrutinized her. Was she messing with me? Not that it mattered. A bear was no match for Mrs. Lanigan's sharp tongue. She could toss a few barbs out and the creature would run back into the forest with his tail between his legs. "All right. I'll be back in a minute."

"Hurry up. I'm thirsty."

Effie was in the kitchen cutting up potatoes. She flashed her sweet smile when she saw me. "Hello, miss. You've managed to get her outside. Well done you."

"Thank you, but I have a problem. She wants a vodka."

She grimaced as she wiped her hands on the front of her apron. "Is it all right, do you think?"

"I think we need to start treating her like she's still amongst the living. She's feeling good. I don't see how one drink can hurt."

"She's nicer after a cocktail," Effie said. "From what I recall."

"She's not so bad once you get past the bark. She said no one can make her drink as well as you."

Effie straightened her shoulders, clearly delighted to have a purpose. "She likes her vodka rocks with five ice cubes and two twists of lime juice, not more, not less. They're the only thing I've ever done she's approved of."

I smiled. "She did tell me you knew how to make them just right."

"Would you like something?"

"A seltzer water for me, if you don't mind. Do you know where Mr. Lanigan is?" I asked.

"He went over to see his brother, Kevan."

I'd told Mrs. Lanigan she could have more letters in exchange for her walk, so I sprinted over to the study to get them. It was important that I keep my promise. By the time I returned with our drinks and a few letters, the sun had lowered.

Mrs. Lanigan turned toward me as I approached. "Please tell me that's a vodka in your hands."

"It is. Do you want me to set it on the table next to you?"

"No, I'll hold it."

"She put it in a tumbler, so it's easier to drink from."

Mrs. Lanigan brought the glass to her mouth and took a tentative sip. "Delicious." She glowered in my general direction. "I want more letters. We had a deal."

"Yes, we did." I sat in the chair next to her and pulled the letters from my pocket. "I've got some good ones here."

Dear Nicholas,

Imagine my surprise to see your name in the newspaper this morning announcing your engagement. Mrs. Purdy reluctantly showed it to me this morning. "Surely there's an explanation?"

I don't understand. How can you say you love me and yet, this? You've said for months now that your father's behavior sickens you. Are you expecting me to be your woman on the side? Is a penthouse suite in my future?

Sincerely,

Augie

. . .

I looked up at Mrs. Lanigan, amused to see her flick an impatient hand at me. "How does he get out of this one?" she asked.

"Just wait and see." I took the next letter from the envelope and read out loud.

Dear Augie,

I had no idea Father had sent the announcement to the paper. Margery and I are not engaged. Our fathers announced our engagement without the consent of either the prospective bride or groom.

My father has had Margery picked out for me since I was a child. Not because he thinks or cares if we're a compatible match. This is about money, as all things are with Father. Margery's father and my family are entrenched in each other's business. They're reliant upon the other but there is no trust between them. Marrying us would ensure things remained in the family.

Margery doesn't want to marry me either. She's in love with someone else. She came by to see me this morning. Her Robert is about to join the Navy and wants her to run away with him. She's afraid of her father, afraid he might lock her up somewhere, like people do with willful daughters. Robert convinced her to come with him tomorrow night. I promised her I'd help her escape. We have an elaborate plan for tomorrow.

I came by earlier today, hoping to catch you before you went to work. I'm now catching a cold, thanks to the bucket of ice water Mrs. Purdy "accidentally" poured out of the upstairs window as I stood there knocking.

Mrs. Purdy and her bucketful of ice water will not deter me. No one will keep us apart.

I've included a box of chocolate to share with the girls and Mrs. Purdy. You might let her know that I now have an awful cold and that she should feel terrible for the way she's mistreated me. I got the caramels she likes in the hope she'll feel even worse for making me sick.

I'll never betray you. Whatever happens, you will always be my true love.

Love,

Nicholas

"Mrs. Purdy dumped a bucket of water on him?" Mrs. Lanigan cackled. "What a spitfire she must have been."

"Because you've been so cooperative, I brought the response."

"How good of you." She said this sarcastically, yet she leaned forward in her chair in obvious delightful anticipation.

When the letter was back inside the envelope, I opened the other.

Dearest Nicholas,

Mrs. Purdy admitted she did throw a bucket of ice water on you from the upstairs window while you waited for someone to answer the door. I'm sorry you now have a cold. In her defense, I'd cried on her shoulder for an hour, thinking you'd chosen someone over me. I explained to her what happened, and she's agreed that you can come calling for me on Saturday evening as you usually do. She said to tell you thank you for the chocolates, but if you ever make me cry again the punishment will be worse.

The thought of you choosing anyone but me hurt more than anything I've ever experienced. I'm afraid, Nicholas, of how you hold my heart in the palm of your hand. Is your love strong enough to walk away from the life you thought you would have?

I'll look forward to hearing how the escape plan went.

Yours,

Augie

Dear Augie,

The escape plan worked. I managed to get Margery and her beau to the station and on their way to California. She knows she'll never see her family again, but it was what she had to do to be with the man she loves. Earlier, I was able to sell several pieces of her jewelry to a pawn shop, so they might have a little cash for their journey and to get started in a new city. They thanked me for helping them and then boarded the train for their new life. I watched as it pulled out of the station my family helped to build. It occurred to me that the family fortune would never be mine, but that what my great-grandfather started would be my salvation. I thought how different life would be if we were not able to escape from the wrong life to the right one.

As I left the train station, I decided to walk for a while to clear my head. I stopped to look through the window of a corner shop. They sold everything from tobacco to candy and newspapers. I watched the owner talk with customers and sneak a free piece of candy to a little girl. Envy washed over me. What would it be like to own a little store and answer to no one but myself? How simple life would be. I compared it to the wicked and complex business affairs of my father and the way we've exploited the small shop owner. Father said I didn't have the stomach for it and he's right. I can't be the man I'm supposed to be and remain here, dealing in the shadows, taking from hardworking men while mobsters run the city. Then, I knew what to do. I'll take you home to Indiana. Somehow, I'll find the money to open a little shop in town. We'll go and never look back. What do you say? Would you still want me if I'm poor? Will you marry me?

If you love me, you do not have to be afraid. Your heart is mine to protect. I will. Always.

Love,

Nicholas

Dear Nicholas,

I love you for your compassionate heart and your sense of humor and gentle touch. I love you for your quick and curious mind. How I feel about you has nothing to do with who your family is or their fortune. If anything, I wish none of it existed so that we were free to love.

I will marry you, under one condition. You have to be absolutely sure that you can walk away from all of it, including your mother and Boyce. If you defy your father's wishes, he will keep them from you. You'll lose them all. Am I really worth it to you?

Love,

Augie

"That's all I have," I said. "But I'll figure out what's next tonight and we'll read them tomorrow."

I folded the letter and put it back into the envelope.

"One time, joking, I asked him if we were related to the railroad Garfields. Father just chuckled and shook his head. 'From what I hear, it's a good thing we're not.' I don't remember if he said anything else about them again. I never gave it another thought."

She was quiet for a moment, taking sips from her drink. "We never think of our parents as people with lives other than us."

"Especially when you lose them young," I said.

"I never had the chance to ask them any questions. Before they died, I was too wrapped up in myself."

"What *do* you remember?"

"Mother smelled of Chanel No. 5 and face powder."

"Classic scent," I said.

"My father bought her a bottle every year at Christmastime."

"That's so romantic."

"Our house always smelled of freshly baked bread. We had this enormous garden with tomatoes and squash and green beans. I'd tag along behind my father when he gardened. He'd let me pick whatever and eat it right there. I drank water out of the hose. Before bed, my mother would read to me."

"What did they look like?" I asked.

"Mother had fair skin and dark hair—light blue eyes in a square face. She was small, barely over five feet tall and quick, in mind and body. Father said the first time he saw her he wanted to put her in his pocket for safekeeping. He was tall with dark, wavy hair and brown eyes. Ciaran looks like him. But his personality was more like Ardan, gentle and quiet. I can't remember him ever raising his voice. They were only a little older than Ardan when they died. Isn't that strange? I thought of them as ancient back then."

"You don't look like either of them?" I asked.

"No, I was blond like my mother's mother. People always said I looked like Doris Day, which infuriated me."

I laughed. "Why?"

"She was cute. I wanted to be beautiful."

I took in her fine bone structure and alabaster skin. "You're still beautiful. Some women are born with a certain elegance and class which never goes away, no matter what age they are. Especially if they toss in a little plastic surgery for good measure."

"Charlotte, what terrible manners you have, insinuating I've had surgery." She hid a smile behind the glass.

"Do you remember your grandparents?"

"Not well. My grandmother passed away when I was just four years old. My grandfather died a year or two later. My mother often said how grateful she was they'd moved back when they did. They had a few more years together." She sipped from her drink. Her cheeks had flushed. The drink was going to her head. I had a twinge of guilt. Maybe giving her a drink wasn't a good idea. She was loose and relaxed, though, which had to be good for her health. "I always wanted curls. I would've piled them on top of my head and let the tendrils tickle my neck."

"I wore it up last night for our date." I clamped my hand over my mouth. Me and my big mouth. I could never have been a spy.

"Date?"

I stayed quiet, as if that would deter her.

"Did my son take you out on a date?"

"Yes. I didn't mean to tell you. It slipped out."

"You've been here a couple of days and you already went on a date?"

"Does it seem too fast? I mean, it is. But we like each other and there's this chemistry when we kissed that made my knees weak, which I didn't think was really a thing, but it is." I really needed to stop talking. Soon I'd be babbling on about soulmates and past lives.

"He kissed you?"

"And I kissed him back." I flushed, remembering all the things we'd done besides kissing.

She smiled wide and almost wicked. "When Edward and I met each other for the first time, we'd spoken for under five minutes before he kissed me." Her eyes sparkled as she continued. Sight remained in her memories.

"I'll have to set the scene first or it won't make sense. San Francisco, late fifties. I was almost twenty years old and I wore this white dress sprinkled with bright blue flowers. My skirt was wide, and the waist tucked. Charlotte, I had such a small waist back then. You should've seen me. My hair was the color of wheat and tucked under a little pillbox hat. I'd just finished work when I caught a packed cable car going up Market Street. I was on the edge, half of me in and the other half off. I held on to that pole for dear life as we started up the hill. The weather was splendid, warm but not hot, without a cloud in sight. I looked back at the bay and it was as blue as I'd ever seen it. I flushed with a sense of well-being in one of those moments where I felt right where I belonged. Just then, the car lurched, and I let out a high-pitched yelp. Very embarrassing. Next to me, I heard this deep male voice.

'Don't worry, miss. I've got you.'

"I looked up to see eyes the color of the bay looking at me. He was tall and wore a dark suit and hat—clean shaven with a thumbprint-sized dent in his chin. Talk about weak knees. I had them in spades." She paused to take a breath.

"What did he say next?" I asked.

"He said, 'I won't let anything happen to you. My job is to keep you safe.'

"I said, 'Now or forever?'

"Without missing a beat, he answered. 'Now until the end of time.'

"We stared at each other all the way up the hill and when the car stopped, he jumped down first and lifted me by the waist and twirled me in a full circle with my feet dangling. He kissed me, right there in front of God and everyone. I was completely caught up in the moment."

"Then what happened?" I asked.

"He took me to dinner and we talked all night. I told him about my parents dying and how alone I'd felt here in the city, knowing I had no one to go home to. He had no one either. His father had died when he was young and his mother when he was eighteen."

"Just like you."

"Just like me. He said, 'From now on, come home to me.' "

"That first night?"

She nodded. "It sounds scandalous, but at the time I was one hundred percent sure this was the man I would be with the rest of my life. We started out making plans from the very first. He was only twenty-two and had just finished university—working as a mechanic. I was a secretary and enjoyed being a working girl, living off my own earnings. Not him. He had big dreams. He had the audacity to think he could build a company out of his passion for engines and technology. Eisenhower had finally gotten the intercontinental highway system sorted out. Soon it would connect us from one side of the country to the other. Edward believed the interconnected highways would change everything. Goods would be transported by big trucks instead of trains. There would be a need for trucks to deliver product from one end of the country to the other. 'Lots of trucks, Riona,' he said. 'And we're going to make them.' He had no money to get started. Only grit, he told me, but he'd figure out a way. A month after we met, we went to the courthouse and got married. On our wedding night, I told him my parents had left me a substantial amount of money. My father's attorney had sold the shop and house and put it all in savings for me. It wasn't a lot in today's terms, but back then it was enough to get us started making all those dreams come true. I'll never forget his face when I told him. His initial reaction was to say no. A man taking a woman's money seemed wrong to him. I said to him, 'We're a team now.' Whatever was mine was his and whatever was his was mine. We built Lanigan Trucking with that money. What an adventure it was, too. Every milestone, we celebrated, knowing we were building something together for our family. Our legacy."

Goosebumps pricked my arms. "Think of the irony," I said. "Trains and trucks."

"Yes. The heir to a fortune made from the railroads walked away to be with the woman he loved. They built a modest life together from hard work and integrity. At the end it was enough to give their daughter the opportunity to build another fortune."

"From trucks, not trains," I said.

"It was the first thing I thought of after you read me those first letters." She paused for a moment to take another sip from her glass. "I wonder if my mother ever believed in the American dream or if her indictment of her parents' new country remained?"

"She and your father built a great life together, despite their rough beginnings, so I suspect the answer is yes."

"I always wished they could see what Edward and I did together from their hard work."

"I have a feeling they did," I said.

"Anyway, Charlotte Wilde, I do not think it's too soon for you and my son. If you're anything like we were, you'll know right away." She shook her drink at me. The ice cubes clanked against the glass. "Finally, I'll have a daughter-in-law who likes me."

"Let's not get ahead of ourselves." I grinned.

"Let's do."

CHAPTER TEN

Ardan

Charlotte had been with us for six weeks. None of us could remember before she arrived to save us all and we didn't want to. Mother continued to improve under her care. Effie had started whistling while she worked again. This morning I'd walked into the kitchen and Effie and Charlotte were giggling over a meme of a cat on one of those robot vacuums like two naughty schoolgirls.

Charlotte filled my house with laughter. She laughed all day long, even in the morning before she'd had coffee or her swim. The minute the woman woke, she bubbled over with the joy of being alive. I hadn't realized how quiet the house had been before she came.

And me? I was a man deeply in love with my favorite person.

For her part, she told me she was writing with a fervor she'd never experienced. By writing during Mother's nap times, Charlotte had finished her third Luci mystery. Although she had little hope for a contract, Mother and I encouraged her to send it off to her agent anyway.

The night before, Charlotte and I had talked at length and

decided it was time to broach the subject of Mother's permanent living arrangements.

Now, I sat with Mother on the couch. "Mother, it's time we talk about the future. I'm in love with Charlotte, and I'm going to ask her to marry me."

"I know all about you and Charlotte. We talk about everything."

"You do?"

"Yes. We've grown remarkably close." Mother said it almost smugly, like it was hard to become close with the sweetest woman in the world. "Not as close as you two, obviously. I'm so very glad for you, dear. To be with the one God made for you is one of the greatest joys of life."

"It seems that way, yes. Here's the thing. We want you to stay here with us permanently."

"I love having Charlotte looking after me. She reminds me of your father. He could always cut through all the nonsense too. That said, I'm worried she'll be burdened if I stay here. She's a young woman. You'll have children, and I'll be in the way. I think you should send me to one of those places."

"That isn't what you really want, is it?" I asked as I took her hand.

She did her sniff and shrug. "It doesn't matter what I want. What's important is for you to put Charlotte first. That's how marriages work best. It's paramount you put each other and your relationship above all else."

"Charlotte won't have it," I said. "You know she can't send you away."

Her bottom lip trembled. "She's such a dear girl. Selfless and kind. Like you." Mother pulled her hand away. "You're making my fingers sweat."

"Did you just give me a compliment?"

"Charlotte says you should give someone a compliment at least once a day. Apparently, it's good for one's health."

"Mother, you're staying here with us. That's all there is to it."

"My greatest fear was to grow so old that I'd become useless and a burden on my children. It seems it's happened."

Mother was a frayed piece of antique lace I wanted to sew back together.

"Charlotte loves you," I said. "She wants you here."

"And you?"

"I know we haven't been close. But I want to be. I want to have what you and Charlotte have. This is a second chance to build our relationship. We can get to know each other in a whole new way."

She'd started to cry, which nearly undid me. Until recently, I'd never seen her cry. Even at the funerals, she was straight and stoic. Charlotte said Mother grieved inwardly, which made her suffering worse.

"I know you kids think I was too tough on you," she said. "With five hooligans it was the only way to survive."

"We've all turned out great, so you must have been right."

"I didn't want you kids to grow up and be worthless. You could've been, given our wealth. Maybe I *was* too hard on you. The others are tough and hard-headed. They needed discipline. But you and Finn…you were born good."

My chest ached at the mention of Finn. "Do you think Father and Finn are together, wherever they are?"

"I'd like to think so. You never talk about either of them," Mother said. "Why is that?"

"It hurts too much," I said.

"I knew when we got the news about Finn that it would be you who suffered the most." Her voice cracked. I gave her a tissue to wipe her damp cheeks. "You loved him with such an intensity I used to worry about what would happen when he moved away to college."

"I followed him, remember?" I'd enrolled in the same college, so we could be together. Those were some of the best times of my life.

"It's not right that someone so good went out that way. The

images of the accident haunt me. I push them away by replacing them with pictures of him when he was little."

"What's your favorite photo of Finn?" I glanced at the family photos on the mantel.

"He's running out of the surf with a toothless grin, carrying that boogie board and sand weighing down his shorts. Do you remember that one?"

"Sure." Father had taken it during a vacation to Hawaii when I was eight. My brothers and I only left the water to stuff a sandwich in our mouth. "Remember the rash I got on my stomach?"

She smiled. "One of my many parenting mistakes. Who knew little boys needed t-shirts for boogie boarding?"

"I loved that vacation."

Her weathered hands shook as she smoothed her hair. "That's the problem of time, Ardan. When I close my eyes, it's the early eighties and we're here on the property. You boys are yelling like banshees over the discovery of one terrified frog under the patio. Steaks are sizzling on the grill. Teagan's running through the sprinkler in that polka dotted bathing suit she refused to give up even though the bottom was so thin her butt cheeks showed through. John Denver is on the stereo. Your father has his arm around my waist as we dance in bare feet on the grass. Where does all the time go? How is it that we continue to move constantly forward, the moment just a second ago lost to us already?"

"It's the way of the world," I said.

"I'd give anything for that moment one more time."

"Mother, you just had it, and you gave it to me. The moment isn't stolen by time if you still remember."

"Everything I was supposed to do I've already done. I'm a useless old woman now."

"You're not useless to me."

"You really want me to stay here?" she asked.

"I really do. Give us this time to make a few more memories."

"Promise me you'll send me away if I'm a burden to Charlotte."

Charlotte appeared in the doorway. "You could never be a burden to me, Mrs. Lanigan."

Mother smiled at the sound of Charlotte's voice.

Charlotte sat next to Mother. "Plus, as my new agent, we have a lot of work to do."

"Both you kids need my business mind if you're ever going to get those books out to the world."

"Speaking of that," I said. "We have something kind of odd to tell you." I launched into describing the book I'd already written before the discovery of the letters. "It came to me in a dream and the story just flew from my fingertips. And then these letters show up that mirror my characters and my story exactly."

"How is that possible?" Mother asked.

"We're not sure," Charlotte said. "Other than divine intervention."

"For some reason, I'm supposed to write their story," I said. "So I did."

A knock on the front door was followed by the voice of Ciaran calling out to us. "Ardan? Charlotte?"

"We're in the living room," I said.

My brother bounded into the room, waving cigars around like a mad man. "We have a new Lanigan. Born this morning. I'm a father to a perfect little baby girl."

I hugged him and slapped him on the back. "Why didn't you call?"

"I thought this kind of news was better in person." Ciaran handed me one of the cigars. "Plus, I had to bring you this. Do you remember Father always said it was a family tradition to bring cigars to announce the arrival of a baby?"

"I'd forgotten that." I said.

Ciaran crossed over to kiss Mother on the cheek. "We named her Carmen Riona."

Mother's hands grappled to find his, and she looked up at him with glassy eyes. "After me?"

"Yes, Mother. It was Bliss's idea."

"What does she look like?" Mother asked.

"A bit like Winston Churchill," Ciaran said. "Bliss says she looks like she did when she was a baby, but all I see is Winston."

"You were a beautiful baby," Mother said. "The most beautiful baby ever born."

"I'm still the best looking," Ciaran said. "Everyone knows that."

I rolled my eyes and slapped him on the back once again. "When can we see her?"

"Tonight, if you can. Bliss slept most of the day, but she said she wants you guys to come by later to meet the baby. She asked if Effie could make her famous lasagna. She's craving it."

Effie, like so often, seemed to appear out of nowhere. "I'd be delighted to. I'll make a salad too. The new mother needs her greens."

CHAPTER ELEVEN

CHARLOTTE

That evening, with the lasagna making the car smell like an Italian restaurant, we pulled into Ciaran and Bliss's driveway. I'd been over a few times to visit Bliss, and I loved their chalet style home that perched on the side of the mountain. I helped Mrs. Lanigan out of the car, and we walked up the smooth driveway to the front door. Since I'd been with Mrs. Lanigan, I'd become hyper aware of surfaces. A smooth one was always welcomed by both of us.

"Remember what we talked about," I said.

"You think way too much of me," Mrs. Lanigan said. "But I'll try my best to be encouraging and complimentary."

Ardan came up behind us with the food. "You can do it, Mother."

Bliss opened the door before we had a chance to ring the doorbell.

"Come in, come in. I can't wait for you to meet her." Bliss wore a black lounging outfit and slippers. Her shiny hair was in a ponytail and her face void of makeup. She looked tired but happy.

We followed her through the foyer to the living room. The

house was all polished wood and high beams, like a high-end ski lodge. I led Mrs. Lanigan over to the couch and helped her get situated just as Ciaran came in with the baby. Tall with dark skin, dancing eyes, and a muscular build, he oozed sex appeal and charm. He was in bare feet and wore loose jeans and a floppy shirt. Ruffled, almost black hair added to his wicked and indolent persona.

"Hello, ladies. Perfect timing. Carmen just woke up from her nap."

"May I hold her?" Mrs. Lanigan asked. "Otherwise, I can't get a sense of her."

"Sure," Ciaran said with a surprised glance at me.

Ciaran placed the baby in his mother's arms. He knelt next to them, lifting the blanket from Carmen's face and guiding Mrs. Lanigan's hand to touch the baby's cheeks. "She has chubby cheeks, Mother. Like a little chipmunk."

"Good. That means she's nice and fat. Bliss, well done."

"Thank you," Bliss said. "I'm also nice and fat."

"You look amazing, baby," Ciaran said.

Mrs. Lanigan put her nose to the baby's head. "She smells like you did, Ciaran."

Ciaran grinned up at his brother. "Can you believe I'm a dad?"

Ardan nodded and smiled. "You're going to be a great one."

Bliss sat in one of the chairs and put her feet on the coffee table. "What I want to know, Mrs. Lanigan, is how you gave birth five times? I'm not sure I have another fifteen-hour labor in me."

"Each time was completely unique," Mrs. Lanigan said. "Your husband shot out of me like he didn't want to be late for a party. Which remained his mode of operation for most of his life."

"Not now, Mother. I'm a boring family guy from here on out."

"Those are the least boring men of all," Mrs. Lanigan said. "What I remember most about the day you were born is how the nurses were so taken with you. They said you were the most beautiful newborn they'd ever seen. For one thing, you were huge. I swear you looked like you were three months old. From the moment they put you in my arms, you wriggled and squirmed and made these hilarious faces that made your father and the nurses laugh. That was just the beginning. You've always been a party. The brightest light in any room. I could never let you know, of course, or it would have gone straight to your head and made you even naughtier than you already were. You made me laugh and laugh. Your father too. One time, you dressed our cat, Mouser, in your sister's baby dress and cap. You paraded him around the neighborhood in his crate with that poor creature yowling. To make it worse, you made kids pay a nickel to see the circus cat dressed as a baby. I asked you, 'What would make you think to do such a thing?' You answered back, 'Mother, how could you *not* think to do such a thing? I mean, look at him. He's hilarious.' I had to bite my lip to keep from laughing. He *did* look funny with that cap tied on his head. The way he looked at you, I was sure he planned to kill you in your sleep the first chance he got. Later, when I told your father, we laughed and laughed while Mouser enjoyed a treat for his trouble.

"Another time, our housekeeper, Sheila, made a batch of cookies for the bake sale at school. I told all you kids they were not to be eaten. I left the room to get my purse. When I came back, you were midway through your sixth cookie—chocolate smeared on your chin. I asked you, 'Why did you do this when you knew you'd be caught and punished?' You looked me straight in the eye and said, 'If Miss Sheila didn't make them so good, I might be able to control myself. So, if you think about it, the whole thing's really her fault.' You made life colorful. I can still feel your glow, even without my sight."

Bliss and Ciaran stared at Mrs. Lanigan like they'd never seen her before.

"I've never heard either one of those stories before," Ciaran said. "I vaguely recall the circus cat incident, now that you mention it. That was some funny stuff."

"How did you punish him?" Bliss asked. "I have a feeling I

may need to have a few tricks up my sleeve if his daughter is anything like him."

"For the cat, I made him give all the nickels back and he was grounded from playing outside with the other kids for a week. That was the only thing he ever cared about. Doing something physical outside."

"Not much has changed," Bliss said. "He thought it was a great idea to teach me to ski."

"His father was like that too," Mrs. Lanigan said. "He was constantly taking the boys on scary adventures I felt certain they would never return from."

"What about Ardan, Mrs. Lanigan?" I asked. "What was he like?"

"Ardan? Let's see. He entered the world gently, without any fuss. The labor was quick, like he wanted to spare me pain. He cried for a second or two when he first came out, but his heart wasn't in it. When the doctor put him in my arms, he stared up at me with the eyes of an old soul. Right away, I thought—he will be like my father—kind, soft-spoken, extremely intelligent. I was right."

"Come on, he couldn't have been that perfect," Ciaran said.

"Every once in a while, he'd surprise us," Mrs. Lanigan said. "When he was eight, we were at the Mason's for Thanksgiving dinner and their little boy said my pie crust was too salty. Arden leaned over the table and punched him in the nose. Your father and I were so shocked we just sat there with our mouths open. We weren't invited back."

"Do you remember that?" I asked Ardan.

He shook his head. "Not at all. Are you sure it wasn't Kevan?"

"No, it was you. If it had been Kevan or Ciaran or even Teagan, it wouldn't have been as memorable. They were always punching things."

"Pie is a serious thing," I said. "As is defending your mother's honor."

"Mother's pies were amazing," Ciaran said. "I wish I had a piece of apple pie right now."

"My mother taught me how to make them," Mrs. Lanigan said. "They were the only dessert I ever made. As Ciaran pointed out, Miss Sheila was a superb cook, so I left it to her," Mrs. Lanigan said. "You must have felt extra protective since I never cooked much else."

"Mrs. Lanigan, do you think you could teach me how to make a pie?" Bliss asked. "I'd like to make an apple pie for Ciaran."

Mrs. Lanigan kissed Carmen's forehead. "I could try. It's been a long time since I made one."

"All my mother taught me was how to roll a marijuana cigarette," Bliss said.

"Is that true?" Mrs. Lanigan asked.

"Not really. She would have, had I asked," Bliss said. "Instead, I focused on getting as far away from her as possible, which meant working hard at school. Neither Blythe nor I had any interest in becoming a useless member of society."

"Good for you," Mrs. Lanigan said. "The other path might have been easier. It takes great character to break the cycle."

"If it hadn't been for my sister, my life would've been much different," Bliss said. "She made sure I had what I needed."

"My son's lucky to have such a resilient, clever woman to go through life with," Mrs. Lanigan said.

Bliss looked over at me and shook her head, as if amazed. "I'm the lucky one." Bliss smiled at her husband. "Growing up, I couldn't have imagined finding a man like him."

"Edward and I were always a team," Mrs. Lanigan said. "Parenting together is harder than being carefree and in love. Just remember to talk through things, include each other in decisions."

"Thanks for the advice, Mother," Ciaran said. "It's nice to have you here."

"I hope you mean that, because I'm staying," Mrs. Lanigan said. "Ardan and I have talked and decided it best I stay with him permanently."

Ciaran's eyes widened as he exchanged a glance with his brother.

Ardan nodded. "Mother's learned how to get around with her cane and knows my house."

"I want to be close to my kids and since you've all decided to live on this godforsaken property, I guess I will too."

Ciaran laughed. "Well, there you go. If you can't beat them, join them, right Mother?"

"Amen," Mrs. Lanigan said.

"Who's ready for some dinner?" Ardan asked. "Effie sent enough food to feed an army."

"I am." Bliss got up and took the baby from Mrs. Lanigan. "Being Carmen's food source is making me hungry."

On the way into the kitchen, Bliss took me aside. "What did you do with my mother-in-law?"

"She was in there all along," I said. "Learning how to be vulnerable sometimes comes through a humbling circumstance. She's keenly aware of the fragility of her life and wants to connect with her children before it's too late."

"You and Ardan *do* belong together."

"Why do you say that?"

"You're better than most people."

"Not really." I flushed at the compliment.

"She actually engaged with me—asked me questions," Bliss said. "Thank you for helping our family."

"I'm the one who should thank you. If you and Moonstone hadn't talked Ardan into the crazy idea to bring me here, none of this would've happened."

"Are you happy?" she asked. "Not just with Ardan, but here?"

"The word is joyful," I said. "And yes."

"Moonstone was right," Bliss said. "I thought she was, but still, like you said, it was a little crazy what we did."

"What a leap we all took," I said.

"Maybe a little crazy is just what we need to make dreams a

reality." Bliss smiled down at her baby. "Like coming to Idaho with a homeless guy and his three-legged dog."

* * *

In her room, Mrs. Lanigan felt for her cane between the mattress and the bedside table, where we'd agreed it should always go when she was in bed. I watched her cross the room with it in front of her and felt like a proud mother when she found the entryway to the bathroom with no trouble. While she brushed her teeth, I prepared her bed for the night by removing one of the pillows and pulling the comforter down to the bottom of the mattress. We'd been over exactly how far down it was so that if she woke in the middle of the night, she would be able to find it easily.

A few minutes later she got into bed. I tucked her in, resisting my impulse to kiss her forehead. I propped some pillows against the back of the bed and pulled back the covers. "I have the rest of the letters. They explain what happened."

Her face lit up. "You were holding out on me."

"Even these letters can't compete with a new grandbaby." It had taken weeks, but I think I finally had the next bit of the story pieced together.

Dear Augie,

I told Mother I intend to marry you. She feels certain Father will follow through on his threat to kick me out. We talked over a plan about what to do and she gave me her blessing. She asked only that I bring her to meet you. Can you be ready tomorrow evening?

Love,

Nicholas

Dearest Nicholas,

I've just returned from meeting your mother. She was exactly as you described, right down to her delicate hands and violet-blue eyes. When we were walking together in the rose garden, she asked that should I ever have a home and yard of my own to please plant a white rose bush in memory of her. I promised her I would but said I hoped it would be a long time before she left us. She squeezed my arm and said she hoped so too. When we reached the end of the garden, she asked if I understood about your father and what it means when we marry. I assured her I did, but that I worried you didn't fully comprehend what it means to our future. She disagreed. "He wants you, not the money. You two can make your own way, like most couples have to."

She told me she has stashed some cash away for us. When we're ready, she will make sure you have it to get us started. "If something happens to me, promise me you'll take Boyce with you, wherever you go. He can't be here alone with his father."

I promised her we would always look after him.

With all my love,

Augie

Dear Augie,

It's nearing midnight and I'm exhausted. However, I wanted to write to you while the details of tonight remained fresh in my mind and to let you know I may not be able to come by for a few days.

After you left, Mother became suddenly ill. We were about to go in for dinner when she collapsed. The doctor came right away. He took me aside and asked where Father was. I told him he was out and that whatever it was, he could tell me. I look after her and my brother. He gave me a strange look, like he knew something I didn't, but proceeded to tell me that Mother's heart is failing. He said she won't have long and to make her comfortable and for God's sake don't let her know how sick she is. Knowing the truth would only make her last days sad.

After I showed him out, I found Boyce crying in the library. "What will we do without her?" he asked.

I told him he would always have me. "I'll never let anything happen to you."

Boyce raised his voice, which I'd never heard him do before. Usually he speaks so quietly I ask him to repeat half of what he says.

"It's Father's fault. He's done this to her. He's broken her heart with his neglect."

We talked for some time about what he wanted to do after Mother passed. I assured him he would always have a home with us, but did he understand how different our lives would be? He said he didn't care. He just wanted to be with me.

We went in to see Mother. She was pale and weak. We sat on either side of her bed. I assumed she was asleep until she reached out for my hand. "Augie is lovely. And smart. She'll be a wonderful mother. You're right to choose her and not the money. Always choose love." She had me open her jewelry box. "My mother's wedding ring is there. She wanted your wife to have it."

I have a ring for you, my love.

She patted my hand and then went on to say she knows she's dying. "I've known for some time. Promise me you'll look after Boyce. Take him with you wherever you go."

"We'll be together, Mother, don't worry."

I'll close now and have Fred bring this over to you.

Love,

Nicholas

Dear Augie,

This morning Father joined me for breakfast. We discussed Mother's health. He said he doesn't believe anything's wrong with her. "It's just another one of her made up illnesses in an attempt to control me."

I wanted to lash out at him, but I knew it would only upset Mother if she heard us arguing, so I kept quiet.

Then, he said it was time for me to earn my keep and stop babying Mother and Boyce. "It's time for you to be a man." He's interested in investing in the moving pictures business, as he believes there will be much growth in the years to come. I'm young, he said, and more suited for it than he. He went on to say he wants me to move out to California and start an office out there. I was taken aback and unsure how to respond. It was the time, I thought, to tell him about you. Maybe, just maybe, he could accept you and we could go to California together.

I should have known better. There was a reason for his sudden interest in me heading up the Hollywood project.

He knows about you.

"You'll have to give up the girl," he said. "Or we're done discussing California or anything else."

"You know about her?"

"I do."

"I love her. I want her to be my wife."

"No."

"Why do you care?" I asked. "What's it to you? She's no threat to you."

"An Irish Catholic who scrubs floors? Really, son, your ignorance and immaturity astound me. Do you really think the girl loves you, or your money?"

"You don't know her."

"I had my boys follow her. I know everything about her, including her route to work."

My mind spun in circles. Was he threatening to have them hurt you? I had to buy time, or I'd be tossed out before I could put our plan together. I pretended to acquiesce. I agreed to the California plan and giving you up. He'll think I'm preparing for a move there, which will give me the opportunity to put some cash together.

"I'll do whatever you want," I said. "But please, don't hurt Augie."

"You keep your word, and all is well."

After what I've learned about his business practices, any misguided hope I had of gaining his love are gone. I no longer care. I'll walk away from all of it with my head held high. The money, my family, everything that could possibly be a barrier to our lives together.

I will fight for you, my love, until the end of time. Nothing else matters. I'll come for you as soon as possible. Until then, I have to stay away for fear Father's thugs are following me. Stay safe, please.

Love,

Nicholas

Dear Augie,

Yesterday was spent organizing my affairs, pretending that it was in preparation for California. I asked Fred to take me to my father's offices, as I had several items I needed from there. Our usual route was blocked by a bank of snow that had fallen from a building, thus he took us downtown instead. We were driving by the Bentley Hotel when I happened to glance out the window at the same time Father came out of the front doors of the hotel. He was with a woman. She had platinum blond hair and wore a long coat with a fur collar. She clung to Father's arm as if she were afraid to fall in her tall heels.

I asked Fred to pull over, which he did. Neither of us spoke for a good minute as they meandered together down the street. The woman's face was animated as they stopped to look into the windows of various storefronts. At one point, he threw his head back, laughing at whatever she'd whispered in his ear. I'd never seen him smile or laugh that way. Seeing them together was like watching something intimate, something I should never see.

After they disappeared into one of the shops, I studied Fred. "Did you know?" They always say a family's driver knows all.

"Yes, sir."

"Who is she?"

"Her name is Miss Prescott. She lives at the hotel. Your father is her sponsor."

I asked him what that meant. He cleared his throat and looked like a rabbit about to be eaten by a boa.

"Do you mean my father pays for her to live there?"

"Yes, sir. She's his close friend."

Close friend? A man does not have a woman as a close friend.

"Do you drive them places?" I asked.

For some strange reason, the thought of Fred having that woman in our car was excruciating. Silly as it is, given that Father has a mistress in the penthouse suite of the poshest hotel in town. Whether Fred drives them places or not is the least of the transgressions.

I needn't have worried. Fred assured me that Miss Prescott has her own driver.

Red fury overtook me. I couldn't see from rage, other than an image of my frail mother telling me she was tedious to her husband.

Fred tried to calm me with some nonsense that it was not uncommon for men of a certain wealth and stature to have women on the side. "It means nothing. Passing fancy," he said. Nothing!

The way he laughed with her and held her arm did not look like nothing. It looked like love.

I didn't know he was capable of love. Apparently, he can't love us, but there's plenty for Miss Prescott.

"How long?" I asked.

"I don't know," Fred said. "Since before I worked for your family."

Fred's worked for us since I was ten years old. Eleven years.

Father and Miss Prescott exited the shop and headed further south.

I leapt from the car and ran down the street toward them, shouting, unable to think of anything but confronting him. When I reached them, they were in front of a bistro. Father gaped at me like I was a ghost. His two worlds colliding right in front of his fat face must have been too much even for him. He propelled Miss Prescott toward the front door like she was a package. "Go inside. I'll deal with this."

This? I was a this.

He put his hand on my arm and had the nerve to speak without any inflection at all. "My personal life has nothing to do with you. I expect you'll keep this quiet."

I cursed at him.

His face turned red and he took me by the collar and shook me.

"You remember your place. Any time I decide, you'll be out on the street. Penniless. And that pansy brother of yours goes too. You hear me? You do as I say when I say it."

"You had the audacity to tell me to give up Augie? And you have this…this whore in a hotel."

He slammed me against the building.

I shoved him, and we fell to the ground where I pummeled his face at least five times. Blood was everywhere. Fred arrived and came between us as my father tried to take hold of my collar. Next, a man dressed in a black tuxedo ran out the front door of the restaurant.

He gave Father a handkerchief for his nose and asked him to come inside. "People are watching."

Fred managed to get me in the car. We drove home without a word. When we arrived, Fred turned around to look at me. "Leave this be. You need to be around to take care of your mother and brother."

I didn't answer for a moment. None of this was Fred's fault, but I couldn't help but be angered by what feels like complacency in the face of evil. Everything's fine because Father's a rich, white man? He can do whatever he pleases without any thought to others?

I came to my senses before lashing out at him. Fred is simply doing a job in order to feed his family. He doesn't have the privilege of a moral high ground.

I thanked him and told him to go home for the night.

I've no idea if Mother knows about Miss Prescott. Would she care if she knew? I don't know the answer to that either. Fred is right. If she did know, it would only hurt her.

The moment I went inside, I headed to Father's liquor cabinet and poured myself a drink. Thankfully, Mother and Boyce were already in bed. I wouldn't have been able to face either of them.

I spent the night packing. This morning, I went in to see Mother to tell her I planned on leaving with you tomorrow. We discussed whether she should send Boyce to us once we were settled or have him go with me now? She wants him to go with us.

Boyce came in and we proposed the idea to him. He cried, saying he wanted to stay with Mother until the end. She begged him to go and he finally agreed.

I bought three train tickets for Indiana, leaving tomorrow afternoon. We will go without a word to Father and never look back.

I'm going to close and have Fred take this letter over to Mrs. Purdy's. Please be ready for tomorrow afternoon.

Love,

Nicholas

Dear Nicholas,

I asked Fred to wait so I could scrawl a quick note back to you. Please, my love, be careful. Your father is a violent man. Get out quickly. Come here to me. I'll be ready.

Love,

Augie

Dear Augie,

I'm not sure how to write this, only that I would never be able to speak the words out loud. This is about Boyce.

When I came home from my last errands this evening, the house was quiet. I checked on Mother. She was asleep. Mrs. Lancaster said she'd had a good evening and had even eaten a little dinner. When I asked after Boyce's whereabouts, Mrs. Lancaster explained that his friend Martin had come for dinner and they were studying together in the library. I knew he was probably saying goodbye to his only friend, not studying.

Noticing how late it was and that Boyce had to pack, I went in search of them. They weren't in the library or anywhere else in the house. Worried, I decided to check the pool house, but they weren't there either. Growing increasingly concerned, I saw a flicker of a candlelight in Mother's hothouse. How sweet and sad, I thought. Boyce and Martin were looking after Mother's orchids one last time.

I found them. They were fast asleep.

Asleep together, Augie, without a stitch of clothing, wrapped in each other's arms.

I'd heard that some men were this way, but I never imagined Boyce to be one of them. Distressed and shocked, I stumbled out of there and ran into the house. I paced for a good hour, trying to decide what to do.

When I saw them heading across the lawn, I ran upstairs. I couldn't see them together just then. Not after what I'd seen.

What should I do? Will you allow him to come with us now? I'm afraid for him. More afraid than I've ever been in my life.

Pray for us, Augie.

Love,

Nicholas

"Oh, dear," Mrs. Lanigan said. "A motive, at last."

"Yes. Do you think he would murder his own son just for being gay?"

"It was a different time. Are there more?" she asked.

"Yes. I've got the rest of them right here."

Dear Nicholas,

I'm shaking from the shock of your letter. We have to take him in, especially now. I wonder if your mother suspected all along. Could this be why she was so adamant he come with us? We can't break our promise to her. I know it's hard to understand, but it's not for us to judge. Only Jesus decides these matters. He is your brother and you love him. Bring him tomorrow. I'll be here.

Love,

Augie

Dear Augie,

Around nine last night, after I'd gotten your letter delivered back by Fred, I was finishing my packing. I heard Father shouting from his study. I ran down the hall and burst through the door. He had Boyce by the throat, choking him. He called him an awful word, over and over. Boyce's face was purple. Father was killing him.

I threw myself onto my Father's back and yanked him away from Boyce. I pushed him to the floor and held him there. Boyce ran from the room. Father and I threw punches at each other and rolled around on the floor until he finally relented and tossed me from him. His face is bruised and purple from our fight yesterday.

How did he find out? Had he seen them together like I had?

"What happened?" I asked him.

There were rumors swirling around about Boyce. Loomis, his arch enemy, was drunk and said it to Father's face, in front of the entire club. Someone had seen him coming out of one of the places they gather.

Father called Boyce a degenerate and disgusting, and he said he wished he had never been born.

That's what he said exactly, Augie.

I ran out of the study and down the hallway. Boyce was in his room, shaking and crying. I put my arm around him and let him sob. When he quieted, he asked if I'd heard what Father called him.

I said I had and that I'd seen him and Martin asleep in the hothouse. He wouldn't look at me. "You told Father?"

"No, no. I would never tell anyone. Someone saw you walk out of that place."

"Are you ashamed of me?" he asked.

I told him I was afraid for him. "It's a dangerous thing to do."

"To *be*," he said. "I tried to change, but I can't. I think Father would've killed me if you hadn't come."

"There are others who will try and do the same. When we leave here, you have to keep it a secret."

He nodded and buried his face into his knees. "I'm sorry. I'm weak."

I went to the window and saw Father's car leave. Going back to Miss Prescott, I thought.

I let Boyce sleep in my room. When I woke this morning, he was gone. I've no idea where he went.

I'll leave this on Mrs. Purdy's front step, so you'll see it right away. If I don't come this afternoon, I'll come tomorrow.

Love,

Nicholas

"Poor Boyce," Mrs. Lanigan said.

"I know." I brought forth the next sequential letter. "Here's what happened next."

Dear Augie,

Please tell Mrs. Purdy thank you for giving you the messages and my notes. I found Boyce at Martin's. I brought him home, knowing Father wasn't there. We're coming for you in the morning. Mother gave me a suitcase full of cash she's been saving for years. It's like she knew one day we'd have to escape. I'll see tomorrow.

Love,

Nicholas

Dear Nicholas,

When you didn't come this morning, I knew something was wrong. I begged Lois's brother to take me over to your house in his car. When we got there, I saw all the police and the medical people. I panicked and ran around the back door. Mrs. Lancaster told me that Boyce was dead and that you were being interrogated by the police. She promised to get this to you. Please come to me as soon as you can.

Love,

Augie

• • •

"Interrogated?" Mrs. Lanigan asked. "Surely they knew he didn't do it."

"The next one sequentially is the very first one we read, telling her they ruled it a suicide. Maybe it was just standard practice to interview everyone. And then there's this one."

Dear Augie,

After the funeral, I brought Mother home and helped her to bed. I knew she would not get out again. She looked up at me with the saddest eyes I've ever seen. "I'll go be with Boyce. I can't let him be alone."

This is the beginning of the end, I thought. Boyce's death was too much for her. She's given up fighting. I sat with her all through the night, listening to her shallow breaths. As dawn broke, she slipped away from me.

I'll bury her next to Boyce and then I'll come for you. This time there is no one left to die.

Love,

Nicholas

"So that's that," she said. "They went to Indiana and I know the rest after that."

"I have another bit to the story that I think you might enjoy," I said. "It's the epilogue of Ardan's book."

"Did he say you could read it to me?" she asked.

"He would like you to read the whole thing," I said. "But you already know the story from the letters, so I'll just read you the part that isn't in the letters. The part about you."

Nicholas called the midwife in the wee hours of a dark February night. She and his wife's mother went inside the bedroom to tend to his wife. His father-in-law joined him in the kitchen and they nodded at each other but did not speak. The wind howled outside his windows, almost drowning out Augie's cries from the pain of labor. He paced the floor and prayed until his father-in-law poured him a whiskey and asked him to sit with him at the table.

"From now on, your heart will forever be at the mercy of your child. There is nothing you won't do for him or her." Mr. Devin placed his weathered, shaky hand on Nicholas's shoulder.

"My heart is already at the mercy of *your* daughter," he said. "There is nothing I won't do for her. I knew the first time I ever saw her that she would be my world."

"It's all a father wants," Mr. Devin said. "Knowing she is loved by a good man, I can leave the world at peace."

"No one leaves today," Nicholas said. "Today our baby comes."

At sunrise, he heard his baby's cry for the first time. Mrs. Devin came out to tell them the baby was a girl and healthy. "Quite fat for a newborn. Augie did well."

They allowed him to come into the room at long last. His Augie looked wan and pale. She held a bundle inside the patchwork baby quilt Mrs. Devin had made. He went to Augie's side and kissed her cheek. "You were brave," he said.

"I wasn't scared." She smiled. "I knew just what to do."

He pulled back the blanket to look at his daughter. He studied her small, determined face. The jutting jaw and clenched fists told him she would grow into a woman of strength and determination.

Augie asked if he would like to hold her. "I'm scared, but I will."

He took her from his wife and held the warm baby to his chest. "Have you decided what she'll be called?" he asked.

"Riona," Augie said.

His gaze returned to his baby. "Riona Devin Garfield, you'll be a force in the world. But first, you'll be my little daughter. I'll teach you how the soil grows tomatoes and of the birds' songs and of the simple pleasure of a hard day's work. And then, I'll send you out into the world and let you make your own life; however you want it—simple or exciting, bold or gentle. For now, you're my precious girl."

He could not know of the future. He knew only that this woman and this child were the reason God had made him. They were worth more than all the treasures in all the world. He did not need to look back to know the truth of his life, only forward.

"How did my boy channel this?" she asked.

"Ardan and I've decided it doesn't matter, only that he did."

"You'll read me the whole thing?"

"As many times as you want."

She grabbed my wrist. "Charlotte, thank you."

"I love you, mean old thing."

"Now don't quote me on this in the morning, but you've saved my life. I didn't think I could live this way, but it turns out I can."

"I never doubted you for a minute," I said. "Now get some rest."

"You're getting bossier by the day," she said.

* * *

That night I fell asleep in Ardan's arms and dreamt of orchids in a hothouse. I moved in damp, thick air, the scent of flowers thick in my nose.

Ardan was there, only he looked different. Dark curls, wire-rimmed glasses, and a fedora. His eyes were the same. "Augie, do you have the tickets?"

"I'm Charlotte."

"I brought your perfume." The flower scent was replaced by Chanel No. 5. "Come home." He smiled and held out his arms.

Yes, I'm Augie. Wife to Nicholas.

I woke with a start. For a few minutes I lay there, half in this lifetime and half in the last. Was it possible? I quickly dismissed the idea. It was the letters. I'd practically lived in their world since I arrived here. This was just my mind playing tricks.

I snuggled closer to Ardan and went back to sleep.

CHAPTER TWELVE

ARDAN

On the first day of June, I asked Charlotte to walk with me to the creek. When we reached the meadow, I spotted a Peregrine falcon. He dove and danced in the air, looking for prey.

An image of my father standing in this very meadow came to my mind. We'd stood together in this same spot and watched a falcon.

"Their strength and grace in combination is what a man should strive for," he said.

I was fourteen that summer, anxious and awkward, my face peppered with acne and braces on my teeth, and I felt neither strong or full of grace.

"You boys hang onto this land after I die. You hear me?"

"Yes, sir."

"Everything you'll ever need is right here."

"Yes, sir."

"Find a girl who loves this land like you do and build a home. Raise a family."

Now, I looked over at Charlotte. She smiled as she watched the falcon ride the wind.

"Do you love it here?" I asked.

She turned her gaze to me. "You know I do."

"And you love me?"

"You know I do."

I reached into the side pocket of my cargo shorts and pulled out the box with the ring in it. I dropped to one knee.

She took a step backward. "What're you doing?"

I opened the lid of the box and presented the ring. The diamond sparkled under the sun. "I'm asking you to be my wife. Moonstone and Bliss brought you here. I want to be the reason you stay. Will you marry me?"

"Yes, yes. I'll marry you."

I wiped her cheeks with my thumbs. Tears evaporated under my touch. We stared into each other's eyes. A sensation passed through my body. Images of faces and times and places I'd never seen before came to me one after the other. Her eyes. They were the same, no matter what lifetime. A hundred lifetimes passed between us. We'd loved each other before. Hundreds of times. Different times, different bodies, but always us.

"It's you," I whispered. "Always you."

"Always us."

CHAPTER THIRTEEN

CHARLOTTE

Just before lunch, I went outside to the patio to call my parents. My mom answered after a few rings, sounding breathless.

"Hey, Mom."

"Darling, how are you?"

"I'm good. Have you been exercising?" I asked.

"No, I just had to run for the phone. We were outside reading when we heard it ringing. I was hoping it would be you. Is everything all right? I've been worried about you."

"I'm fine. Better than fine. Can you get Dad and put me on speaker?"

"I'm already here, sweetheart." I warmed at the sound of my dad's baritone.

"Hi, Dad. I called to tell you that I'm getting married. Ardan and I are getting married."

Silence on the other end of the phone.

"I know it's been fast, but we're in love and we just know it's right. We've spent a lot of time together and we're just so happy. Like soulmates."

My mother spoke first. "It *is* fast, but if you're sure, then we're pleased."

"More than pleased," Dad said. "It was that way with your mom and me. We knew after our first date, didn't we, honey?"

"I think it took me until the third date," Mom said. "But yes, we knew. When you know, you know."

"Do you have a date set?" Dad asked.

"That depends on you two," I said. "We want to do it this summer. When can you get here?"

"Why so soon? Are you pregnant?" Mom asked.

"No, Mom, it's not that. We're just ready. We feel like we've been waiting for this day all our lives. Mom, I want you here to help plan the wedding and pick a dress and all that."

"We can come anytime," Dad said. "It'll take a week or two to get there from Florida, but it's no problem."

"Ardan's family property is big. There's room for your Airstream," I said. "More than enough room."

"Good," Dad said. "I'll be there to give you away."

"We want to do it here on the property—on the spot where we first met."

"How romantic," Mom said.

"When you get here, Dad, Ardan wants to ask your permission."

"It's a bit old-fashioned," Dad said. "The only permission he needs is yours."

"I know, but that's how he is."

"I think it's wonderful," Mom said. "Shows respect."

"I did a little research on the Lanigan family," Dad said. "Sweetheart, do you understand how rich they are?"

I laughed. "Yes, Dad. Even so, they're completely down to earth. You'll like them."

"It's not the money, is it?" Dad asked. "You love him for him?"

"Head over heels. I'd live in a ditch as long as it was with him," I said.

"As long as you're sure," Dad said.

"How's Mrs. Lanigan doing?" Mom asked.

"Better." I told her about how independent she was becoming. "Mom, she'll love you."

"Everyone loves your mother," Dad said.

I smiled. "True. But I mean you have a lot of the same interests. It'll be good for her to have another friend."

We talked for a few more minutes before I had to go. Minutes after I hung up, my mother sent the first link to a wedding dress. By the end of the day, there were a dozen of them.

* * *

For dinner that evening, Ardan and I convinced Mrs. Lanigan she should join us in the dining room. We wanted to tell her together about our engagement.

"What're you wearing?" she asked as we walked toward the dining room.

"I'm wearing a yellow sundress with a white cardigan."

"I bet you look lovely," Mrs. Lanigan said. "What's the occasion?"

"We have something exciting to tell you," I said.

"Did that dolt of an agent sell your book?"

I almost laughed. Only Mrs. Lanigan would assume we were celebrating a business success and not a personal one. "Just wait and see."

Ardan was already in the dining room when we arrived. We'd gotten in the habit of me describing what people were wearing.

"He's wearing fancy jeans, a light blue shirt, and a blue jacket."

"No tie?" she asked.

"No tie. But shiny brown shoes."

"That's something, I guess."

Ardan kissed his mother on the cheek and led her over to a chair. Effie had set one end of the table with china, cloth napkin, three kinds of wine glasses, and a bouquet of deep pink peonies. I described all this to Mrs. Lanigan.

When Ardan and I were seated, Effie arrived with a bottle of champagne and poured us each a glass.

"The sound of champagne bubbles," Mrs. Lanigan said with a smile. "Another reason to live."

"Mother, there are reasons to live besides adult beverages."

"Books on audio," she said. "And Charlotte."

"Speaking of Charlotte," Ardan said. "She's agreed to be my wife."

Mrs. Lanigan clapped her hands together. "Didn't I tell you? And you're sure, Charlotte?"

Why did everyone keep asking me that? They should ask Ardan that question. He was the one with all the money.

"I've never been more sure of anything in my life," I said.

"Me either," Ardan said.

"How did your parents take the news?" Mrs. Lanigan asked. "Were they worried it was too soon?"

"My mom said when you know, you know," I said.

"I can't wait to meet them," Mrs. Lanigan said. "When can they come?"

CHAPTER FOURTEEN

ARDAN

The next evening, we mingled with my brothers and their wives in Kevan and Blythe's living room. Kevan had opened a nice bottle of wine. As we sipped from our glasses, Blythe came out with a platter of appetizers. Charlotte was already half finished with her glass, and we'd only arrived five minutes ago.

We learned Blythe's daughters were in Seattle, visiting their father for the first week of summer vacation. They'd be here later in the summer.

Blythe, looked like her sister, Bliss, only she was shorter and more petite. They shared the same dark blond hair, the color of sun-kissed honey, and amber eyes. However, their personalities were wildly different. Bliss was lively and quick whereas Blythe was serene and nurturing.

Over the past few years, I'd gotten to know both my sisters-in-law well. I adored them. They'd despaired with me at my lack of luck with women and were on the constant hunt for the woman of my dreams. When Moonstone had suggested Charlotte, Bliss had jumped at the chance.

Charlotte tightened her grip on my hand. "Do it now and get it over with."

I'd tried to reassure her on the way over that they'd all be excited for us, but she was worried they'd think we were rushing into things.

"We have an announcement," I said, trying not to wince from the death grip from my fiancée. "Charlotte and I are engaged."

Bliss and Blythe squealed. Charlotte held up her hand as the ladies rushed over to see the ring.

"I knew it," Bliss said. "Didn't I tell you, Ciaran?"

"Yes, dear." Ciaran rocked Carmen's car seat with his foot. "You called it."

My brothers hugged me one after the other.

"Happy for you, little brother," Kevan said.

"It's about time," Ciaran said. "We thought you were going to die alone with a cat."

"Me too," I said. "Maybe two cats."

"When's the wedding?" Bliss asked.

"End of the summer," I said. "Charlotte's parents are coming from Florida to help plan the wedding."

"We want something small," Charlotte said. "Just family."

"Here on the property," I said.

With Carmen asleep in her car seat, the party divided between men and women. My brothers dragged me outside to smoke cigars and drink good scotch. The women had already pulled out a laptop and were looking at wedding dresses.

While Kevan poured us drinks, Ciaran handed me a cigar. "What got into you?" Ciaran asked. "You afraid to lose her so you put a ring on it?"

"No, it just felt right." I took the drink from Kevan. "We've spent a lot of time together since we first met. I'm sure it seems fast to you guys, but to me it feels like I've waited my whole life to find my soulmate and she's finally here. We don't want to waste another minute apart."

"I guess Moonstone was right," Kevan said. "I thought it was a little crazy to bring her out here, but it was obviously the right thing."

"She's been great for Mother," Ciaran said. "But you don't think it was the power of suggestion, do you? Like Moonstone told you she was your soulmate and so you started to think she was?"

"No, it wasn't like that." I took a tentative sip from my glass of scotch. "But I'll tell you what did happen. Given the off chance that she was my soulmate, I behaved like she was. I was bold and flirtatious. I made a move right away instead of second guessing myself for months and losing the opportunity. It gave me a sense of the inevitable. Let me tell you, after that first kiss, there was no doubt in my mind. This is going to sound crazy, but I swear, it's like we were together in another lifetime. She's so familiar to me."

"I get that," Kevan said.

"I do as well," Ciaran said. "As much as I tried to resist Bliss, it was impossible, like a force pulled me to her."

"That's it exactly," I said. "I was going to wait and propose to her in Italy, but I decided a honeymoon in Europe was a better idea. She's never traveled and wants to. I want to give her everything. Every experience. Every opportunity."

My phone buzzed inside my jean pocket. A quick glance told me who it was. Felicity. This was the fourth time she'd called in the past few weeks.

"What is it?" Kevan asked.

I shoved my phone back in my pocket. "You won't believe it. Felicity's been calling me. She never leaves a message, but she's called at least half-dozen times."

"When was the last time you heard from her?" Ciaran asked.

"I haven't talked to her since the whole thing blew up with Melanie. I just needed to purge her from my life."

"You and me both. She got psycho there at the end. I told you I had to block her, right?" Ciaran asked.

"That's what drove her to my house that night," I said. "She was out of control."

"I feel bad, but I couldn't have her calling and texting a thousand times a day with Bliss right there. You know Bliss. She wouldn't have taken kindly to that."

We all chuckled.

My phone buzzed again.

"Dude, maybe answer it and get it over with," Ciaran said. "She obviously wants something."

I told them about Moonstone's prediction. "The minute she said it, I remembered the phone calls. She wrecked my last relationship. I can't lose Charlotte."

"You won't," Kevan said. "You'll see. Once you find the right person and you agree to fiercely protect each other, no one can pull you apart."

"I hope you're right." As if she heard me, the phone buzzed again. "For heaven's sake. Excuse me. I'll just go out by the cars to talk to her."

I had to answer. I would simply tell her I had no room for her in my life and to stop calling.

"Hello," I said.

"It's Felicity."

"I know. Jesus, you've called a hundred times. Can't you take a hint?"

"I'm sick, Ardan. Cancer. I'm dying."

My stomach lurched. "Dying?"

"The cancer's spread all over. There's nothing to be done. I only have months, maybe weeks."

No, this couldn't be happening. "God, Felicity, I'm so sorry."

"I've made peace with it except for one thing. I have a baby. She's a year old. Isabel. I named her Isabel after my mother."

Her words were like someone head butted me in the chest. "Are you married?"

"No. The father's a sperm bank donor. When I was four months pregnant, I found out I had ovarian cancer. I would've had to abort in order to get treatment. I didn't want to do that. Not with this baby. My miracle baby."

I couldn't feel my legs as I did the math in my head. "You got pregnant not long after I saw you?"

"That's right."

"What're you going to do?"

"I need to come home, Ardan. I want to die in Idaho where I was happy. I want you to spread my ashes by the side of the creek."

"You want to come here?"

"Yes, and I want you to take Isabel. I want you to raise my daughter."

* * *

I staggered back to the table where my brothers were smoking their cigars.

"Pour me another drink," I said.

"Crap. What did she do?" Ciaran asked.

"She's dying of cancer. Not only does she want to die in my house, she wants me to raise her one-year-old baby."

"What the hell?" Ciaran asked.

"Where's the father?" Kevan asked.

"Sperm donor." I shared with them what she'd told me about the pregnancy.

"I hope you shut that idea down," Kevan said. "You're getting married. As sad as it is, you can't take her or her child in. How is she your responsibility?"

"What did you tell her?" Ciaran asked.

"I told her I had to talk to my fiancée first."

"Good man. Do not fall into her trap again," Kevan said. "She's done enough damage to your life as it is."

"Seriously, Ardan, you're finally happy with the right woman. Don't let her wreck it. Charlotte's not going to want to be saddled with all this. You guys have a wedding to plan."

"A honeymoon to go on," Kevan said.

"I know you're right. It's just that she's so sick and she has no one."

"Brother, don't do this. Please." Ciaran gestured toward the inside of the house. "Your loyalty is to that sweet girl in there. Not some woman who chose me instead of you."

"I get it," I said. "I do. I won't mess this up."

CHAPTER FIFTEEN

CHARLOTTE

I knew the moment we got into the car to go home that something was wrong. His brothers must have given him a hard time about the engagement. I didn't want to ask. I didn't want to know. The night had appeared to go so well. The toasts and camaraderie had seemed completely real.

We were in the house by the time I had the courage to ask him. "Did something happen with your brothers?"

"What? No, no. They're so happy for us."

"Then what's wrong?"

"Felicity called again. My brothers convinced me to answer."

"What did she want?" A shiver went down my spine. This woman was trouble.

He slumped against the counter. "She's dying. Cancer. There's nothing to be done. She has only months, maybe weeks to live."

Cancer? The answer was so unexpected, I just stared at him.

"She wants to die here where she was the happiest," he said.

"Here? Like your house?"

"She'd probably prefer Ciaran's, but yes."

"I…I don't even know what to say." For once I was speechless.

"She has a baby. A twelve-month-old baby girl named Isabel. And get this. She wants to leave the child with me."

A brick dropped from my throat to my stomach. "You? Why you?"

"She said I'm the only one she can trust to raise her like she would." He picked up a spoon from the counter and tapped it against the palm of his hand. A drop of coffee dripped on the table. I wanted to wipe it away with my thumb. Make it disappear so the granite was perfect once more.

"What did you say?"

"I told her about you and that we're starting a life together. But she wants to come here." His voice wavered. "She wants to die here where her happiest times were."

"But what about the baby?"

"I told her to come and bring Isabel, and I'll help her figure out what to do. There are agencies we can contact to find couples who want to adopt. She agreed to talking about it when she arrives."

"What else? There's something you're not telling me."

"I'm worried. Moonstone warned me. She told me she had a dream about a fragile, blond woman threatening our relationship."

I couldn't think about that just now. I needed more details.

"Where's the father?" I asked.

He cleared his throat. "The pregnancy was via a sperm donor. She's in her late thirties and decided she wanted to have a child, even though she was single at the time. After she became pregnant, she was diagnosed with ovarian cancer. Rather than abort and have the cancer removed, she continued with the pregnancy. After the baby came, they operated right away, but the cancer had spread. To her lungs. She's had chemotherapy, but it's done nothing to shrink the tumors."

My mind spun. A baby?

"But what about family?" I asked. "Isn't there anyone to take her?"

He shoved his hands into the pockets of his jeans. "There's no one else. She has no family. Her parents were killed ten years ago in a small aircraft crash. You may remember seeing it on the news. Her father was a Hollywood producer—Wayne Spinner. His wife, Felicity's mother, was an actress back in the day."

"Your Felicity is Felicity Spinner?" I asked.

"That's right."

I remembered the story well. Wayne Spinner had produced some of the most popular shows in the late eighties and early nineties. His wife had been the star on one of his sitcoms. Felicity had been their only child. I flashed upon a photograph snapped by the tabloids of a stunning blond woman coming out of the church after her parents' memorial service. Felicity Spinner was known for her philanthropic work, mostly with children's causes.

"I take it from the look on your face, you know the story," Ardan said.

"It would be hard not to." Felicity Spinner was a shiny head of blond hair and formal dresses most women wore once for their senior prom and once for their wedding. She was American royalty with her slender, aristocratic bearing. Insecurity that minutes ago had seemed like a distant enemy, roared through me.

"Don't look like that," he said. "No one is as beautiful or special as you. Not to me."

"Oh, Ardan. This is so sad."

"She's a sweet person, but she's lost. She always has been. I'm afraid of the havoc she'll bring to our house."

"But if she wants to come here, you can't turn her away."

"She said she's hired a private hospice nurse willing to come here."

I fidgeted with the necklace that nestled in the hollow of my throat. What could I say that wouldn't sound either dumb or trite? I bit my thumb nail before yanking it from my mouth. Biting my nails? I hadn't wanted to do that since I was in college.

As if he could read my mind, he took my hands and kissed them. "I'm sorry this is happening. I wanted everything perfect for you."

"What if we're supposed to take the baby?" I asked.

"I don't understand what you mean. You mean like it's preordained?" The muscles below his cheekbones flexed. He pressed my hands against his chest. I felt his heart beating.

"Yes, like we knew about each other?" I asked. "Will it be obvious?"

"It's not the same thing."

Images of a baby splashing in a farmhouse sink came to me. "We've done this before," I whispered. "Raised a daughter."

"What?"

I blinked. "Nothing. Just a weird feeling."

"That we've been together before? Like in other lifetimes?"

"Yes."

"I've had them too. Mostly in dreams," he said.

I wrapped my arms around his neck and he held me close. "Whatever happens, we'll be together," I said.

"That's all we know for sure."

"That's all we need to know," I said. "The rest will become obvious."

CHAPTER SIXTEEN

ARDAN

A member of the airline staff brought Felicity out to the gate in a wheelchair. I would not have recognized her if I hadn't been expecting her. Only hints remained of the striking blond beauty she had once been. Her eyes were the same, although they peered at me from a thin face. In contrast, on her lap was a plump, pink baby with golden curls and her mother's eyes. She waved a toy in front of her face and babbled.

I approached, fighting tears and having a stern talk with myself. Keep it together. Be strong. Don't let her see how shaken you are.

"Hi, Ardan," she said.

I leaned down to kiss her thin cheek. "Hello." I smiled at the baby. "And this is Isabel."

"Isn't she pretty?"

"She is. She looks like you," I said.

"Sir, would you like me to escort you to baggage?" The attendant was a young man with a military cut and a chipped front tooth.

"No, we can take it from here," I said. "But thank you."

"I can walk," she said as soon the attendant was out of earshot. "They insisted I use this wheelchair, but I'm fine."

"How about if we just get to baggage and then you can walk to the car?" I'd parked close to the entrance. The Hailey airport was small, thankfully.

By the time we were out of baggage claim, she'd shared the details of her affairs, including the sale of her condo and the trust she'd set up for Isabel. Her father had left her hundreds of millions, which would now go to Isabel.

The next thing out of her mouth shouldn't have surprised me, but it did.

"How's Ciaran?"

I took a second to answer, thinking through the best way to talk to her about a sore subject between us. "He's married."

"I know. I saw it in the papers."

"They just had a baby."

She made a sound like I'd punched her in the stomach. "I didn't know that."

"You can't possibly still care?" How could she still be thinking of my brother when she was facing death and leaving her daughter?

"I'll always care." Her voice was dull and listless. "He's the only man I ever loved. Now, as I'm nearing the end, I know it more than ever."

I didn't respond. What was there to say? Unrequited love was the most painful of all its forms.

"Tell me about Charlotte," she said as we began the climb toward Peregrine.

"She's everything I've ever wanted and more."

"How long have you known her?"

"Long enough to know she's the one."

"Which is?" she asked with a smile.

"A couple months."

She turned in her seat to look at me and winced in obvious pain at the sudden movement. "That's all?"

"Yes."

"Then you barely know her," she said.

"Wrong. I know her."

"When and where did you meet?"

I shared how it had happened, including Moonstone's prediction.

"You guys hired her because a supposed psychic said to?" Felicity asked.

"She's not supposed. She *is* psychic."

"And you fell in love with this Charlotte in a few months?" she asked.

"Actually, at first sight."

"What if she's just after you for your money?"

"She's not like that." I told her about Charlotte's writing and her upbringing. "She's turned Mother around. Before she came, Mother wouldn't even get out of bed."

"I wanted you to raise Isabel, not some stranger," Felicity said. "Charlotte changes things."

"I thought you would say that." I glanced over at her. She stared out the front window with glazed eyes. "None of this is my business, but I really think you need to consider looking for a couple who wants to adopt."

"I want you."

"Felicity, Charlotte and I are starting a life together. We have plans. Ones that don't include adopting a child."

"You don't want Isabel?" Her voice had raised an octave. From the backseat, Isabel babbled.

I gripped the steering wheel. "How could you ask me to do this? It's too much."

"We go way back. We're practically family."

"I'll keep in touch with her, like an uncle would. I can manage the trust until she turns eighteen. I can promise you I'll make sure she's all right. But she needs a couple who wants her. Do you know how many infertile couples there are out there?"

"Would you be saying this if it wasn't for Charlotte? Is she the one who doesn't want her?"

"If you want to know the truth, Charlotte said we should meet her and see how it feels, like if it's right that we take her. I wouldn't have taken her, with or without Charlotte. Especially without Charlotte. I was a single guy. What would I know about raising a little girl?"

"You're gentle and kind. And you're a Lanigan."

"What does that mean?" Was this about her obsession with Ciaran?

"I want her to be with your family. I want her to have what I couldn't."

"You want her to be a Lanigan? That's funny."

"Funny?" she asked. "I'm serious."

"My family's far from perfect."

"You were. Before Finn died anyway," she said.

"You were on the outside looking in."

"I know what I know." She crossed her arms and turned away to look out the window. Isabel had fallen asleep with her head tucked into her neck. A beautiful child.

Not yours.

It was my father's voice.

Not yours to keep.

"Felicity, I'll help you find the right family for her. But it's not me."

"Wait and see. You'll fall in love with her. Everyone does," Felicity said. "She's special."

Not yours.

CHAPTER SEVENTEEN

CHARLOTTE

I sat with Mrs. Lanigan on the patio basking in the late afternoon warmth. Effie had already brought Mrs. Lanigan her cocktail and left to make dinner and homemade apple sauce for the baby. Mrs. Lanigan sipped her drink as I read to her from my second Luci manuscript. After I finished the chapter, she clicked her tongue. "Why that agent can't sell this one is beyond me." She closed her eyes and lifted her face toward the sun. "I've been thinking of my parents. How devoted they were to me."

I set aside my laptop to give her my full attention.

"Do you know I can't even remember what Teagan and I last fought about?"

"You could send her an email," I said. "Invite her to come home for Ardan's wedding."

"It *would* be a good excuse," she said.

I opened my laptop and logged into Mrs. Lanigan's email account. I'd been checking for her each day to see if she had any mail. I picked *Teagan Lanigan* from the contact list. "What do you want to say?"

She puckered her lips. "What *should* I say?"

"Just say you're sorry and you want her to come home."

"That seems too simple."

"Sometimes simple is best." I typed into the computer, while speaking out loud.

Dear Teagan,

This is Charlotte Wilde. I'm writing on behalf of your mother. She wants you to know how sorry she is for the misunderstandings between the two of you. She'd very much like it if you'd come for a visit and bring Christopher.

"Tell her that it's my fault—everything. I'm a stubborn old woman and I want to make amends before it's too late."

I typed the rest without speaking out loud.

Your mother's contrite and humbled. Being vulnerable has changed the way she views her relationships with her children. She feels a sense of urgency to fix things between you. She's doing much better than when I arrived. She's up and moving—healing and learning to cope with her lack of sight. I know it might be hard to let go of the anger and resentment but think how much better it would be if you were able to reconcile now, rather than live with regret.

"You're typing a bunch. What're you saying?"

I looked up. "I simply told her that you're feeling unsure of your future and that you'd like to reconcile before you go."

"That about sums it up," she said with a stubborn set of her jaw.

"Should I hit send?"

"Yes."

I glanced at my words one more before hitting the send button. When I looked up, I realized Mrs. Lanigan was crying.

"What is it?" I asked, alarmed. I set the computer aside and grabbed a handful of tissues from my pocket.

"I wasted all this time being angry with Teagan and now I won't know what my grandson looks like."

I placed a few tissues in her hand and took in a deep breath, her pain, my pain. "I'll be here the whole time. I'll describe him to you. Every detail. You'll be able to hear his voice and feel his face and skin and smell his hair. You'll still know who he is. His true essence isn't what he looks like. Souls are felt, not seen."

She sniffed and dabbed her cheeks. "I thought the eyes were the windows to the soul."

I thought about Ardan's eyes, how they had seemed that way to me the first time I looked into them. "There is more than one pathway to the soul. All you need is quality time with him. You'll see."

"What if he doesn't like me?"

"He'll like you. Everyone loves their grandmother. You might consider taking your sharp tongue down a notch, though. He's only six."

She let out a shaky laugh. "I can't be you."

"No, but you can be 'fun grandma' "

"How? I can't do anything with him. Not without my eyes."

She had me stumped. It did seem that activities a six-year-old would be interested in weren't necessarily a good fit with Mrs. Lanigan.

"What is this? For once you don't have an answer?" she asked.

"We'll think of something. Once we meet him, we'll know."

"You're a ridiculous optimist."

"Who else could put up with you?"

"I have proof I'm not a good grandmother." Her voice sounded raspy. "Rori, Kevan's daughter, and I don't exactly have the closest relationship. As far as I can tell, she thinks I'm a horrid old lady."

"Do you want me to send her an email?"

"Let's call her instead. I'd like to hear her voice."

"Did you remember to put your phone in your pocket?" I asked.

"I'm blind, not senile." She reached in and found it easily. I took it from her outstretched hand.

"You're doing well."

"Don't sound so pleased with yourself. It's very unbecoming."

"See there? You saw right into my soul by deciphering the tone of my voice."

She shook her head. "You think too much of yourself."

I pulled Rori's name up from the contact list and pushed the call button.

A second later, Rori answered. "Hi, Grandmother."

"Hi. You're on speaker phone," Mrs. Lanigan said. "Charlotte's here with me."

"Hey, Charlotte. Uncle Ardan texted that you guys are getting married. That's so awesome." She had a sweet, almost raspy voice. "I'm excited to meet you. All the girls in my dorm are passing your book around. Uncle Ardan sent a few paperbacks out to me."

"I didn't know that," I said.

"Everyone loves it," Rori said. "Even though it's kept a few of us up too late reading when we should be studying."

"Will you be home for the summer?" Mrs. Lanigan asked.

"For sure. I wouldn't miss the wedding. Plus, my boyfriend and I want to spend the summer with my family."

"Same boyfriend?" Mrs. Lanigan asked.

"Yes, same one. Cole."

"Isn't it time you moved on from him?" Mrs. Lanigan asked.

"Moved on?" A sharp edge crept into Rori's voice.

I tapped Mrs. Lanigan on the knee. "Be nice," I whispered.

She ignored me.

"His mother's a drug addict," Mrs. Lanigan said. "He wasn't exactly raised in the most stable environment. Is he the man you want to be the father of your children?"

"Cole and my dad are super close," Rori said. "We're all the family he needs."

"Sure. With all the money we have, who wouldn't want to be close to us?" Mrs. Lanigan said.

"Grandmother, you have no idea what you're talking about."

"Isn't your father paying for his college?"

"So what?" Rori asked. "My dad offered. He believes in him."

"What's he like?" I asked, hoping to defuse the tension.

"He's a computer genius," Rori said. "Super smart, funny, sweet. We've been together for years now. He wants to get married after I'm done at the University of Oregon."

"Oh, brother," Mrs. Lanigan said under breath.

"He sounds great," I said. "I look forward to getting to know you both."

"Me too," Rori said. "But hey, I need to go. Lots to do."

"Bye, Rori," Mrs. Lanigan said.

"Bye, Grandmother. Bye, Charlotte." She hung up.

"What was that?" I asked.

"Can't I share my opinion?"

"No, you can't. Not when it sounds like criticism."

"I worry. Cole's mother is about as trashy as you can get."

"Do you see how you alienated her?"

"Well, excuse me for looking after my own granddaughter."

"You know full well that wasn't the way to do it."

"Fine. You're right. I'm a work in progress."

"You can say that again," I said. "If we can get Teagan to visit, you have to hold your tongue. Not everyone needs your opinion and most don't want it."

"What about you?" she asked. "You're always asking for my opinion."

"That's because we're close. We've established trust. We understand each other."

"Why can't everyone be as easy as you?" she asked.

"It's easier because we're not family. There's no history there.

No easily uncovered scars. The closer you are to people, the more they can hurt you."

We were interrupted by the sound of a car in the driveway. I drew in a deep breath. As much as I'd tried to convince myself otherwise, I was frightened. Felicity Spinner was an unknown. Despite my bond with Ardan, he went way back with her. He'd once fancied himself in love with her. He'd admitted how many times she'd wreaked havoc on his life. Would this be yet another occurrence?

Mrs. Lanigan shook her glass at me. The ice rattled like the thoughts in my head. "You do what's best for you and Ardan. This baby is not your responsibility."

The sound of the patio door opening stole any chance of further discussion. I had a feeling it was the first of many.

Ardan carried a baby on his hip. Fine blond hair stuck up in tufts on top of her perfectly round head. Big blue eyes seemed to take everything in at once. The woman next to him was not the same woman I remembered from television footage of her parents' funeral or from the society section of Vanity Fair. She was as thin as the pages of Augie's letters. Her once long and shiny blond hair had been replaced with a pink scarf. I silently cursed cancer.

I stood to greet them as Ardan introduced us. "Felicity, this is Charlotte Wilde, my fiancée."

"Welcome," I said as I held out my hand.

She gave it a quick but faint squeeze—frail and weak. Why did it have to be this way? "It's nice to meet you." Felicity's smile was warm and inviting. Even cancer couldn't strip a woman of her beautiful smile. Felicity knelt closer to Mrs. Lanigan and kissed her on the cheek. "Mrs. Lanigan, it's nice to see you."

"You as well," Mrs. Lanigan said. "And Isabel, of course. Charlotte, what does she look like?"

"She has white blond hair and big blue eyes."

"What color blue?" she asked.

"Cornflower."

"Like her mother," Mrs. Lanigan said.

"Yes. She looks like me," Felicity said. "She has my fair skin too. And, Mrs. Lanigan, she adores Ardan already. Just like I knew she would."

Fairly manipulative. Good to know.

"Ardan told me about your sight," Felicity said. "I'm sorry."

"Don't you spend any time feeling sorry for an old lady. I'm fine."

Effie appeared, all hustle and efficiency, and performed a slight curtsy for Felicity. "I'm the housekeeper, ma'am. Please let me know if you need anything at all. I have a room ready for you and the little miss." She smiled at Isabel and was rewarded with a slobbery grin. I spotted four adorable teeth.

Ardan helped Felicity into a chair. I sighed with relief as I sat myself. I'd wanted her to sit. Her legs were as thin as a child's. She reminded me of a glass ornament that could shatter from the slightest movement.

Felicity winced as Ardan arranged a pillow behind her back. "I need a pain pill and a glass of wine."

"Should you?" Ardan placed the baby on Felicity's lap. "I mean, are you up for it?"

"Darling, I'm dying. There's not much it can do to me now."

"I thought you might like to rest before dinner," he said.

"I slept on the plane. I'd rather get to know Charlotte." Felicity kissed her baby as Isabel snuggled into her chest.

Ardan asked Effie to open a bottle of white wine and bring enough glasses for all. He sat next to me and spoke quietly into my ear. "Are you all right?"

"A little shaky," I whispered back.

"I am too." He looked into my eyes and we didn't have to say anything further. All was well.

"What a long day it's been already," Felicity said as she adjusted the scarf on her head. "Isabel did better than I thought she would. She'd never been on an airplane before, and without Nanny Dee. She has a family of her own in the city, which made it impossible for her to come with us. Quite the teary scene this morning when we had to say goodbye." She spoke lightly but the husky undertones told me how excruciating it must have been for all of them.

"Anyway, I don't have much time for small talk," Felicity said. "There are a few things I need to settle, like what happens to Isabel." She glanced at me. "I understand you and Ardan are going to make the decision together?"

"That's right," I said.

Effie came out with the wine and a platter of cheese and crackers. "Would you like me to take the baby for a while?" she asked Felicity.

"She's sticky," Felicity said.

"I'll give her a bath," Effie said.

"Are you sure?" Felicity asked.

"I practically raised my baby brothers, miss. It's no trouble at all."

"Let her take Isabel," Ardan said to Felicity. "It'll give us a better chance to talk."

Felicity agreed. Effie took the baby from Felicity's arms. "Hello, moppet. Aren't you a pretty one?" Isabel squealed and tugged the ends of Effie's hair as they set off for the house.

Ardan poured us all wine.

"Charlotte, Ardan tells me you're a writer," Felicity said.

"She has an amazing talent," Mrs. Lanigan said. "Unrecognized by the world as of yet, but another few books and everything will fall into place for her."

"Mother's going to become Charlotte's agent," Ardan said.

"Are you interested in having children someday?" Felicity asked. "Given your ambitions, I suspect the answer is no."

"To tell you the truth, I haven't thought about it much," I said. "Ardan and I have been wrapped up in each other. We have plans to travel and write. Children might come, but later. I'm still young, so I have a few years to decide."

"I, on the other hand, don't have any time to waste," Felicity said.

I winced. *I'm an insensitive heel.*

"When I decided on Ardan, I assumed he would say yes," she said. "I didn't realize there was a woman in his life."

"Does that change things for you?" I asked.

"I suppose it does." Felicity smiled. "It's just that I imagined her growing up with Ardan as a single dad. It never occurred to me to think otherwise. That probably sounds short-sighted. It does to me now, as I say it out loud."

"There are plenty of people out there who want a baby," Mrs. Lanigan said. "Perhaps you should put her up for adoption and help pick the parents you want for her."

"I want her here. In Idaho. With your family," Felicity said.

"Why?" Mrs. Lanigan asked. God bless Mrs. Lanigan for being here, asking the hard questions.

"Because Ardan's the finest person I know. And I've always loved your family—wished I could be part of it. This way Isabel can."

"It's a lot to ask," Mrs. Lanigan said. "And these two are just getting started. They will want to have their own family."

"I understand that," Felicity said. "I'm at their mercy." She turned to Ardan and me. "I can only hope you two will fall in love with her before I die."

I wanted to cry. How could we not take Isabel? The wish of a dying woman? An innocent baby? What kind of people would we be if we sent her away?

"*That's* the plan?" Mrs. Lanigan asked. "Just hope these two to decide to take her?"

"That's the plan." Felicity's hands shook as she sipped from her wine.

I glanced over at Ardan. He stared at the ground, his wine untouched.

"It seems manipulative and misguided," Mrs. Lanigan said.

"You haven't changed," Felicity said. "Always upfront with your opinion."

"Honestly, I don't mean to be unkind," Mrs. Lanigan said. "But what an absurd thing you've done. Coming here? Expecting Isabel to be taken in by our family?"

"Mother, let's give Felicity a chance to relax." Ardan picked up his glass and took a swig of wine.

"No, it's all right," Felicity said. "Mrs. Lanigan, I'm dying. As a mother, surely you can understand that I want to leave this earth knowing my daughter is with the right family. If it can't be me, I want it to be Ardan, with his brothers as Isabel's uncles."

"I'm sorry you're sick," Mrs. Lanigan said. "However, that doesn't give you the right to guilt my son into taking your child."

"Guilt? I've no intention of guilting him," Felicity said. "I simply want to give him the opportunity to see what a special child Isabel is. If he chooses to keep her, then I can die in peace. If not, she'll have to go to strangers."

"Strangers who would be wonderful parents," Mrs. Lanigan said.

"We don't know that," Felicity said.

Mrs. Lanigan looked in my direction. "Charlotte, would you help me to my room? I'm suddenly tired."

"Yes, of course." I stood and offered my hand. "I'll get her settled and come down later."

Ardan grabbed my hand and brought it to his mouth. "See you soon."

I took Mrs. Lanigan upstairs and helped her get ready for the night. When she was safely in bed, I told her to sit tight while I fetched her dinner.

"Charlotte?" she said, when I reached the doorway.

"Yes?" I returned to the bed and sat beside her.

"I'm sorry I made everyone uncomfortable, but this is ludicrous. You and Ardan have no business taking that baby, and she has a lot of nerve to put you two in this position."

"What if it's meant to be? Like Ardan and me?"

"You and Ardan are not supposed to save the world."

"What if we're just supposed to save one baby?" I asked.

"Dear, you're a good person with a big heart, but I swear, sometimes you're as dumb as a sack of rocks."

I laughed. "Mrs. Lanigan, you're a mean old thing."

"Well established."

"Felicity's thin as paper," I said. "I feel terrible for her."

"She's always been a bit of a wounded bird. When they were young it was always her with the bee sting, or almost drowning in the creek or falling off the horse. But it's not your job or Ardan's job to take care of her or that baby."

"What would you do?" I asked.

"If I was young like you and just starting out with Edward?"

"Yes. Would you take the baby?"

"We had enough children of our own. All he had to do was look at me and I was pregnant again. But I had several friends who couldn't have a child. They would've given a lot to be able to adopt."

"Ardan and I wanted to travel next year. He thinks it would be good for my writing."

"It would."

"I'll be back with your dinner."

She grabbed my hand. "Thank you for putting up with me."

"I love you, mean old thing," I said.

"You silly girl. Loving an old bat like me."

I slipped from the room as she turned the television on.

As I passed through the living room, I glanced outside. Ardan and Felicity appeared to be in a heated argument, given the way their hands were flying. I decided it would be best to head to the kitchen.

Effie was there with Isabel. Felicity must have brought a portable high chair with her because Effie had secured it to a chair and was now feeding the baby mashed avocado.

"Hello, miss. Mrs. Lanigan's supper's there on the counter." A plate of spaghetti and a side salad, plus a glass of milk, were on a tray.

I drew closer to inspect Isabel more closely. She *was* adorable.

Her cheeks were pink from her bath. Damp curls stuck to her neck. She wore a bib over a pink onesie, which seemed an exercise in futility, as avocado was smeared over her face and clothes.

"Maybe you should've given the baby a bath *after* dinner?" I asked.

"I'll just wipe her down. The important parts are clean."

"I don't know anything about babies. I didn't even babysit as a kid." I'd worked in the local bookstore instead where everything was clean and smelled of new books. What *were* the important parts of a baby?

I picked up the tray and headed toward the doorway.

"Miss, don't forget this is your life. You don't let anyone push you into anything."

I bit my bottom lip. Sweet Effie didn't miss much. "She's kind of manipulative. I can see why Ardan had trouble disentangling himself from her. When she wants something, she's used to getting it."

"We can't blame her for wanting the best for Isabel," Effie said. "But there are better ways, in my opinion, than this."

I moved my gaze once more to Isabel. She had her fingers in her mouth, sucking off the last remnants of avocado.

"You'll see, miss, everything will work out as it should."

How could she say that when Isabel's mother was dying? Surely that wasn't how it was supposed to be?

I thanked her before heading back through the living room with Mrs. Lanigan's dinner. I stole a glance outside. Ardan's neck was bent in concentration as she talked, gesturing with her hands to emphasize some point I couldn't hear.

I jerked away from the window and strode down the hallway, spilling milk onto the tray. Should I cry over spilled milk? I wanted to cry over something.

Mrs. Lanigan was sitting up in bed, listening to the television.

"Good job finding the remote," I said.

Mrs. Lanigan smiled. "Remote at noon. And you were right.

These shows with the description narration are quite good. It's almost like reading a book."

She paused her show using a voice command. I put the tray around her lap. "It smells good," she said. "Spaghetti?"

"Yes. It's covering the entire plate. A bowl of salad is on your right. A glass of milk is on the left."

She already had her fork in hand. "Is it hot?"

"No steam, so I don't think so. Effie had it dished up when I went down there."

She took a tentative bite. "Good. I'm hungry after you made me walk around the pool fifty times."

"It was only twelve. Which is a new record. Yesterday we only did ten."

"I need to start counting. I don't know if I trust you," she said.

"It won't do any good. I'm ruthless."

Her phone buzzed with a text. "You have a new message," I said. "It's from Teagan."

Her fork froze in midair. "What does it say?"

I read it to her.

Thanks for your email. I was glad to hear from you. I'm finishing up a job in a few weeks and would like to come home for a visit. Ardan called me about Charlotte. I'll be there for the wedding.

"She never was one for many words," Mrs. Lanigan said.

"Short and to the point," I said. "She's coming home. That's all you need to know."

"It's a start," she said.

I put the phone back in its holder.

"Do you think Nicholas ever regretted walking away from all that money?" I asked Mrs. Lanigan.

"What makes you ask that?"

"I don't know. I'm curious, that's all."

"I don't believe he ever was."

"How can you be sure?" I asked.

Her features softened, like she was watching a cherished movie. "One night when I was about ten, I got up to go to the bathroom. We lived in this old house and everything creaked. I heard music coming from the living room, so I walked down the hall to see what was going on. They had the record player on and were dancing. Her cheek was against his chest and his chin rested on the top of her head. They barely swayed to the music. For the rest of my life, I thought of that moment as the first time I understood what it meant to experience total joy and peace with another person. What it meant to be truly in love forever. You know how you said souls can be felt not seen? That's how you and Ardan feel to me when you're together. Like my parents. Would you do whatever it takes to be with him?"

"Yes."

"Same was true for them."

I realized tears had dampened my cheeks. I sniffed and grabbed a tissue, unable to speak.

"All right go on now. I have my show to finish."

I was almost to the door when she called out to me.

"I love you, nice old thing."

CHAPTER EIGHTEEN

CHARLOTTE

The afternoon after Felicity arrived, while most of the house napped, I wrote, stretched out on a chaise under the shade of an umbrella. Other than Effie, who was making pizza dough for later, and Ardan who had gone into town for supplies for the baby, the house was quiet. Today was in the low seventies with clear skies. A glass of iced tea sweated on the table next to my chaise. I had my sunglasses off, so I could see the computer screen. When I occasionally glanced up from my work, I squinted into the afternoon sun.

I was about to finish writing the sixth chapter when Felicity appeared. Dressed in jeans and a black cardigan sweater, she greeted me with a weak smile. She tightened her sweater around her waist. "May I sit with you?"

"Yes, I was just finishing up." This was a lie. I could have spent the rest of the afternoon writing. Interruptions in this house were numerous. For a second, I thought longingly of my quiet apartment with nothing but my elderly neighbor next door to worry about.

She gingerly lowered herself into the chaise next to mine.

"How are you feeling today?" I asked.

"Not great. I told Ardan it's time for the nurse to come. I don't think there's much time left." She closed her eyes and seemed to sag from fatigue.

"Should you be resting in your bed?" I asked.

"I'd like to stay outside." She winced. "But I need another pain pill."

"I'll get you one. Where are they?"

She told me where they were in the house and I ran to get them, along with a glass of water. By the time I came back outside, she was shaking. "I'm so cold," she said before swallowing the pill.

I moved the umbrella to allow the sun to warm her before heading inside to grab a throw blanket from the couch. After I had it tucked around her legs, she asked for sunglasses. I gave her mine.

"Sit with me?" she asked.

I sat back in my spot, careful to close my laptop.

She turned toward me with a slight smile. "You're a sponge. An observer. People love to talk about themselves to you, don't they?"

"I guess so." Unsure where she was going with this, I waited.

"Tell me about Bliss Heywood," she said. "You must know her well."

Not what I expected. "I do. Or, did. It's been several years since we worked together. A lot has happened to her since then."

"From what I've gathered, she's like Superwoman or something," Felicity said.

"She used to work too much. But that was before she met Ciaran."

"Right. Falling in love changes a person," she said. "Or so I've been told."

I picked at a hang nail on my thumb, causing it to bleed.

"Ardan told me they had a baby."

"That's right."

"Isabel will grow up with Ciaran's child." She said this like a delirious child with a fever. I wondered if the pain pill had kicked in.

"Is that important to you?" I asked.

"No. Just a statement."

"Would you like some more water?" I asked.

"No, I need a favor."

I prepared to get to my feet. "What can I get for you?"

"I want to see Ciaran one last time. I have things I have to say to him. The doctors said months, but I can feel my body shutting down. It's weeks away, not months."

"Why, Felicity? Won't it just hurt to see him?"

"Ah, so Ardan told you?"

My misshapen reflection in the sunglasses stared back at me. "Ardan and I have no secrets."

"You've known each other for like five minutes."

I shrugged. It would not be the first time someone called me out on this. "It's between us, but there's a soul connection."

"I felt that once. With Ciaran. Only he was too immature to know what to do with it."

Nerves fluttered in my stomach. I picked at skin on my other thumb.

"I let it go on too long. I see that clearly now." Felicity's fixed her gaze on the pool. I had a feeling she didn't see what was in front of her. She was visiting the past. "When he was in town, he called. I answered. And every time I thought—this time will be the one where he sees how right we are together. Would you arrange for us to see each other?"

"I'm happy to, but wouldn't it be better if you contacted him yourself?"

"I can't." She mumbled this. "He blocked me from his phone and email and everything else two years ago."

"Blocked?"

"You can save the judgment. I had trouble letting go. When

Ciaran told me he'd fallen for someone seriously, I went a bit unhinged. Don't look at me that way. It's not like I tried to burn down his house or killed his bunny. I just sent him a million texts." She took off the sunglasses and laid them in her lap.

"I see." I *did* see. This obsession Felicity had with Ciaran was about fifty shades of unhealthy.

"All I'm asking is for you to call him and see if he'd come by," she said. "What harm can come from it?"

"As long as you're sure."

"I just want a chance to say goodbye to the man I loved for twenty years. No one needs to feel threatened or afraid. I can barely lift a toothbrush."

"It's not that," I said. "I'm thinking of you and how you want to use your energy."

"Did Ardan tell you how we all met?"

"Here, during summers, right?"

She tightened the blanket around her legs and leaned her head back and closed her eyes. "When I was sixteen, my father bought a house adjacent to this property. We were to spend all summers and vacations out here. He told me it was because he wanted to learn to fly fish and look at the stars without the lights of L.A. drowning them out. The real reason was more complicated. He wanted to get my mother away from her boyfriend."

I must have flinched because she looked over at me and let out a bitter laugh. "It happens in a lot of marriages when a much younger woman marries an old guy. When she meets him, he's fifty and she's twenty. He's still sexy, aided by a personal trainer and the huge bank account. Even ugly guys are sexy when they're rich. But after sixty he starts to become an older man married to a thirty-year-old woman. The next decade he's seventy and she's forty and they have a teenaged daughter who they think doesn't know what's going on. I knew. My mother was a young woman. No amount of Viagra was going to make them a good match. She started bonking the gardener. Then, ironically, her personal trainer. Next thing I know, we've moved to Idaho."

"I'm sorry. That must have been rough." I had an image of my parents dancing in the kitchen to a Celine Dion song. The smell of beef Bourguignon simmered on the stove while I did my homework in the breakfast booth. How insulated and lucky I was.

"It was just how things were," Felicity said. "And then came the Lanigan family." She closed her eyes and gritted her teeth. "I need another pill."

I shook one into her hand and handed her the glass of water on the table between us.

After a minute or so, she continued. "The first morning we were here, I wandered outside and across the meadow until I reached the edge of our property. A fence separated our property from the Lanigan's. I hear this whoop, like a Native American war cry. Here come the Lanigan brothers, all four of them on horses and all four gorgeous. Ciaran and Kevan with dark, shiny caps of thick hair. Finn and Ardan with hair the color of sun-bleached straw. They lined up their horses in front of me—I don't know if they did it on purpose or not—but they lined up from youngest to oldest. I looked at them one after the other, landing on Ciaran, the youngest, last. And that was it, Charlotte. I was done. Those laughing brown eyes looked right at me and everything else faded from view. For the next twenty years, it was only him. I dated others, but no one ever lived up to the summers I spent here with Ciaran. He was my first and my last. Until he married your friend Bliss, I never gave up hope. I could recall every moment we spent together when we were kids. They were magical. I could never figure out how he didn't see it or feel it. I guess I'll never know why. These last few years, being sick, I've spent a lot of time thinking about my life. All the ways it went right and wrong. Every one of them led me right back to the Lanigans.

"It wasn't just Ciaran I wanted, either. It was his family. They'd have these family dinners and Mrs. Lanigan would always invite me to stay." She gestured toward the direction of Kevan and Blythe's home. "The old house was here then, and it was a big, rambling thing with an enormous back deck. There was this long table with benches on either side. Two of the boys would sit on one side and two on the other. Little Teagan and I would sit next to our favorite brother. Mine was Ciaran, of course. Teagan's was Kevan. Mr. and Mrs. Lanigan sat on the ends. I swear to you, Charlotte, those evenings with the loud, messy Lanigans were the best of my life. They'd argue over everything from music to who spit the watermelon seed the farthest to who looked best in a pair of jeans. It was family. The type of family I wanted. It wasn't just that I loved Ciaran. I loved them all."

"Is that why you want Isabel with them?" Now it seemed obvious. *Backstory always explains everything.*

"Yes. I want her to know this ground, this sky, these trees. I want her to be a Lanigan. I never got to, but she might. I want her to grow up in a loud, messy family."

"Ardan told me he and his siblings found their parents strict and a little critical."

"They were. But there were five of them, all with huge personalities, all stubborn and opinionated. Mrs. Lanigan had to be that way, or they would have run wild. Especially Ciaran."

"What about Ardan?" I asked. "What was he like back then?"

"The same as he is now. Quiet and steady. Smart and sensitive. He always noticed everything. Every detail. If I trimmed an inch off my hair, he would be the only one who noticed. He was in love with me, unfortunately. Not that he ever told me, but I knew. Women always do, don't you think? He suffered mostly in silence. Buried his nose in a book every time I came by to get Ciaran to go into town or for a ride." She let out a raspy laugh. "He disapproved of us back then. Ciaran and I were wild. Always sneaking booze out to the swimming hole and skinny dipping. Making love in a sleeping bag." Her voice had turned wistful. "Sometimes when I'm in pain, I think about those times. I replay them in my mind. I can't help but wonder, why not me? What is it that Bliss has that I don't? Even before her, I wondered if I'd been taller or thinner or darker or a hundred other things—would that be what tipped him over to loving me like I loved him. I wish it had been different. I wish he'd wanted me. I might not even be sick."

I didn't say anything. Not that I was an expert, but I was pretty sure cancer didn't care who you were or who you loved or who loved you.

She turned her head to look at me. Tears glistened in her eyes. "Charlotte, I know it's a lot to ask. But Ardan's the finest person I've ever known. He would make sure Isabel grows up with values and discipline and family. If you and Ardan have kids, she would have siblings. Cousins. If I knew this, I could leave peacefully. My last thoughts would be imagining her here with all of you under the sun, eating watermelon or swimming in the pool."

"I understand now," I said. "I see why it's Ardan you want."

"But you don't want her?"

"We have plans to travel and write before we have kids. We want to do all the things we didn't get to do before."

"Before?"

I shook my head. "I don't know why I said it like that. I meant, all the things we want to do but haven't had a chance to do yet. I haven't seen much of the world, and Ardan thought it would inspire me and open me up to a whole new level of creativity."

"And a baby just isn't in that picture?" she asked.

"Right. At least not yet. But we haven't decided. You just got here. Let's give it a little time."

"That's just it. My time is running out."

"I know. Just give us a few days to talk it through. We're getting married in a few weeks. Or that was the plan anyway. Now, I'm not sure when."

"I've ruined the party for Ardan. Just like I have so many times before," she said.

"We'll figure out what's best for Isabel. You just focus on enjoying her."

"Knowing the end of my life is near makes everything quite clear." She gestured toward the sun. "You never waste the chance to sit in the sun on a spring afternoon. Remember that, after I'm gone. When you look at the sun, think of how precious every moment is. I wish I'd done more of that."

Effie stuck her head out the back door. "Miss Felicity, the baby's crying."

"I'll get her." I stood. "You rest. I'll change her and bring her out. You can have a moment in the sun with your baby."

Felicity smiled up at me. "Thank you, Charlotte."

* * *

Isabel was screeching by the time I reached her. When she saw it was me and not her mother, she stopped for a split second then started up again with added vigor. I reached into the crib and pulled her into my arms. Her diaper smelled ripe. "You're a stinky one."

She threw back her head and screamed in what my mother would have described as bloody murder.

I set her on the changing table and got her out of the dirty diaper and cleaned her up. By the time I had her chubby bottom in a new diaper, she'd stopped howling. Instead she stared at me with her enormous blue eyes, drops of tears stuck in her thick lashes.

"I'm Charlotte," I said. "Mommy's friend."

No response.

I lifted her from the table and held her at arm's length. She wore a legless onesie scattered with ducks. "Will you be warm enough in that?"

She babbled an answer, then scrunched up her face like she was going to cry again. "Now, let's not do that. Let's have a bottle instead."

"Baba."

"Ah, I see you know a word. Excellent." I secured her onto my hip and scurried down the stairs and into the kitchen. Effie already had a bottle of formula made. "How did you know?" I asked.

"That was a 'dirty diaper and I'm hungry' cry."

"Right you are."

Effie handed me the bottle, but Isabel was having none of that. She grabbed it with her two chubby hands and tipped it back like a cowboy drank his favorite beer.

"All right, then," I said. "She's a girl who knows what she wants."

Effie sniffed her head. "That smell. Reminds me of home."

"Do you want a baby someday?" I asked.

Her eyes widened. "I've done enough raising of the wee ones, miss. No child will ever pass from these hips."

I kissed Isabel's cheek. "She's such a sweetie though, isn't she?"

"Yes, she is." Effie fluffed Isabel's curls.

"I'll take her outside to her mama."

Felicity was asleep in the chaise. I sat and let Isabel finish her bottle, my mind tumbling from one thought to another. Would Felicity live to see her baby take her first steps? If she was right about how long she had left, she would not. This fact made me want to cry. And her wish to see Ciaran? Was it the right thing for her to do? It was understandable to want closure and to say goodbye. Yet, I worried she would only be hurt all over again, especially when she saw him with Bliss. Everything she'd wanted with him, he now gave to another.

Felicity looked peaceful sleeping in the sun. But I'd promised her I would talk to him and I would keep my promise. I decided to visit Bliss and Ciaran this afternoon. Surely, he wouldn't deny a dying woman her chance to make amends. Like Felicity had said, she was no threat to anyone. Bliss wouldn't have the heart to turn her away.

She stirred just as Isabel finished her bottle. Her gaunt face lit up at the sight of her daughter. I tucked Isabel next to her on the chaise. "I'll go check on Mrs. Lanigan now," I said. "Effie's just inside if you need anything."

Isabel put her hands on the sides of her mother's face. "Mama."

"Charlotte, she said it! She said mama. That's the first time."

"She sure did." *Good girl Isabel. You gave her a first before she has to go.* I said a silent prayer for a few more of those moments as I headed up the stairs to check on Mrs. Lanigan.

She was up and dressed, sitting in the chair by the window. Classical music played on the stereo. She turned when she heard the door open. "Charlotte."

"It's me."

Her brow wrinkled. "Has something happened? You're fretting."

"How do you know?"

"Your voice sounds higher than usual."

"Did you know that Ciaran and Felicity spent time together over the years?" I asked.

"By *time* you mean sex?"

I coughed. "Yes."

"Yes, I knew. Ciaran was quite the playboy before Bliss stole his heart."

Making sure to keep my voice low, I relayed my conversation with Felicity from earlier, including her obsessive behavior. "Felicity asked if I'd talk to Ciaran for her. She wants to see him. It's awkward for several reasons, one of which is my friendship with Bliss." I hesitated, picking again at the piece of skin on my thumb.

She patted my knee. "Let's go see him in person. I'll go with you."

"Really?"

"Yes. You can count on me, just as I've counted on you."

* * *

A half hour later, Mrs. Lanigan and I arrived at Ciaran's home. Bliss asked us to come in and make ourselves at home in the living room.

"The baby's asleep," Bliss said.

"That's okay," I said. "We actually came for another reason."

Ciaran greeted us as he entered the room. "Charlotte, great to see you." He shook my hand before leaning over to kiss his mother on the cheek. "Mother, you're looking pretty."

"Charlotte took me to town for a cut and color," she said.

"With Heather?" he asked.

"Yes, she mentioned you right away," Mrs. Lanigan said. "What did she call him, Charlotte?"

I flushed. "A snack."

"Ew, she used to babysit me," Ciaran said.

"She overheard some girl in her shop refer to you that way," I said.

Bliss laughed from the bar where she poured glasses of lemonade. "Ciaran's more like a full course meal."

"Honey, my mother's here." Ciaran winked at his wife.

"For heaven's sake," Mrs. Lanigan said. "You've been married for a year already. Isn't it time to start acting like adults rather than randy teenagers?"

"Mother, never," Ciaran said.

Bliss handed me a glass of lemonade and encouraged me to sit.

"How's the baby?" I asked.

"Exhausting," Bliss said.

"It's a good thing Carmen's cute," Ciaran said. "Because she's kicking our butt."

"Why in God's name haven't you hired a nanny?" Mrs. Lanigan asked.

"We want to do it ourselves," Ciaran said. "At least for now."

"Don't forget to make time for each other," Mrs. Lanigan said. "Your relationship has to come first or the children will suffer."

Ciaran and Bliss exchanged a look.

We talked about other benign topics for a few minutes until Bliss mentioned the reason for my visit. "You said over the phone you had something you wanted to talk to us about?"

"Right. Yes." I fidgeted with the bottom button of my blouse. "It's about Felicity."

"We're here because that poor girl's dying, and she wants a word with Ciaran before she goes," Mrs. Lanigan said.

Subtlety wasn't Mrs. Lanigan's strong suit.

"We didn't exactly part on good terms," Ciaran said.

"We realize she acted rather badly," Mrs. Lanigan said. "But she's no harm to you now."

"I was always honest with her," Ciaran said. "She knew I wasn't interested in anything serious. Why don't women believe men when they tell them the truth?"

"Because we want it to be different," I said.

"How sick is she?" Bliss asked.

"The doctors said months," I said. "She thinks less."

"How awful," Bliss said. "That poor baby."

"She's asked Ardan to take the baby," Mrs. Lanigan said.

"It's Felicity's dying wish," I said. "She wants him to raise Isabel."

"What the hell?" Ciaran asked. "The woman's always taken advantage of Ardan. This is just one final ask in a series of out of line asks."

"She wants Isabel to grow up here, with all the Lanigan clan," I said.

"Why?" Ciaran asked. "I don't get it."

"Because the best times of her life were spent here with you. All of you," I said.

"That's sad," Bliss said.

"I think so too," I said.

"What does she want with me?" Ciaran asked.

"She just wants closure. Whether it was returned or not, she thinks of you as the love of her life," I said.

"It's pitiful," Mrs. Lanigan said. "What a waste."

"Honey, you have to go see her," Bliss said.

"Yes, okay. I'll go. You ladies are right. She's dying. The least I can do is tell her I'm sorry about how I acted. I was a pig back then. She deserved better. When should I come?" He directed this last question to me.

"Would now work for you?" I asked. The sooner the better. When we'd left the house just now, I'd popped in to her room to check on her. She was curled up on the bed with Isabel, both asleep. The image of that plump healthy baby in the arms of her frail mother would not leave me soon.

CHAPTER NINETEEN

ARDAN

I arrived home earlier than anticipated from my trip into Hailey. The clerk at the baby store had been knowledgeable and I left with a crib, changing table, and bookshelf, along with a stuffed dog I couldn't resist. I'd called Moonstone earlier to see if she could send Sam over to the house to help me put the furniture together. When I pulled into the driveway, he had already arrived. On his knees, he weeded a flower bed. Sweetheart chewed on a bone while staying near his beloved master. Sam's red toolbox was by the door. I greeted him and asked him to help me carry the boxes inside the house.

When we had everything in the bedroom I intended for Isabel, Sam took a small notebook and pencil out of his pocket. He wrote something before showing it to me. "I'll do it."

I nodded and thanked him. Sam liked to work alone. I wasn't sure if it was his lack of speech that made it more pressure to have someone near or if he thought I'd be in the way. Rescuing beautiful women from a herd of elk was one thing. Putting furniture together was quite another.

I wandered to the kitchen. Effie was at the counter cutting up vegetables. "Miss Felicity doesn't want anything but soup broth, so I'm making it as healthy as I can."

"Where's Charlotte?"

"I'm not sure, Mr. Lanigan. I saw her and Mrs. Lanigan leaving together. They didn't tell me where they were going."

I ambled without purpose to my study. There were items in my email to attend to, but I couldn't concentrate. I had just shut down my laptop when I heard a car pull up. A quick glance out the window told me it was Charlotte and Mother back from wherever they'd been. Seconds later, my brother's car pulled up. I went to the front door as the three of them came in.

"What's going on?" I asked Charlotte.

"Felicity wanted to see Ciaran," she said. "So, your mother and I went over to talk to him."

I shoved my hands in my pockets and rocked back on my feet. "She wants to see him. For what purpose?"

"She wants closure," Charlotte said apologetically. Why should she apologize? None of this was her fault.

"She's in her room. I can tell her you're here." I put my arm around Charlotte's shoulder. She snuggled into me. All was right with the world when my Charlotte was with me.

Mother waved her cane. "Yes, Ardan, you tell Felicity that Ciaran's here. No one needs this to drag out. Charlotte, can you take me to my room? I need a respite."

Charlotte moved away from me and took Mother's arm.

As they walked away, Ciaran put his hand on my shoulder. "Let's talk for a moment."

We went into my office. Ciaran shut the door. "Don't screw this up with Charlotte."

"I won't."

"Don't take this baby. Put yourself and Charlotte first," he said. "The child can be adopted to a nice couple. You guys had plans."

"We're running out of time."

"You tell her no," Ciaran said. "It's as simple as that."

"It's not simple. Not something like this."

"Brother, you deserve to be happy."

"I know." I raised my arms in exasperation. "I just don't know if either one of us can say no to her."

"She's already gotten to Charlotte," Ciaran said. "That much is obvious."

"Charlotte has a huge heart."

"So do you. Sometimes to your own detriment," Ciaran said.

"Let's put a pin in this," I said. "I'll go get her."

I walked down the hall to Felicity's room. She was on the bed, dressed and wearing lipstick that matched her pink scarf. Isabel was playing with a toy on Felicity's lap.

"Ciaran's here," I said. "But I suspect you know that."

"Don't be mad at Charlotte. I practically forced her to do it."

"If it's what you want, I'm not going to stop you."

"Are you angry at me?" she asked.

"Of course not, other than I don't want to see you get hurt. Just like always." I took the baby from her lap. Isabel snuggled her head against my chest.

Felicity adjusted her scarf. God help us, she looked too weak to get off the bed. I held out my hand and assisted her to her feet.

She let out a moan as we crossed the room. "Can you give me another pain pill?"

I ran back into the room to grab the bottle and a glass of water from the bedside table. She swallowed it quickly before looking into my eyes. "I just need to say goodbye, that's all."

"I know. You do whatever you need to do."

Ciaran stood by the fireplace with his back to us. When he turned to face her, Felicity looked like someone eating their first meal after near starvation. Ciaran, on the other hand, paled at the sight of her. She was not the same woman he'd left behind two years ago.

Ciaran held out his arms and Felicity disappeared in his embrace. "I look awful, I know," she said.

"I had no idea you were sick."

"I thought I could beat it. You know me, always unrealistic about the most important things. Can we talk alone? In Ardan's study?"

"Sure."

The two of them walked together to my study and shut the door behind them.

The baby babbled and rubbed her downy head on my chin. She was a beautiful child. Would I ever be able to love her like she was my own? *Would* she be better off with someone else? Or were Charlotte and I her destiny, as we'd been for each other?

I took Isabel into the kitchen. Effie was at the island cutting turkey into small pieces. "Sam brought the high chair in," she said.

Isabel kicked her legs, clearly excited for dinner. I'd helped when Rori was little. From what I could tell, not much had changed when it came to high chairs. I set her inside and fastened the belt, then slipped the tray into place. "Does she wear a bib?" I asked.

Effie glided over with a pink bib with "Mommy's Girl" on the front. She tied it around Isabel's neck.

Effie placed a pile of turkey on the tray, followed by soft chunks of cooked carrots. Isabel grabbed several turkey pieces at once and stuffed them into her mouth. I pushed a carrot toward her. She squashed it between her fingers, managing to get only half of it in her mouth. The rest smeared across her face.

"Mr. Lanigan, are you feeling all right?" Effie stared at me with a worried furrow of her brow.

"Yes, I'm fine. Just sad."

For the next fifteen minutes, I supervised Isabel's eating and chatted with Effie. She'd made pizza dough earlier and was now rolling it out to put onto cookie sheets. Charlotte came down and joined us, having gotten Mother settled.

She came over to me first and leaned against me. I wrapped an arm around her waist.

"Is my brother right?" I asked. "Have mother and child gotten to you?"

She laughed. "Is that what he said?"

"Is he right, miss?" Effie asked.

"She shared with me more about why she wants Isabel to be a Lanigan. I understand better now about her lonely childhood and how happy she was here with your big, messy family."

"That's because she didn't really have one," Effie said.

"I agree," I said.

"Maybe," Charlotte said. "Because I'm enamored with you Lanigans myself." Charlotte went to the refrigerator and pulled out a bottle of wine. "I want a big fat glass."

"Me too," I said.

While she poured us some, Charlotte looked over at Effie. "Tell us the truth. Is the life we planned for the next few years completely off the table if we take Isabel?"

"Pretty much," Effie said.

I heard the front door slam shut. "They must be done," I said. "What do I do?"

"Go check on her," Charlotte said. "I'll stay here with Isabel."

Felicity was on the couch in the living room with a blanket wrapped around her shoulders, staring into the unlit fireplace.

I asked if she was all right. "Do you need anything?" She looked at me, her face so thin I could see the outline of her cheekbones.

From the kitchen came the sound of Isabel's laughter, followed by Charlotte's.

"How did it go?" I asked.

"He told me about the woman who stalked him all those years—that he was afraid to love anyone because he wasn't sure he was going to be around."

I sat next to her. "Does that make you feel better?"

"Not really, no. Bliss was enough to get him to change his mind." She wiped tears from her cheeks. "I've wasted so much time loving him."

"Did you get closure?"

"Stupid closure everyone's always talking about isn't as great as it sounds. But yes, I said I was sorry. I told him I've never stopped loving him and that my times here with him were the highlights of my life. We had a few laughs remembering some of our antics. He told me he was sorry for how he treated me. I deserved better than to be just one of his girls." She paused as she took a rattling breath. "God, it still hurts so much that he chose someone else."

"Your pain will be over soon," I said. "You'll have the chance to start over or be in heaven. All this will be done, finally."

She tilted her face toward me. "You didn't love me that way, did you? I know you loved me when we were kids, even though you never said. I'm not the reason you haven't married?"

"No. I just hadn't met the right person yet."

"And you feel certain it's Charlotte?"

"I do."

"I'm sorry about Melanie. I've never properly apologized."

An image of Melanie's face when she saw us on the sofa flashed before my eyes. I waited for the familiar pain and embarrassment of that night to wash over me. It didn't. There was only a smidge, like the leftover peanut butter on the bottom of a jar. Charlotte had changed me. She was my world now.

"It doesn't matter now," I said.

"I was sick with grief over Ciaran's rejection. I should never have come to your place."

"Don't give it another thought."

"Did you tell her we didn't have sex?" she asked.

"Melanie never gave me a chance. She'd been cheated on before and she thought I was a guy she could trust. When she saw us like that, it was all over."

"I've always brought the drama, haven't I?" she asked.

"You *do* have a gift for it," I said gently.

"I know I don't deserve it, but I'm desperate. I'm dying, Ardan. You have to take Isabel."

"Charlotte's part of my life now. I have to make the decision with her, not in a vacuum with you."

"A vacuum?"

"That's what it's like with you—you pull me into the Felicity vortex until all I can see is you. I can't do it this time. I have to choose myself first. I've made promises to Charlotte that I intend to keep."

"Isabel needs you."

"It doesn't have to be me."

"It does. You have to do this for me."

"See, that's the thing, I don't. I owe it to myself and to Charlotte to do what's right for us. I don't love Isabel. Until you came here, I didn't even know she existed. I'm not the person to leave her with."

"You'll grow to love her. I know you."

"Felicity, this is all wrong. This isn't how it's supposed to be."

"I know. God, Ardan, don't you think I know that? I'm not supposed to be dying." She turned away, tears sliding down her face. "I hate her."

"Who?"

"Bliss. I hate her with every ounce of what's left of me." She sobbed as she spoke. "I hate that she's healthy. I hate that she has Ciaran's baby. Why couldn't it be me? I loved him first. No one's ever loved him as much as I did."

My stomach churned. How could this still be on her mind? Out of my peripheral vision, I saw Charlotte standing at the foot of the stairs.

Charlotte approached, her face contorted in sympathy and sat on the other side of Felicity. "Come here now." She cradled Felicity's head in her lap. "It's all right. Let it out."

"It's not fair." Felicity continued to sob. "You were right. Seeing him made it worse. He was tired from being up all night with her baby. Not mine."

"I know," Charlotte said.

"Why am I left with no one at the end?" Felicity asked.

"You're not alone," I said. "We're here."

Felicity quieted. Charlotte stroked her shoulder.

"You'll let Isabel stay?" Felicity asked. "I want her to know how much I loved her. Please, promise me you'll take care of her."

"Isabel will be loved," Charlotte said.

"You'll keep her?" Felicity asked. "Ardan?"

All my life, I've prided myself on being honest. God forgive me, I couldn't this time. I had to lie to her, so that she might have peace. We had to fib so she could let go of this world and enter the next.

I anchored my eyes to Charlotte. She gave me a slight nod.

"I promise you," I said. "Charlotte and I will look after her. You don't have to worry any longer."

"You'll make sure she gets to roam the woods and swim in the creek and all the other stuff we did?"

"Yes. We'll make sure she has a good life," I said.

"Your job is just to let go now," Charlotte said. "We'll take care of the rest. Where you're going, you'll be at peace."

"Do you think so?" she asked. "I won't be punished for wasting my life?"

"You haven't wasted it," I said. "Think of all the people you've helped with your philanthropy work."

"I wish I had longer. I'd do so many things differently." She moaned as a wave of pain overwhelmed her. "I need pills."

"It's time for you to rest," Charlotte said. "We'll bring Isabel to see you."

"Let's get you to bed." I stood and picked her up as gently as I could. Her head flopped against my chest.

"I'm sorry, Ardan. I've been a burden to you."

"Shush now," I said. "We're going to tuck you in, all cozy."

Seeing Ciaran one last time had cost her weeks. She had to do it, yet it caused her impetus into final decline.

She was nothing but bones as I carried her back to her room. I placed her on the bed and covered her in blankets. Charlotte gave her two pills, holding her up so she could drink from the glass.

"It's time. Time for the nurse to come," Felicity said.

"I'll get her here tonight." I helped her lay back against the pillow, then sat in the chair next to the bed. Charlotte tucked the blankets around Felicity.

"Don't leave me," Felicity said. "Stay until I fall asleep?"

"Of course." Charlotte sat next to her on the bed. "We'll be right here the whole time."

Felicity closed her eyes. "Ardan, do you remember the time we found the kittens in that old barn?"

"Sure." We'd found a litter of four kittens without their mother. We assumed she'd been killed while scouting for food.

"Whatever happened to the kittens?" Felicity asked. "I can't remember that part."

"Mother brought them inside and we took care of them until they were big enough to be adopted," I said. "We ended up keeping two of them."

"Which ones?" she asked.

"The tabby and the tuxedo. The others went to one of the ranching families," I said.

"I wanted to keep one, but my mother said no," Felicity said. "Please, get a kitty for Isabel when she's older. That way she won't be so alone."

"She won't be alone," Charlotte said. "But we'll get her a kitten. Maybe two."

"Two is better. Everyone should be in pairs." Felicity drifted off to sleep.

Charlotte stood, brushing tears from the corners of her eyes. "I'll go check on your mother and the baby."

I nodded. "We'll talk later," I whispered.

She leaned in and kissed me lightly on the mouth. "We'll work it all out. We're a pair."

"Always."

I stayed for a few minutes, watching Felicity take ragged breaths, knowing in my gut she didn't have long. What if she'd allowed herself the chance with the right man? She would have had years and years of happiness instead of her last bitter moments thinking about the man she'd never had in the first place.

An image of her when we were young floated before my eyes. She was on one of our horses. They'd stopped in the middle of the meadow, waiting for the rest of us to catch up. Her long blond hair blew about her face. She was laughing. At what, I couldn't recall. Probably something Ciaran said.

I would remember her that way—describe her to Isabel just this way—not the ravaged woman before me. Damn you, cancer.

I went down on my knees and prayed harder than I've ever prayed in my life.

Please God, end her pain. Give her peace. Guide Charlotte and me. Tell us what you want us to do.

CHAPTER TWENTY

CHARLOTTE

I stood outside. The sky presented in the unique shade of blue that comes just after twilight. A howl of a coyote somewhere in the thick forest echoed in the night. I shivered. I'd forgotten to add coyotes to the list of wild animals that could possibly eat me. Were the elk safe from coyotes? I would have to ask Ardan.

I turned when I heard the doors to the patio open. Ardan stood there with his hands in his pockets, looking drawn and pale.

"Hey," I said softly.

"Effie's with the baby. She thought we might need some time alone." He reached for me and I dissolved into his arms.

The coyote's howl penetrated the still night.

"What do we do?" I asked.

"Ever since you arrived here, I've been hearing my father's voice in my head, like guiding me. He keeps saying, 'Not yours.' "

"You think it's about Isabel?"

"I do. I'm not supposed to have her. We've trusted this voice guiding us from the moment we first met. I have to believe that we should continue to do so."

Effie burst out the French doors, out of breath. "I'm sorry to bother. But I think something's wrong with Miss Felicity. Her breathing's dodgy. I think we need to call the nurse."

* * *

The hospice nurse arrived within an hour, along with a hospital bed and other equipment. The nurse, Candace, was middle aged with wiry salt and pepper hair and a nurturing persona. She hooked Felicity up to oxygen, a morphine drip, and other machines I didn't understand.

Candace confirmed our fears. Felicity was fading quickly.

Effie had Isabel ready for bed by eight, having brushed her little teeth and put her in pajamas with feet. Ardan and I put Isabel to bed in her new crib. She was a good baby, according to Effie, and accustomed to sleeping in her own bed alone. Before we put her down, I held her on my lap and read her a story about a giraffe who learned to dance. She sucked on her pacifier and snuggled against my chest. Her hair smelled like flowers and baby powder. When I turned the pages, she grunted and pointed at the animals in the pictures.

After the story was over, I put her into the crib with her special blanket. She hugged the blanket and looked up at me with those big blue eyes. Did we stay until she fell asleep? Ardan turned on the baby monitor and pointed toward the door. I kissed Isabel on the forehead and walked away, holding my breath. No crying. When I peeked back at her, she'd closed her eyes.

We walked down the hallway holding hands. "We did it," I said. "Baby in bed, check."

"Effie said she should sleep through the night but wakes before six," Ardan said.

"Thank God for Effie."

As we passed Felicity's room, the sound of the oxygen machine droned an eerie tune.

Ardan and I had abandoned our glasses of wine earlier. Neither of us had eaten. When we came into the kitchen, Effie was just taking a sausage pizza out of the oven. The scent of sausage and red sauce made my stomach rumble.

Ardan refreshed our wine glasses and asked me to join him at the table. We both sank onto the benches at the breakfast booth, weary.

"We need to have a family meeting," Ardan said. "Effie, stop moving around for a minute. I need you to be part of this."

"Me?" She pointed at herself with the pizza cutter.

"Yes, you're part of this family," he said. "Bring the pizza and some plates and come join us."

"Yes, Mr. Lanigan."

Effie cut the pizza before bringing it to the table. We all took a slice and ate a few bites. Ardan took a long sip from his wine and looked at me, then Effie. "We have to decide what to do. Felicity won't be here much longer. Charlotte and I just lied to her and promised we'd take Isabel."

"Oh, dear," Effie said.

"We couldn't let her suffer any more than she already is." I hesitated as I worked through what to say next. "Effie, you know how much work a baby is, right?"

She nodded. "But they bring a lot of joy to the house. Joy like no other."

"She *is* sweet," I said. "And smells good."

"We could bring the baby with us on our travels," Ardan said. "We could hire a nanny to go with us."

"I don't know," I said. "That's not the kind of mother I want to be."

"What do you mean?" he asked.

"My mother was always there," I said. "She raised me, not a nanny."

"But miss, you have your work," Effie said. "I'm here to help. We might not need anyone else, Mr. Lanigan. The three of us could do it together."

"What are you two saying?" Ardan asked. "You think we should do this?"

I peered into the bottom of my glass. If only there were answers in there like tea leaves in a cup. "I'm not sure any of us are ready, but there's a baby who needs us. And, we promised Felicity. We're all perfectly capable of loving a child."

"Yet, my gut says no," Ardan said. "Like it's not meant to be."

"If my mum were here, she'd say we're knackered and to eat our supper, go to bed, and say our prayers. The answer will be there in the morning if we leave it in God's hands."

"Amen." I picked up my glass and clinked Ardan's. "To answers."

* * *

That night I dreamt I was in Nicholas's store. I snacked on popcorn and watched as he put magazines on shelves.

"Did you ever learn what happened?" I asked.

"Martin was the only one who knew the truth."

I woke up in a cold sweat. Next to me, Ardan slept, snoring softly. The clock read 5:00 a.m. I'd never get back to sleep. I dressed in Ardan's warm robe and went downstairs to his study.

Martin was the only one who knew the truth. Martin, the lover. How would he have known?

What had happened to him after Boyce's death? There had been so little information about him. He must have been at the funeral, yet there was no mention of him. I pulled that letter from the stack and read it again. Martin Boomer.

I opened my laptop and typed Martin Boomer and the year 1938. Nothing. I took out 1938 and searched on his name and Chicago. An obituary from 1991 popped up.

Martin Louis Boomer, 73

Martin Louis Boomer passed away from unknown causes on March 24, 1991. He was born in 1918 to Alexander and Mary Boomer in Chicago, Illinois. He spent most of his career as a professor of

Drama at Northwestern University. His life was devoted to the theatre, his students, deep dish pizza, and growing orchids in his greenhouse. He's survived by his wife of fifty years, Celine Trane Boomer, 68, sons Boyce Julian Boomer, 47, and Michael Daniel Boomer, 45; daughters-in-law, Susan Boomer, 47, and Michelle Boomer, 44; grandchildren Blake Ward Boomer, 20, and Louisa Grace Boomer, 16.

I shivered with anticipation. This had to be him. That he was married to a woman gave me pause, but the rest of it appeared to fit. A theatre professor who grew orchids like Nicholas's mother. A son named Boyce. Had he married to hide his sexuality or had his time with Boyce been an experiment? From what gay male friends had shared with me, that seemed unlikely. It was more probable, given the time period, that he had married because of societal pressure.

I typed in *Louisa Grace Boomer, Chicago.* A Facebook and Instagram profile appeared. I looked at her Facebook wall first. She lived in a suburb of Chicago and appeared to be about the right age. In her biographical information, she listed a website: LouisaBoomerChef.com. I clicked on the link. A personal chef, she was available for parties or in-home cooking. For queries into her services, she listed an email address. Bingo. Should I send an unsolicited message? I'd come this far. What harm could come from asking?

Dear Louisa,

I'm writing on behalf of a friend looking for information about your grandfather, Martin Boomer. He was good friends with her uncle, Boyce Garfield, back in the late thirties. I know it's a slim chance you have any information regarding Martin and his friendship with Boyce. It's been a long time and your grandfather was only sixteen at the time of Boyce's death. It was ruled a suicide by poison. However, his brother, my friend's father, felt certain he was murdered. We're reading through old letters to see if we can solve an old mystery. If you have any information, please write to me at Charlotte-

Writes@smail.com Or call at 555-483-9677. I understand this is a long shot, so forgive me for your trouble.

Sincerely,

Charlotte Wilde

I hit send and searched the brother's name but found nothing. About the time I decided to make a cup of coffee, my phone buzzed with a text.

Hi, Charlotte. This is Louisa Boomer. We should talk. Please call whenever possible.

My hands shook as I clicked the call button. She answered on the first ring.

"Hello."

"This is Charlotte."

"Yes. That was fast." I detected a slight midwestern accent.

"I happened to be right by my phone." *And I'm a weird obsessed mystery writer.*

"I'm not sure where to start," she said. "What do the kids say these days? It's complicated?"

"I'm in no hurry."

"I'll try and be succinct. My grandfather was a closeted gay man. He died of AIDS in 1991. Until he got sick, my grandmother had no idea. He worked as a drama professor and over the years, apparently, there were many affairs. As she said later, he was a great actor."

"Did she get sick too?"

"No. She was never infected. I'm assuming they didn't have much sex, as you might imagine."

"Right. The gay thing."

"Yes. Once he was diagnosed, he told her everything. She said it was the least he could do since their entire marriage had been a lie. The only thing he'd been truthful about is why he wanted to name my father, his first son, Boyce. It was in memory of his best friend growing up, Boyce Garfield, who died when they were sixteen."

"My friend's uncle," I said. "Like I said in my email, his death was ruled a suicide."

"That was my grandmother's understanding as well. My grandfather was from a wealthy family. They ran in the same circles as the Garfields. My grandmother, however, was from working class people, and to her own admission, rather plain. Until she learned the truth, she'd always considered herself lucky to have won the heart of handsome, rich Martin Boomer. After the truth came out, it made more sense. He needed a beard."

"Do you know he and Boyce had been lovers?" I asked.

"Yes, he told my grandmother everything, including that they'd been in love. When the true nature of their relationship became clear to the Garfield family, Boyce's older brother, Nicholas, hatched a plan to get them away from their violent father. Nicholas was afraid for Boyce's life."

"That's clear from the letters. They were terrified of him," I said. "Which is why we're fairly certain, Boyce was murdered by their father."

"I can see why it seems that way. But that's not what happened."

I held my breath, waiting. Had Martin killed him?

"The boys had been reading *Romeo and Juliet* at school," she said. "They fancied themselves rather like the doomed lovers. When they thought they'd be separated forever, they made a suicide pact. My grandfather bought the poison. They were to take it together the night before Boyce was supposed to leave. At the last minute, he changed his mind. Boyce had already taken his dose, so my grandfather only pretended to drink his. Boyce died in his arms, believing they were going together."

"Then he left?" I asked.

"That's right. He carried the guilt around with him for the rest of his life."

"How awful."

"He said it was the great tragedy of his life. He'd loved Boyce with all his heart."

"But not enough to die with him," I said.

"They were young and melodramatic. The suicide pact was decided in a moment of panic over being parted. He just couldn't go through with it."

"Boyce's family knew he was gay," I said. "That had to influence his decision as well. Not only did he have to leave Martin, he was facing a life of exile and shame. Even if he'd married a woman, his brother would always know the truth. I imagine that must've felt unbearable."

"At the end of his life, my grandfather asked my father if he would find Nicholas and tell him the truth. He'd wished he'd done so long before. My dad tried, but there was no trace of him. It was like he disappeared off the face of the earth."

"Nicholas had been dead for a long time by then. Even if he'd figured out where they went after they left Chicago, it was too late," I said. "He and his wife died in a car accident when their daughter, my friend, was only eighteen."

"We didn't know he'd had a daughter. When I got your note, I wanted to get in touch with you right away. I'm glad she'll know the truth."

"Reading these letters—it's remarkable how closed-minded everyone was. If only they'd lived in today's world, things would've been so different for them."

"My brother's gay," she said. "When Grandfather's story came out, so did my brother. My parents were shocked at first, but having heard Boyce and Martin's story, they never wanted him to suffer for who he was. Now, he's married to a wonderful man. They adopted two little girls—orphans because of the AIDS crisis in Africa."

"So, in a way, redemption," I said.

"That's how I've always thought about it," she said.

"What happened with your grandmother? Was she all right?"

"Oh yes, she was fine. She said that although it broke her heart to learn the truth, she would not have changed a thing because she wouldn't have had her sons and grandchildren. She lived another sixteen years after his death, and if you can believe it, married again."

"Really?"

"Yes, and get this. Raymond was her next-door neighbor, also widowed. She'd had a secret crush on him for like thirty years. He'd been secretly in love with her for decades. But they were both married, so they never acted on it. They were couple friends who played cards together and that kind of thing. On the surface, they appeared to be happy couples. My grandfather was gay and Raymond's wife was a heinous bitch who treated him terribly. Neither knew how miserable the other was until their spouses died. Apparently, no one on that street was having sex with their spouses. So here they were, both newly single in their late sixties. They got together, married, and had fifteen great years together. She told me she knew from the moment she met him, he was her soulmate."

"Soulmate? But forbidden. How tragic."

"Exactly. They were best friends all those years, sure it would always remain platonic." She laughed. "One time my grandmother told me you could never be too old to experience hot sex."

I joined her in laughter. "So, once again, redemption."

"And, justice."

I thanked her profusely for talking to me. "Mrs. Lanigan will be happy to know the truth at last."

"Wherever my grandfather is, I'm sure he's feeling at peace now."

We said our goodbyes and hung up. I sat there for a moment, absorbing what I'd just learned. Finally, we had answers. I went off to find Mrs. Lanigan.

* * *

"It was suicide after all." Mrs. Lanigan said. "Not exactly as presented, but suicide just the same. And can you imagine the shock Martin's wife must have felt after all those years? How could she not know?"

"She was only eighteen when she married him, probably sheltered and virginal."

"The poor girl." Mrs. Lanigan's fingers played with the edges of the throw blanket I'd placed on her lap. "I wish my dad had known the truth. Do you think he and his father would've reconciled if he'd known?"

"I doubt it. There was too much between them. Too many betrayals."

A knock on the door startled us. I looked over to see a tall, angular redhead dressed in black leggings, riding boots, and a tight black tank top standing in the doorway.

"Who is it?" Mrs. Lanigan asked.

"Mother, it's me." She shook her wild mane of chestnut hair and flashed that Lanigan smile with the perfect teeth. She wore almost no makeup, other than slightly pink lip gloss and a subtle stroke of eyeliner and mascara.

Mrs. Lanigan smiled. "Teagan? Home at last?"

A dark-haired little boy that looked remarkably like his uncle Ciaran peeked out from behind Teagan's legs. Brown eyes stared at me. "Yes, and I've brought Christopher. Can you say hello to your grandmother?"

He came forward, his eyes moving from me to his grandmother. "Hello, Grandmother."

"Christopher, come closer," Mrs. Lanigan said. "What does he look like?"

"He looks like Ciaran," I said. "Same thick brown hair and mischievous eyes."

"I think so too," Teagan said as she held out her arms. "You must be the angelic Charlotte. I have to hug you."

"I *am* Charlotte," I said. "Not sure about the angelic part." We embraced quickly then drew apart. Intense eyes the color of steel wool stared into mine.

"Ardan didn't lie about how pretty you are," Teagan said.

"He greatly exaggerates," I said. "But thank you."

"We didn't know you were coming today," Mrs. Lanigan said. "The wedding's still weeks away."

"It was unexpected," Teagan said. "Ardan called to tell me about the wedding, then I got Charlotte's letter. Ardan said he wants to take his bride on an extended honeymoon. Christopher starts first grade next fall. I turned down a movie offer and decided to come home for a while. I'm ready to get my house built. If it's all right, we'll stay here and look after you, Mother, while the lovebirds go off on their world tour."

"That would be wonderful, but there's no school here," Mrs. Lanigan said.

"I'll drive him into Hailey, like the other families here do," Teagan said. "We're ready to set down some roots, right buddy?"

Christopher nodded. "Mom says it's time to get away from the phonies and come home."

"We've got a bit of situation here," Mrs. Lanigan said. "Did Ardan tell you?"

"He did," Teagan said. "We already met the baby and Effie."

"That's one fat baby," Christopher said.

I laughed. "She's fat and cute."

"If you like babies," Christopher said. "Which I don't."

"What do you like?" I asked.

"Trucks, dogs, video games, soccer."

"I like dogs too," I said.

"Chris is ready to meet some kids his age. What do you think, Charlotte? Do I have soccer mom potential?"

The question could be asked of me as well. Did I have mom potential at all?

"You'll be a great soccer mom," I said.

"We're going to have our own house," Christopher said. "Mom has the plans and everything."

"I had an architect friend of mine design our perfect house," Teagan said. "Construction starts tomorrow."

"This is all so sudden," Mrs. Lanigan said. "What's really going on?"

A flash of irritation crossed Teagan's face. "I told you. I've got to get Chris in school. It's time for us to be with our family," she said. "Time to start making memories."

Christopher touched Mrs. Lanigan's arm. "Grandmother, do you want to come swim with me?"

"I won't be able to swim, but I can come out with you. Charlotte can fix the umbrella so I'm in the shade."

"Cool. Mom said if I was good in the car I could swim when we got here. I love swimming."

"He's a fish, like Ardan," Teagan said. "Chris, go find your swim trunks in the suitcase. We'll meet you down there."

"Will do," he said and took off running.

"Where will we put you?" I asked. "We're a little full at the inn."

"No problem. Kevan said we could stay at his place. We know you've got your hands full here."

"Are you going to tell us the truth or not?" Mrs. Lanigan asked. "Why are you here?"

"Mother, you're always so suspicious."

"You love your career. Settling down here is not your style."

"I would've said the same about you," Teagan said.

"I was forced to come here because of my eyes. What force brought you here?" Mrs. Lanigan asked.

Teagan flopped onto the bed. "Fine."

Fine? Wasn't that Mrs. Lanigan's "go to" word? Amused, I watched, almost wishing I had some popcorn.

"Fine what?" Mrs. Lanigan asked.

"I had a little fling with Wyatt Black and I had to get out of town before I made a complete fool out of myself by falling in love with him."

"Wyatt Black?" I asked. "The country singer?"

"Yes. He's starring in the movie I was supposed to work on and we met to talk about costumes and one thing led to another."

"By fling do you mean one night?" Mrs. Lanigan asked.

"No. Like a month. And then he left for a few concert dates and I got the heck out of dodge," Teagan said. "There was no way I was going to be there when he got back."

"You quit the movie because you were afraid to fall in love with him?" Mrs. Lanigan asked.

"Don't make it sound like I'm crazy," Teagan said. "People have turned down movies for lesser reasons."

"Why is Wyatt Black acting in a movie?" I asked.

"It's a movie about a country singer down on his luck," Teagan said. "He'll mostly be singing."

"I love those kinds of movies," I said.

"You would. Charlotte's a hopeless romantic," Mrs. Lanigan said. "Basically, the complete opposite of you."

"I'm not unromantic," Teagan said. "I just don't believe in love."

"Why don't you want to fall in love with Wyatt Black?" I asked.

Teagan lifted her head and looked at me before flopping back into her prone position, hair splayed out about her like runaway flames. "Because he's a bloody musician. Think about it, Charlotte. Always on the road. Booze and women everywhere. Recipes for bad choices and broken hearts. *My* broken heart to be exact."

"You actually like him? I can't believe it," Mrs. Lanigan said. "Charlotte, Teagan's never liked anyone ever."

"That's not true. There was Evan Sevens in third grade."

"He grew up to be gay," Mrs. Lanigan said.

"Well, that's sad for all womenkind," Teagan said. "He was such a nice dresser."

"Speaking of gay, have we got a story for you," Mrs. Lanigan said.

* * *

The next afternoon, I sat next to Felicity's hospital bed. The nurse had asked for a break and I'd offered to sit with her. She was not in pain, the nurse assured me, but if she wakes, simply push the morphine pump button. "Our job is to keep her comfortable until the end comes."

The nurse had been gone a few minutes and I was at the window looking out at Blue Mountain when I heard a soft moan. I turned. Felicity's eyes were open. "Charlotte, is that you?"

I quickly returned and took her hand. "It's me."

"How's Isabel?"

"She's good. Effie's with her right now. Do you want me to bring her?"

"I want to kiss her." Her voice was so faint I had to lean closer to hear her.

"I'll get her," I said.

She closed her eyes. I thought she'd drifted off again until she shook her head. "Bliss. Not Bliss."

"Just rest. Don't think about any of that."

She faded away again. The dark room seemed to close in on me. I stumbled over to the window and adjusted the blinds to let a little light into the room. Through the slats I watched Effie and Isabel playing in the swimming pool. Effie twirled Isabel in a circle. Their laughter penetrated through the closed window.

Felicity stirred and called out for me. I immediately went to her. She stared up at me with glassy eyes. "Don't let her have Isabel."

"Who?"

"Bliss. I want Isabel close to her father."

"What father?" I asked.

"Ciaran. Ciaran's baby," she whispered before falling back to sleep. My stomach dropped to the floor.

Ciaran's baby.

CHAPTER TWENTY-ONE

ARDAN

While Effie and Isabel played in the pool, I took care of a few administrative tasks in my office. The doorbell rang just as I finished an email to my attorney about Isabel. I was surprised to see Moonstone at the door.

"You're here. Good," she said. "I need to talk to you."

"Sure. Come on in." I ushered her into the living room.

"It's about Isabel."

"Have a seat."

Her legs seemed to collapse as she sank into the couch, clutching her tie-dyed purse against her chest. "I had a vision this morning. It was a series of texts on a phone from Felicity to the father of her unborn child. Like reading a long script, the messages flashed before my eyes." She took a piece of paper from her bag. "I wrote them down as best as I could."

I looked down Moonstone's notes, scrawled in purple.

I need to see you.

. . .

I can't. I'm at the Idaho house all winter.

I'll come there. It's urgent that I speak with you.

Is this about the photographs of Hope and me?

No. I know those are not real.

Listen, I've met someone I'm getting serious with. I'm sorry, but don't contact me again.

There was a space on the page in between that group of correspondence and the next. "The next thing I got was the second chunk," Moonstone said.

Why won't you return my texts?

Are you there? Please call me back.

Felicity, this is the last time you'll hear from me. I'm blocking you from my phone. Seriously, you've texted me a thousand times. You need to get some help. I told you I'm in love and I can't have you blowing up my phone any more. Good luck.

. . .

Ciaran, please don't do this. I'm pregnant. It's yours.

This contact has blocked your number.

I looked up at Moonstone. "Oh, crap."

"I could be wrong, of course. It happens," Moonstone said. "But these were so clear."

"Ciaran's Isabel's father?" My insides lurched like I was on a fishing boat. "Why would she do this?"

"I don't know," Moonstone said. "Did you have your heart set on the baby?"

"No. If you want to know the truth, something's felt off. My gut kept telling me I wasn't the one who should take her. I had no idea why."

I put my hand to my mouth, remembering suddenly, the night she'd come to my house and tried to seduce me. "The night she came to me, she must have been pregnant already. She was trying to make me think the baby was mine."

"Dear me," Moonstone said. "What a tangled web."

"Why me? Why not just ask Ciaran to take her?"

"When I asked the same question, I got the color yellow," Moonstone said.

"Yellow for jealousy?"

"I believe so. This was about Bliss. She doesn't want her to have Isabel."

CHAPTER TWENTY-TWO

CHARLOTTE

The nurse returned a few minutes later. "Are you all right, Charlotte? You look like you've seen a ghost."

"Yes, I'm fine." I smiled to reassure her. "I might be a little hungry."

"Go on and have your lunch. I'll let you know if anything changes."

I headed down the hallway in a daze. *Ciaran's baby* repeated in my mind a thousand times.

My feet took me to Mrs. Lanigan's room. I tapped on the door. "It's Charlotte."

"Yes, come in."

She sat in the chair near the window. Her headphones were on her lap.

"Am I interrupting?" I asked.

"Not at all. I was listening to a book."

"I need to talk to you." I took my usual chair and tried to think of how to start.

"Have you been running? You sound out of breath."

"I've had a shock." I crossed my legs, then uncrossed them.

"Is it one of your parents?" she asked.

"No, they're fine. It's about Isabel. I think Ciaran might be her father."

She recoiled like I'd slapped her in the face. "No, it can't be."

I told her about Felicity's strange utterings. "She said she didn't want Bliss to have her, which didn't make sense until she told me Isabel was Ciaran's baby."

"She must've gotten pregnant right before he met Bliss," Mrs. Lanigan said.

"Yes, and once she realized she was pregnant, she tried to get in touch with Ciaran, but he blocked her calls. Desperate, she went to Ardan and tried to seduce him, so he'd think the baby was his."

"To use him like she always did." Mrs. Lanigan tightened her cardigan around her waist. "She didn't want Bliss to raise her child, so she set up this lie to get Ardan to do it."

"This way Ciaran would be part of her life, but Bliss wouldn't be her mother." As I spoke out loud, the truth became all too clear. "Ardan was the only man who had ever been loyal to her without asking anything in return. He was also her child's uncle."

"Making him the perfect choice."

"It's so twisted." I realized both my hands and voice were shaking. "All this time he's said he didn't think we were meant to have her. This must be why. What do we do now?"

"We tell the boys. Ciaran can take a DNA test to be sure. I should tell them. I'm their mother. It should come from me."

"I already know." I whipped around to see Ardan standing in the doorway. "Moonstone saw it in a vision last night. She just came by to tell me."

He was as white as the sheets on Mrs. Lanigan's bed. I was afraid he might faint. I led him over to the chair and made him sit.

"She's Ciaran's." His eyes were dull and flat, like a worn doll's. "I was ready to take her. You were ready to take her." He bowed his head and closed his eyes. "I didn't even think of this as a possibility, which now seems stupid."

"I wonder if she got pregnant on purpose?" I sank to the floor next to his chair.

"All this time she knew, and she was going to have me raise Ciaran's child. Mother, what if we'd repeated the same thing that happened with Finn and Kevan?"

"But we didn't," Mrs. Lanigan said. "The truth's out now."

"I didn't think she was capable of such deception," Ardan said. "I really didn't."

"Unrequited love makes a person do things they wouldn't normally do," I said.

"We have to tell Ciaran and Bliss," Mrs. Lanigan said.

For the first time, I thought about Bliss. "She just gave birth. And suddenly she has another?"

"What a mess," Ardan said.

"Your brother will have to step up," Mrs. Lanigan said.

As would Bliss. I ached for my friend and the shock that was about to come her way.

"They will," Ardan said. "Once he knows the truth, he'll want her. I know my brother. But Mother, I should tell him. It's better coming from me."

Both Ardan and I jumped when his cell phone rang. "It's the nurse."

I held my breath, knowing it was bad news.

Ardan nodded. "Yes, thanks for telling me. We'll be right there."

"Is she gone?" Mrs. Lanigan asked.

"Yes. She took her last breath a minute ago." He looked down at his hands, his words strangled in his throat. "I should've been there with her, so she didn't have to go out alone."

"It's all right," Mrs. Lanigan said. "She's in the right place now. No more pain."

I started to cry. Despite my complicated feelings for the woman who had caused such havoc in our lives, she was a friend. Her little daughter would never know her mother. Ardan pulled me against his legs and stroked my hair. "Mother's right. Now we need to make sure Isabel has what she needs."

I wiped my eyes and rose to my feet. "She's with Effie. I'll go to them. Effie and I will look after her until we get everything sorted out."

Mrs. Lanigan held out her arms. "Come here and give me a hug before you go."

I knelt by her legs and let her arms encircle me.

"You're a good girl," she whispered in my ear. "It'll be all right."

* * *

Effie cried when I told her. We were in the breakfast booth. Isabel was on Effie's lap, oblivious to the sadness of the adults around her.

"The poor lady," she said. "Leaving her baby."

"I just hope she's at peace now. She had a troubled life."

"I always figured rich people had no problems until I came here," Effie said. "Now I'm thinking I didn't have it so bad, even though we were poor."

I nodded. She spoke the truth. "Love is what we need, not money."

"What about poor Isabel? Have you and Mr. Lanigan decided?"

"I think I know what's going to happen with Isabel." I shared what we'd just learned.

Her tears stopped as her eyes widened. "Ciaran is her father? What will happen now?"

I played with one of Isabel's curls. "Hopefully she'll go where she belongs. With her dad."

"I'll miss her."

I smiled. "Me too. But we'll get to see her as much as we want."

"This means you and Mr. Lanigan can make all your dreams come true. You can travel and see the world. But you'll come back to me, won't you?"

"Maybe you'll come with us for some of it," I said. "You know I can't cook. You'd like to come to Italy, wouldn't you? Think of all the vegetables."

"Yes, miss. I would like that very much."

"Now we have to plan a wedding."

"I'm glad for you, miss. What would've happened to us had you not come?"

"You would have been fine without me, but I'm not sure I would have been. Everything's changed for me because of all of you."

"Even me?"

"Even you, Effie."

CHAPTER TWENTY-THREE

ARDAN

I didn't call my brother before I went to his house, afraid my voice would betray me. This was not news to share over the phone. I couldn't predict exactly how my brother would react, other than I knew only this: he would never turn away from his child. We are Lanigans. No matter how messy family gets, we're still that: family.

Bliss answered the door, wearing sweats and an old t-shirt. Her usual impeccable appearance made her nearly unrecognizable. Her hair was matted. Deep circles under her eyes were evidence of sleepless nights. From inside, the cries of a baby penetrated the quiet afternoon.

"Is everything all right?" Bliss asked as she gestured for me to come inside.

"Felicity passed."

She put a hand on my arm. "I'm sorry. Are you all right?"

"Yes. I'm glad she's out of pain and somewhere she can be free. I need to talk to my brother."

"He's with the baby. We had a rough night. She has colic, which basically means she never stops crying. We're both exhausted."

I followed her into the house. Ciaran was by the window with the baby in his arms. Since I'd first arrived, she'd stopped crying. "I finally got her to sleep." He set her in the cradle by the couch. My brother looked worse than his wife—unshaven face, greasy hair, and spit up on the shoulder of his shirt. "What's up?"

Unsure of how to proceed, I stood with my hands in my pockets.

"Felicity's passed," Bliss said.

"I'm sorry to hear that." He raked his hands through his hair. "I don't know what to say."

I should tell them both, not just Ciaran. Saving him from the torture of telling Bliss was the least I could do. "I have something I need to tell you guys. You better sit down."

Bliss sank into the couch and yawned. Ciaran sat next to her as I took the chair.

They both looked so fatigued I almost turned back around and drove home. How did one share this kind of news?

"What is it?" Ciaran asked with a hint of impatience. His brown eyes had lost their humor and playfulness.

I swallowed and began. "Before she died, Felicity told Charlotte the truth about Isabel's father. She was delirious from the morphine, but her last words to Charlotte were fairly clear." I'd save the part Moonstone played in this until later the conversation. "She wasn't conceived via a sperm donor. Ciaran, she said you're Isabel's father."

"What did you say?" Ciaran blinked, like he wondered if he were seeing visions.

"It appears that the last time you were together, before you met Bliss, she got pregnant," I said.

"Oh, God," Ciaran said. "But we used a condom. I always did."

"Sometimes they break," I said. "Or sometimes people poke holes in them. Charlotte believes she did it on purpose."

Ciaran had turned gray. He pressed his fingers against his

mouth like he might be sick. "Yes, the last time we were together was right before I met Bliss. I was in the city for the weekend and ran into her at a charity function."

"Does the math work?" I asked.

"Yes. I suppose it does," Ciaran said.

"Why wouldn't she have told him?" Bliss asked. "Why now?"

I shared with them Mother and Charlotte's theory. "It seemed she wanted Isabel to be part of Ciaran's life, but not you, Bliss."

"Let me get this straight." Bliss's eyes snapped with such force I could practically hear them crackle. "She wanted her near Ciaran but didn't want me raising her? Is that what're you're saying?"

"That's what we think, yes."

"Did she know about Rori?" Ciaran asked.

"No. She had no idea." I hadn't seen Felicity since before we discovered the truth about who Rori's father was.

"We might have repeated the same pattern," Bliss said.

"Except we all know Isabel isn't mine," I said. "But yes, we would never have known the truth."

"Should we do a DNA test?" Bliss asked.

"Sure, to be certain. Also, Moonstone came by this morning." I shared the details of what she saw.

"I remember," Ciaran said. "She wouldn't stop texting me and I'd just met Bliss. I told her I'd met someone and blocked her."

"Felicity learned about the cancer when she was pregnant," I said. "And must've decided to raise her alone."

"But then realized she was dying," Bliss said. "And came up with the idea of you."

"That's right," I said.

Ciaran stared straight ahead.

"Ciaran?" I asked. "You all right?"

He blinked, like he hadn't remembered there were other people in the room. "What do we do here?" He turned to his wife. "Bliss, what do I do?"

Bliss took his hand. "She's your daughter."

"Baby, I'm sorry. I had no idea. This was before you. Before I knew what love is."

"I know, honey. It's going to be fine. We'll work it out." The reassuring tone of Bliss's voice didn't match the look of terror in her eyes. I knew what she must be thinking. How could they take another baby on when their infant daughter was only weeks old and wouldn't stop crying?

"I can send Effie over to help with the transition," I said. "She's really good with Isabel and knows everything about babies. We'll help you hire a nanny. Charlotte's a good judge of character. We'll find someone great."

"Yes, we'll need help," Bliss said. "Is she an easy baby?"

I smiled, thinking of Isabel's little grin. "She's very flexible and totally sweet. The nanny she had was very good. She goes down at night without a fuss."

"That poor, desperate women," Bliss said. "How excruciating it must have been to leave her."

"Will you have Charlotte bring her over?" Ciaran asked. "I want to meet her."

"She's already on the way."

As if on cue, the doorbell rang. I sprinted to the door. Charlotte stood there with Isabel on her hip. "You guys ready?"

"It's still sinking in, I think. But they want to meet her."

I heard footsteps behind me and turned to see my brother with tears in his eyes. Charlotte stepped into the house. Isabel smiled when she saw me and clapped her hands. Ciaran drew closer, his gazed fixed on his daughter.

"She's beautiful," Ciaran said. "Would she let me hold her?"

"She might," Charlotte said. "If she fusses, I'll take her back."

He held out his arms. "Hello, Isabel. I'm your daddy."

She smiled and babbled something. I could swear it was *dada*.

I glanced at Charlotte. From her wide eyes, I guessed she'd heard the same thing.

Charlotte handed Isabel over to Ciaran. "Here you go, Daddy."

"Hello, doll," Ciaran said.

Isabel smiled as big as the sun as Bliss came to stand beside them.

"She's so pretty," Bliss said. "She reminds me of my niece at that age. She had gold curls too."

I caught Charlotte's eye. With a tilt of her chin, she indicated we should go outside and give them time alone.

"We'll go out for a little walk and come back in a few minutes," Charlotte said.

They nodded, absently, too enthralled with Isabel to take much notice of us.

* * *

A trail led into the woods adjacent to Ciaran's house. Charlotte took the lead, with me following closely behind, enjoying the curve of her calves. I told her of my conversation with Ciaran and Bliss and how they had immediately made the decision to take Isabel. "I knew they would," I said. "But still, it was impressive how they didn't hesitate."

"Bliss is taking it hard," Charlotte said. "I can see it in her eyes."

I agreed that I'd sensed the same.

"But it's impossible not to love Isabel," she said.

I nodded. "They will make a wonderful family for her."

"Bliss told me she wanted more babies, but didn't think it would happen, given her age," I said.

"Why did everything work out except for Felicity?" I asked.

"There's no answer to that question."

We came out of the woods to the meadow where Ciaran and Bliss snowshoe in the winter. Today, tall grasses swayed gracefully in the breeze. Wildflowers were dashes of colors, scattered in between. Above us, a cloudless Idaho sky promised a warm afternoon.

"We're free, Charlotte."

We clasped hands.

"Is it wrong I feel relieved?" I asked.

"No, I don't think so. We had prepared ourselves for an instant family. We would have stepped up. We *had* stepped up. But knowing we can take our time and enjoy each other for a few more years feels pretty good."

I played with the engagement ring on her finger. "We'll have a family, but for now I'll keep you all to myself. I've waited a long time for you to come," I said. "And now that you're here, I can't remember the time before you."

"Soulmates."

"Soulmates." I kissed her. The hawk above did one final swoop and disappeared into the shadow of Blue Mountain.

CHAPTER TWENTY-FOUR

CHARLOTTE

I found Bliss outside on the patio. She sat with her arms crossed over her chest, staring at Blue Mountain. Light green needles at the end of the firs' branches displayed the new growth that had come since my arrival in Idaho.

"Hey," I said. "You need anything?"

She lifted her face toward me. Tears glistened in her lashes. "Just taking a moment."

I sat in the chair next to her. The sun hovered just above the mountain, casting shadows across the yard. A blue jay squawked from the tall fir tree next to the patio. "What can I do?"

"That's you, always asking how you can help. It made you a great assistant and a great friend. It'll make you a great wife and mother."

I settled back into the chair. "I've learned since I've been here that sometimes there's nothing to be done to help another person." I sighed as a gentle breeze brought the scent of fir. I imagined it was the smell of the shiny new growth.

"Did I ever tell you about my mother?" Bliss asked.

"I didn't even know you had a sister until that day you fell and hurt your head," I said.

"So, I guess that's a no?" A weary smile lifted the corners of her mouth.

"What was she like?"

"Not like yours," Bliss said. "Blythe was more of a mother to me than our real mother. Our mom was always about herself instead of us. I always figured I was the same, not cut out for motherhood. I loved being Auntie Bliss to the girls, but that was easy. In and out, bring gifts and tell funny stories. None of the hard stuff. Then I met Ciaran and everything inside me changed. Suddenly, I was split wide open with this overwhelming love I felt for him. I wanted to make a family with him. When I found out I was pregnant, Ciaran was thrilled. For me though, all those old feelings came rushing back. What if I was like my mother? What if I didn't have the qualities needed to love a child? But when I looked into Carmen's eyes for the first time, I knew. This was exactly what I was made to do. I was made to love Carmen Riona Lanigan with everything I am. But this—loving someone else's child—what if this is something only women like my sister or you can do?"

"You're the type of woman who can do anything," I said.

"Not when it comes to matters of the heart. That's you and Blythe. Loving stray cats and stray people, even those no one else can love, is like breathing to you. I'm not that way."

"You brought a homeless man and his three-legged dog to Thanksgiving in Idaho. Your heart's big enough for this baby. Give it a little time. You're still in shock."

"I've never been good with surprises," she said.

"This is one heck of a surprise. Go easy on yourself."

"She's an innocent child who needs parents to love her unconditionally. Here I am, healthy and more than capable of taking on the child of a woman who lost her life. *I'm* the one with Ciaran. I should be grateful. Instead, I feel confused and frightened and completely out of my element. I don't understand how this happened. Or why."

"All that's completely normal. I've struggled to understand how God could let that little girl's mother die. I don't know why some of us get to stay longer than others. I don't know the answers. But I know one thing. No mother could wish for a better woman than you to raise her daughter."

"She didn't want me to," Bliss said. "She lied to Ardan to make sure I didn't raise her daughter. How am I supposed to look that little girl in the eye knowing that?"

"Because Felicity wasn't in her right mind. Jealousy made her act irrationally."

"I have to do this for Ciaran," Bliss said. "I don't know how to do that without feeling resentful."

"What Ardan and I have together—what you and Ciaran have—makes sacrifice for the other seem less like sacrifice and more of an act of love." I shared with her about the letters between the long-ago lovers. "What he gave up in order to be with her was great, yet he never questioned it. He never looked back. From then on, his world was her world."

"It's true I would do anything for that man," she said.

"You would, and you will." I smiled. "I have a little secret. I've already fallen a little in love with Isabel. She's going to giggle her way right into your heart."

"What if I can't forget who she came from and why?"

"You have to. For Ciaran. And for that sweet little girl. Anyway, I'm not worried. I know how brave and clever and tenacious you are. Look what you've done with your life so far."

"Nothing prepared me for this," she said.

"That's where you're wrong. Everything that came before prepared you for this very moment. All the struggles and triumphs made you the exact woman to raise Isabel. She's your destiny, just as Ciaran was. The same woman who took in a homeless man and his three-legged dog—a woman who called her former assistant to come to Idaho simply because her friend had a vision—is a woman who can fall in love with a motherless baby."

She reached over and squeezed my hand as the sun disappeared behind Blue Mountain. "Do you ever wonder what it would be like if we could be the person others think we are?"

"I do." I thought of my sweet Ardan and how he made me see my own beauty every time he looked at me. "Sometimes it takes another's view of us to see the truth of who we really are."

CHAPTER TWENTY-FIVE

CHARLOTTE

The presence of Teagan and Christopher had helped to purge some of the sadness from the house after we lost Felicity. Although her time with us had been short, we were all deeply shaken by her arrival in our lives and subsequent abrupt exit from this world to the next. Ardan and Mrs. Lanigan and Effie had seemed to move on more easily than I. After we let Felicity's ashes drift into the swimming hole as she'd asked, I could see the burden lift from Ardan's shoulders. He was ready to move on to the next chapter of our life. Mrs. Lanigan was focused on repairing her relationship with her children and grandchildren.

During the days, I faked it well, busy with plans for the wedding. Effie and Teagan had taken on the project with great zeal. Teagan insisted on designing and making my dress. Effie had every detail of the wedding planned, including food, flowers, music.

Christopher was a ray of light. The sound of his footsteps running through the house and shouts of glee while playing in the pool should have brought me joy. Especially given that his companionship had brought Mrs. Lanigan even more to life. He'd convinced her to venture into the shallow end of the pool. The water felt good to her old bones, she'd told him, igniting his chivalrous nature. Each day they did their "grandmother" exercises together, which comprised of laps walking around the shallow end while chatting about trucks, dogs, video games, and soccer.

My parents had called earlier to say they would arrive tomorrow afternoon. Normally, I would have been excited. Instead, I felt bad. Why did I have so much, including my parents, when Felicity was dead, and Bliss was still reeling from the addition of another child in her life?

If that wasn't bad enough, my agent called. By some miracle, she'd sold books two and three of my Luci series. I was marrying the man of my dreams at the end of the summer. I should be dancing jigs down the hallway.

Instead, I had fallen into a heavy case of survivor's guilt. I couldn't write. I woke in the middle of the night thinking I heard Felicity's oxygen machine, only to discover it was the wind. I'd started dreaming of Roberta again, reliving that awful day in various nightmarish versions of a recurring dream where I tried to save her but couldn't.

Once again, I'd survived when my peer had to go.

I knew Ardan and Mrs. Lanigan sensed my moroseness but weren't sure what to do.

The night before my parents arrived, Teagan and Christopher had gone to Kevan and Blythe's for dinner. It was just the three of us, like old times. I hadn't told either of them about the books, even though I'd gotten the news yesterday. I'd wanted to tell them together, but somehow it hadn't yet felt right.

We'd finished eating, although I hadn't done much but move my food around my plate.

"Sweetie, we're worried about you," Ardan said.

"Against our better judgment, we've decided to play armchair shrink," Mrs. Lanigan said.

I teared up and pretended to examine the bottom of the salad bowl.

"You're guilty because everything you've ever wanted is happening," she said. "Perfectly understandable, given the loss of your friend when you were young."

"My agent sold books two and three." I blurted this out, then burst into tears.

Stunned silence met me from either side of the table.

Ardan recovered first. "Sweetie, that's incredible."

"Finally, that twit comes through," Mrs. Lanigan said.

"Why me?" I sobbed. "Why do I get it all? Wonderful parents? This deep friendship with you, Mrs. Lanigan? And now a book deal when I'm about to marry someone with gobs of money? And mostly, you, Ardan. I am marrying the love of my life and I'm so happy and yet there's so much sadness. Roberta's dead. Felicity's dead. Bliss has a baby she doesn't want. Mrs. Lanigan, you've struggled so."

"For heaven's sake," Mrs. Lanigan said. "Don't you know by now we don't have any idea why these things happen? Our job isn't to know the answers. You two hippies have been telling me that for months now. We're supposed to take it as it comes and lean into the darn mystery. Isn't that what you told me?"

I started laughing through my tears. "I might have said something like that."

"My love," Ardan got up from his chair and knelt next to mine. "Has it ever occurred to you that you deserve good things because you've been so good to others?"

"Like cranky old ladies, for example," Mrs. Lanigan said.

"And manipulative, albeit dying, young ladies," Ardan said. "No one I've ever known has a bigger heart than you."

"Or worked harder," Mrs. Lanigan said.

"Or taken leaps of faith and looked at challenges as a possibility for something better rather than an inevitable acceptance of doom," Ardan said.

"But here's the thing," I said. "If good things happen because we're good, then why don't bad things only happen to bad people? And we all know that's not true."

"Well, we're going to ask God that the minute we get up there," Mrs. Lanigan said. "For now, we're going to savor the nectar of every sweet moment from this mysterious life, and endure and adjust as we're forced to. Charlotte, you brought this house to life…heck, me, back to life. Please, let yourself be joyful."

Ardan looked into my eyes. "I'm so proud of you and so damn lucky I'm the one who gets to grow old with you."

"You know I feel the same," I said. "I'm sorry I've been down."

"Don't apologize," he said. "It's completely understandable."

"Not even you can be chipper every moment of your Pollyanna life," Mrs. Lanigan said. "We love you however you wake up in the morning, but we want you to be happy because you've made us so happy."

"I love you, mean old thing," I said.

"I'll tell you what we need," Mrs. Lanigan said. "We need a reason to live."

Ardan laughed. "Mother, are you hinting at champagne?"

"She has a book deal. Charlotte, Luci has another chance to find the readers she desperately deserves." Mrs. Lanigan slapped the table. "Damn right we're having champagne."

Effie came around the corner with a bottle and three glasses. Clearly, she'd been listening at the door.

"Miss, we're so proud of you."

Ardan leapt to his feet and popped the champagne cork. "Effie, get another glass. You're joining us tonight."

"No sir, I couldn't."

"Please, Effie," I said. "You don't want me to cry again, do you?"

"No, no. Please don't."

While Effie ran to get another glass, Ardan poured for the three of us. "I have other news. Other reasons to live."

Effie was back, eyes sparkling. Ardan filled her glass and they both sat.

"I don't know if you two had forgotten, but we had one last mystery to solve about the Garfields. What happened to the money? Was there anyone around to inherit the money? I hired a detective and I now have answers."

"And?" Mrs. Lanigan asked.

"Charlotte was right. Ivy, Randolph's sister had two sons, contemporaries of Boyce and your father, Nicholas. They're named John Garfield and Lucius Garfield. Upon the death of Randolph, Ivy inherited everything. When she died, her sons received equal portions of the estate. John married Lila Thorton and had two daughters about your age, Mother. Lucius had no children. From what the detective gathered, he was gay. He died last year at age sixty-nine. However, the two daughters of John, Hattie and Hannah, are alive and well. They're both widowed and have two children each. As it turns out, we do have long lost cousins. Hattie and Hannah inherited almost the entirety of the estate, as Lucius left his money to them as well."

"Have you contacted them?" Mrs. Lanigan asked.

"I have. They live together in a posh retired community outside of Chicago and are both spry, although they're in their mid-seventies."

"That's incredible," Mrs. Lanigan said.

"They said they're excited to meet you and want to come visit."

Mrs. Lanigan raised her glass. "Yet another reason to live."

We all toasted.

"Think of it, Charlotte. There could be two more just like me." Mrs. Lanigan beamed a wicked smile from across the table.

"No one could be just like you," I said. "You're one of a kind."

"For which we are thankful," Ardan said.

We were all laughing when the doorbell rang. Effie jumped up to find out who was at the door. A few seconds later, my father's voice echoed through the house. I screamed and ran out of the dining room and into the foyer.

Effie was staring at my father like most women do when they first meet him but managed to tear her gaze from him to step back and announce them in her cute accent. "Miss, your parents are here."

"Surprise, darling. We're early," Mom said.

I rushed into her arms and the familiar scent of her perfume. She wore a red and blue polo dress and white sneakers. How did anyone look this neat and put together despite all the hours riding co-pilot in an Airstream?

I threw myself at Dad who pulled me into a hug like only he could give. "I thought you'd be here tomorrow," I said.

"We made good time," Dad said. "And your mother was anxious to get here."

"Me?" Mom asked. "Your dad broke every speed limit law from Florida to here."

"I wanted to see my little girl. A cop would've understood. Had I been stopped, which I wasn't." Dad smiled his dentist smile and put his arm around Mom. "You look beautiful. Glowing."

"Sun-kissed," Mom said. "Idaho agrees with you."

Ardan joined us. I introduced them. "This is my Ardan." When he and my dad shook hands, I had to blink back tears. *Savor the nectar of every sweet moment from this mysterious life.* What a time we would have tonight. Catching up. Hearing their stories from life on the road.

We led them back to the dining room to meet Mrs. Lanigan. She'd waited, not exactly patiently, given the tapping of her fingers against the table top. She stood when we came in the room. Mom, being the person she is, rushed to her and hugged her. "We're glad to meet you, Mrs. Lanigan. Charlotte has told us all about you."

"She highly exaggerates. I'm sure you know that," Mrs. Lanigan said.

"She always sees the good in people," Dad said. "Sometimes that's gotten her into trouble."

"Not this time," I said.

Ardan put his arm around my shoulder. "We're celebrating tonight, as you can see. My fiancée has exciting news."

I told them about the book deal.

"That malnourished agent finally sold them," Mrs. Lanigan said. "It's a miracle."

"How wonderful." Mom hugged me again. "I'm thrilled for you."

"We thought Mother was going to have to become her agent," Ardan said.

"From what Charlotte tells us about you, Mrs. Lanigan, it sounds like a good idea," Dad said.

Mrs. Lanigan turned her face to the sound of his voice and smiled. "Please, call me Riona."

Even women without sight swooned when my dad was in the room.

Effie had brought out two more glasses and another bottle of champagne. "I've made a chocolate cake, miss. Should I bring it out?"

I realized she was asking me, not Ardan or Mrs. Lanigan. I was the mistress of the house now. "The answer to cake is always yes," I said.

"And more champagne," Mrs. Lanigan said.

We gave my parents a tour of the house while Effie helped Mrs. Lanigan to the living room. Mom couldn't stop exclaiming over the house. "Charlotte, Ardan has just our taste."

"I know. Weird, right?"

"The designer I hired had just your taste," Ardan said. "She did most of it."

When we settled into the living room, Dad made a toast to Ardan and me and our engagement. Mom, next to Mrs. Lanigan on the couch, tapped her glass with her own. "To future grandchildren." Mom said this in Mrs. Lanigan's ear, but everyone heard her.

Mrs. Lanigan nodded and smiled. "Hopefully I'll still be alive by then. All this travel nonsense has Charlotte distracted."

I laughed. "Mrs. Lanigan wants me to travel. She says I need to find more stories and traveling is the way to do it."

"Did I say that?" Mrs. Lanigan asked. "I need to learn to keep my big mouth shut."

Mom and I laughed.

"I see where Charlotte gets her lovely laugh," Mrs. Lanigan said to Mom.

"How kind of you to say," Mom said.

"Charlotte's been helping me to become a Pollyanna like her," Mrs. Lanigan said. "It's nauseating but effective."

Mom laughed again. "You're even funnier than Charlotte described."

Mrs. Lanigan smiled like a satisfied cat. "My sense of humor has been greatly exaggerated."

"We understand you're traveling for part of next year?" Dad asked Ardan and me.

"That's right, sir." Ardan was perched on the arm of my chair with one hand on my shoulder. "My house in Italy is centrally located. Charlotte wants to see Europe. We'll leave after the wedding and spend the fall there."

"Paris in October. How romantic," Mom said.

"So that's where she gets it," Mrs. Lanigan said under her breath.

"But we'll be back by Christmas," I said. "We want to spend our first Christmas in Idaho."

"It's beautiful here in the winter," Ardan said.

"Mom, it'll be a white Christmas," I said. "Just like you always wanted. You and Dad will plan to be here, won't you?" I gestured toward the big window. "Ardan says he puts his tree right there. See the mantel? We can decorate it with fresh branches from our own property."

"Darling, it's perfect. You won't be able to keep us away," Mom said.

"We noticed some 'property for sale' signs on our way out here," Dad said.

I studied him. Was he hinting around that they might like to stay?

"We'll have room for your Airstream anytime, Doctor Wilde," Ardan said. "We have enough land that you can pick your favorite spot and spend as much time as you want here."

"Or stay with us," I said.

Mom's fingers plucked the stem of her champagne glass. "We were thinking of something more permanent. Like you, we might like to intersperse our travel with a more permanent residence."

"Mom, what are you saying?" I told myself not to get my hopes up, but it was too late.

"We might like to build a little house of our own," Dad said. "Near our only daughter."

"Darling, we missed you and now that you're getting married into a large family, like we always dreamt of, well, it's cruel to think of being anywhere but here with you."

"We'll still travel some," Dad said. "But your mother missed having a home."

"Cooking beef Bourguignon is just not the same in the Airstream," Mom said.

"Completely dodgy," Effie said as she handed Dad a piece of cake.

"We have plenty of room for another house on *our* property," Ardan said. "There's only one spot spoken for by Teagan. The rest of the acreage has great locations for houses. It would be silly to buy another piece of land when we have all this."

"I don't know. That feels like a freeloader type of move," Dad said.

"You're family now," Ardan said.

"Plus, the closer the better," I said.

"There's a house already built," Mrs. Lanigan said. "That's sat empty for too long."

Ardan jerked back, like she'd smacked him. "Are you talking about Finn's house?"

"They won't have the memories we have," Mrs. Lanigan said. "It won't be painful for them to be there. We can have it gutted and remodeled, but the house itself is spacious with tall ceilings and the most wonderful kitchen that looks out over the valley." She said this last part to my mother.

"Since we've retired early, we can't really afford a big remodel," Mom said. "We were thinking a small cottage."

"Dear, we're Lanigans. Enough money is not our problem," Mrs. Lanigan said.

"But it's too much," Dad said.

"Charlotte came and waved her Pollyanna dust and fixed us," Mrs. Lanigan said. "The least we can do is give her parents their dream home."

Next to me, Ardan shifted.

I looked up at him. "Is it all right with you?"

He smiled with a hint of sadness. "Finn would love the idea of the smell of beef Bourguignon filling that house. I think it's a great idea." He turned to my dad. "Mr. Wilde, it would make your daughter happy, which means it makes us all happy. Please, think about it."

"I will," Dad said. "Thank you."

"Now that we have that settled, my glass is empty," Mrs. Lanigan said. "And where's my cake?"

* * *

After everyone finally went to bed, Ardan and I grabbed a blanket and went out to the patio to snuggle in a chaise. A full moon hovered over Blue Mountain. An owl hooted from the woods. Billions of stars lit the sky.

"Tell me again why the stars shine so brightly?" I asked.

"To remind us of our purpose."

"Which is to love."

"Do they still shine as brightly for you as they did that first night?" he asked.

I nodded against his chest. "Just like when you walk into a room, my stomach does the flipflop dance. Some things will never change."

"I've loved you for at least a dozen lifetimes. I'll love you for the rest of this one and the one after that and the one after that."

"I'll find you. Wherever you are, I'll find you," I said.

"And I you."

The stars shone so brightly in that moment, the dark sky feared for its existence. I understood then that all the ways in which we love each other nourishes the stars, just as they nourish us. Love would always outshine the darkness if we remembered our purpose.

Our only purpose. To love.

To love so fiercely and fearlessly that hate shrinks and cowers and disappears.

The End

ALSO BY TESS THOMPSON

Miller's Secret

Duet for Three Hands

The Santa Trial

The River Valley Series

Riversong

Riverbend

Riverstar

Riversnow

Riverstorm

A River Valley Christmas: Tommy's Wish

The Blue Mountain Series

Blue Midnight

Blue Moon

The Legley Bay Series

Caramel and Magnolias

Tea and Primroses

The Cliffside Bay Series

Traded: Brody and Kara

Deleted: Jackson and Maggie

Jaded: Zane and Honor

Marred: Kyle and Violet

Tainted: Lance and Mary

ABOUT THE AUTHOR

Tess Thompson writes small-town romances and historical fiction. Her female protagonists are strong women who face challenges with courage and dignity. Her heroes are loyal, smart and funny, even if a bit misguided at times. While her stories are character driven, she weaves suspenseful plots that keep readers turning pages long into the night.

Her desire is to inspire readers on their journey toward their best life, just as her characters are on the way to theirs. In her fiction, she celebrates friendships, community, motherhood, family, and how love can change the world. If you like happy endings that leave you with the glow of possibility, her books are for you.

Like her characters in the River Valley Collection, Tess Thompson hails from a small town in southern Oregon, and will always feel like a small town girl, despite the fact she's lived in Seattle for over twenty-five years. She loves music and dancing, books and bubble baths, cooking and wine, movies and snuggling. She cries at sappy commercials and thinks kissing in the rain should be done whenever possible. Although she tries to act like a lady, there may or may not have been a few times in the last several years when she's gotten slightly carried away watching the Seattle Seahawks play, but that could also just be a nasty rumor.

Her historical fiction novel, *Duet for Three Hands* won the first runner-up in the 2016 RONE awards. *Miller's Secret,* her second historical, was released in 2017, as were the fourth and fifth River Valley Series books: *Riversnow* and *Riverstorm*. The sixth River Valley book will (hopefully) release in the latter part of 2018.

Traded: Brody and Kara, the first in her new contemporary, small town romance series, Cliffside Bay, released on February 15th, 2018. The second in the series, *Deleted: Jackson and Maggie* released May 7th. The subsequent three Cliffside Bay books will released every couple months in 2018.

She currently lives in a suburb of Seattle, Washington with her recent groom, the hero of her own love story, and their Brady Bunch clan of two sons, two daughters and five cats, all of whom keep her too busy, often confused, but always amazed. Yes, that's four kids, three of whom are teenagers, and five cats. Pray for her.

Tess loves to hear from you. You can visit her website http://tesswrites.weebly.com/ or find her on social media.